"[This is] a terrific series of French noir novels, a Marseilles trilogy of sun-baked bad guys and beautiful women, smart cops and mean situations. Mr. Izzo was a marvelous food writer in addition to being a poet of violence and regret. His books are filled with winning descriptions of Provençal meals run through with the flavors of north Africa, Italy, Greece."
—Sam Sifton, *The New York Times*

"Caught between pride and crime, racism and fraternity, tragedy and light, messy urbanization and generous beauty, the city is for Jean-Claude Izzo a Utopia, an ultimate port of call for exiles. There Montale, like Mr. Izzo himself perhaps, is torn between fatalism and revolt, despair and sensualism."—*The Economist*

"What makes Izzo's work haunting is his extraordinary ability to convey the tastes and smells of Marseilles, and the way memory and obligation dog every step his hero takes."—*The New Yorker*

"In Izzo's books . . . Marseilles is a *'ville selon nos coeurs,'* a city in tune with our hearts, as we can read in the penultimate sentence of *Total Chaos*. A cosmopolitan, maritime city, greedy, sensual and warm, but undermined by racism, hatred, money, mafia, and religious fundamentalism—and passive complicity in the face of these scourges."—Michel Samson, *Slow Food*

"Jean-Claude Izzo's Marseille trilogy . . . delve deep into the guts of multiracial Marseilles, a city that is at once a hopeful symbol of the Mediterranean's rich cultural past and an urban dystopia burdened by unemployment, racism and violence . . . Noir at its finest: compelling, sophisticated literature with a biting social edge."—Hirsh Sawhney, *The Times Literary Supplement*

"Like all tragic noir heroes, Montale treads a dangerously narrow line between triumphant savior and doomed avenger."—*The Village Voice*

"*Total Chaos* is undeniably literature . . . Part of this is due to Izzo's amazing characterization . . . Izzo takes a convention of noir—the lost soul who finds himself in vengeance—and packs it with enough realism to make it utterly lifelike . . . *Total Chaos* is a noir through and through, but it feels so real that it reminds us that the clichés of noir were originally drawn from real life."—*The Quarterly Conversation*

"A few years ago I was planning a trip to Madrid and Paris from Los Angeles. I was also deep into Jean-Claude Izzo's *Total Chaos* . . . By the time I finished the book, I had replaced the Paris leg of my trip with Marseilles. I'd found Lagavulin, the main character's scotch of choice. (Mine was always Laphroaig.) And a whole lot of interesting jazz . . . The story had leapt out from the book and into my life."—Valla Vakili, CEO, Small Demons

"Like the best American practitioners in the genre, Izzo refrains from any sugarcoating of the city he depicts or the broken and imperfect men and women who people it."—*Publishers Weekly*

"Jean-Claude Izzo's *Total Chaos* is a marvelous noir novel in which passions and feelings are thrown into the narrative mix without reserve and without gratuitousness."—*La Repubblica*

"*Total Chaos* . . . draws from the deep, dark well of noir . . . Izzo's plot is labyrinthine, but his novel is rich, ambitious and passionate, and his sad, loving portrait of his native city is amazing."—*The Washington Post*

TOTAL CHAOS

Jean-Claude Izzo

TOTAL CHAOS

*Translated from the French
by Howard Curtis*

Europa
editions

Europa Editions
214 West 29th Street
New York, N.Y. 10001
www.europaeditions.com
info@europaeditions.com

Translation by Howard Curtis
Original Title: *Total Khéops*
Translation copyright © 2005 by Europa Editions
Eulogy for Jean-Claude Izzo © 2006 by Massimo Carlotto,
translation from the Italian by Michael Reynolds

First published in 1995 in France by Éditions Gallimard

This work has been published thanks to support from
the French Ministry of Culture – Centre National du Livre
Ouvrage publié avec le concours du Ministère
Français chargé de la Culture – Centre National du Livre

Library of Congress Cataloging in Publication Data is available
ISBN 978-1-60945-440-1

Izzo, Jean-Claude
Total Chaos

Book design and cover illustration by Emanuele Ragnisco
www.mekkanografici.com

Prepress by Grafica Punto Print – Rome

Printed in Italy at Arti Grafiche

CONTENTS

EULOGY FOR JEAN-CLAUDE IZZO
by Massimo Carlotto

Recalling the work and the person of Jean-Claude Izzo will forever remain painful for those who knew him. Izzo was first and foremost a good person. It was impossible not to feel warmth for that slight man who always had an attentive, curious look in his eyes and a cigarette in his mouth. I met him in 1995, in Chambery, during the Festival du Premier Roman. Izzo was there to present *Total Chaos* (*Total Khéops*). I bought the book because its author stirred my interest: he seemed a little detached in many of those cultural gatherings, as if faintly annoyed by them, as he was most certainly annoyed by the quality of food and wine offered by the organizers. I read his book traveling between Chambery and Turin, where the Salone del Libro was underway. I found it a superb, innovative book, an exemplar in a genre that was finally starting to establish itself here in Italy. I recommended it to my publishers. And not long after Izzo arrived in Italy. A few sporadic meetings later, I went to Marseilles for a conference. Izzo was not there. He was in hospital. Everyone knew how serious his illness was. Marseilles was rooting for its noirist. Every bookshop in town filled its display windows with Izzo's books. Then, on January 26, Jean-Claude left us. He wasn't even fifty-five. He left us with many fond memories and several extraordinary novels that convincingly delineated the current now known as "Mediterranean Noir."

Autodidact, son of immigrant parents, his father a barman

from Naples, his mother a Spanish seamstress. After lengthy battles as a left-wing journalist, having already written for film and television, and author of numerous essays, Izzo decided to take a stab at noir, penning his Marseilles Trilogy, *Total Chaos*, *Chourmo* and *Solea*. The protagonist: Fabio Montale; a cop.

Montale, son of immigrant parents, like Izzo, and child of the interethnic mix that is Marseilles, defiantly stakes out his ground in the city that gave birth to the *Front National*.[1] In *Solea*, Izzo writes:

> It was good to be in Hassan's bar. There were no barriers of age, sex, skin color, or class among the regulars. We were all friends. Whoever came there to drink a *pastis* sure as hell didn't vote for the *Front National*. And they never had, not once, not like some others I knew. Here, in this bar, every single one of us knew why we were from Marseilles and not some other place, why we lived in Marseilles and not some other place. Friendship mixed with the smell of anise and filled the place. We communicated our feelings for one another with a single look. A look that took in our fathers' exile. It was reassuring. We had nothing to lose. We had already lost everything.

Izzo's writing is political, in the tradition of the French neo-polar novels[2], and the writing of Jean-Patrick Manchette. But compared with Manchette, who does not believe in direct political action inasmuch as he believes it is ineffective and doomed to failure, and who limits himself to using noir as an instrument with which to read reality, Izzo goes further. His

---

[1] The party was founded in 1972 by Jean-Marie Le Pen and is currently led by Marine Le Pen. It is generally considered to be of the far right, although its leaders deny this qualification.

[2] Neo-polar: the 1970s-80s version of the French mystery novel, after the rebirth of the genre following May '68. Often a politically-oriented novel with a social message.

use of the noir genre is not limited simply to description but penetrates deep into the heart of the incongruities, leaving room for sociological reflection and for a return to his generation's collective memory, and above all, gives sense to the present day. Via Montale's inner journey, Izzo declares his inexorable faith in the possibility of transformation, both individual and collective. The point that matters most to Izzo, politically speaking, that is, the point that cannot be abandoned, is the existence of a united culture. From the defeats of yesterday come the losers of today. From this perspective, Montale is an extraordinary figure. Son of marginalization, he joins the police so as to avoid the criminal margins. He abandons his group of childhood friends, a group that embodies multiple ethnic differences, but he will never forget his roots. This becomes a source for his feelings of guilt when faced with his role as cop in a society that is becoming increasingly intolerant. An internal gestation and growth obligates him to leave the police force and to become a loner in search of the justice that is not furnished by the courts. What gets him into trouble is the ethic of solidarity and the desire, common to culturally and ethnically mixed milieus, to find a place and a moment in which he can live peacefully.

On Mediterranean Noir

Solea, the concluding installment in Izzo's Marseilles Trilogy, is flamenco music's backbone, but also a song by Miles Davis. Indeed, music is one of the author's passions. Particularly jazz and the mix of Mediterranean rhythms that characterize contemporary southern European and North African music. In Izzo's writing, however, music does not simply represent rhythm and a source of nostalgia, but also a key to understanding generational differences. Montale contemplates the merits of rap music. He doesn't like it much, but his reflections represent a kind of understanding as to its intrinsic worth:

> I was floored by what it said. The rightness of the intentions behind it. The quality of the lyrics. They sang incessantly about the their friends' lives, whether at home or at the reform school.

With *Solea*, Jean-Claude Izzo gives substance to the political intuition that is the cornerstone of Mediterranean Noir. He understands that the sticking point the movement must face consists in the epochal revolutions that have transformed criminality. Babette Bellini's investigation[1] does not result in the typical affirmation of the Mafia's superiority and organized crime's collusion with higher powers. Izzo defines the outlines of Mediterranean Noir when he introduces into his novel the principal contradiction present in the crime-society dyad: the annual income of transnational criminal organizations worldwide is US$10,000 billion, a sum equal to the GDP of many single developing countries. The need to launder this mountain of dirty money is at the root of the dizzying increase in the corruption of institutions, of police forces. It is also the catalyst for strategic alliances between entrepreneurs, financial policing bodies, politics, and organized crime. The society in which we live is criminal inasmuch as it produces crime and "anti-crime," resulting in an endless spiral in which legal and illegal economies merge in a single model. Call it, if you will, a socio-economic "locomotive," as in the case of northeast Italy.

Mediterranean Noir, in this sense, departs from the existing conception of French Noir, and likewise from the modern police novel. The novel no longer recounts a single "noir" story

---

[1] Babette Bellini: a character in the Marseilles Trilogy. Journalist and activist, friend of Fabio Montale.

in a given place at a given moment but begins with a precise analysis of organized crime.

Another of Izzo's intuitions was his having individuated the Mediterranean as the geographical centre of the universal criminal revolution. There is a rich fabric of alliances in this region between new illegal cultures emerging from the east and from Africa. These alliances are influenced by local realities, which they in turn absorb into themselves. As a result, they possess the means to pursue direct negotiations with established power structures.

This is what Mediterranean Noir means: to tell stories with a wide swath; to recount great transformations; to denounce but at the same time to propose the culture of solidarity as an alternative.

for Sébastien

There is no truth, there are only stories.
JIM HARRISON

PROLOGUE

Rue des Pistoles, twenty years after

All he had was her address. Rue des Pistoles, in the old neighborhood. It was years since he'd last been in Marseilles. But he didn't have a choice. Not now.

It was June 2nd, and it was raining. Despite the rain, the taxi driver refused to turn into the back alleys. He dropped him in front of Montée-des-Accoules. More than a hundred steps to climb and a maze of streets between there and Rue des Pistoles. The ground was littered with garbage sacks spilling their contents. There was a pungent smell on the streets, a mixture of piss, dampness and mildew. The only big change was that even this neighborhood was being redeveloped. Some houses had been demolished, others had had their fronts repainted ocher and pink, with Italian-style green and blue shutters.

Even on Rue des Pistoles, maybe one of the narrowest streets of all, only one side, the side with even-numbered houses, was still standing. The other side had been razed to the ground, as had the houses on Rue Rodillat, and in their place was a parking lot. That was the first thing he saw when he turned the corner from Rue du Refuge. The developers seemed to have taken a breather here. The houses were blackened and dilapidated, eaten away by sewer vegetation.

He was too early, he knew. But he didn't want to go to a bistro and sit drinking one coffee after another, looking at his watch, waiting for a reasonable hour to wake Lole. What he wanted was to have his coffee sitting comfortably in a real apartment. He hadn't done that for months. As soon as she opened the door, he headed straight for the only armchair in the room, as if it was something he'd often done. He stroked the armrest with his hand, sat down slowly, and closed his eyes. It was only afterwards that he finally looked at her. Twenty years after.

She was standing. Bolt upright, as always. Her hands deep in the pockets of a straw-colored bathrobe. The color made her skin look browner than usual and emphasized the blackness of her hair, which she was wearing short now. Her hips may have grown thicker, he wasn't sure. She'd become a woman, but she hadn't changed. Lole, the Gypsy. She'd always been beautiful.

"I could use a coffee."

She nodded. Without a word. Without a smile. He'd dragged her from her sleep. Maybe from a dream in which she and Manu were hotfooting it down to Seville, not a care in the world, their pockets bulging with cash. She probably had that dream every night. But Manu was dead. He'd been dead three months.

He sprawled in the armchair, stretching his legs. Then he lit a cigarette. The best in a long time, no question.

"I was expecting you." Lole handed him a cup. "But not this early."

"I took a night train. A train full of legionnaires. Fewer checks. Safer."

She was staring off into the air. Wherever Manu was.

"Aren't you going to sit down?"

"I drink my coffee standing up."

"You still don't have a phone."

"No."

She smiled. For a moment, the sleep seemed to vanish from her face. She'd dismissed the dream. She looked at him with melancholy eyes. He was tired, and anxious. His old fears. He liked the fact that Lole didn't say much, didn't feel the need to explain. It was a way of getting their lives back in order. Once and for all.

There was a smell of mint in the room. He looked around. It was a big room, with unadorned white walls. No shelves, no knick-knacks or books. Furniture reduced to the bare essentials. A table, chairs, and a sideboard that didn't match, and a single bed over by the window. A door led to another room, the bedroom. From where he was, he could see part of the bed. Rumpled blue sheets. He'd forgotten the night smells. The smell of bodies. Lole's smell. When they made love, her armpits smelled of basil. His eyes were starting to close. He looked again at the bed near the window.

"You could sleep there."

"I'd like to sleep now."

Later, he saw her walking across the room. He didn't know how long he'd slept. To see the time on his watch, he'd have had to move, and he didn't want to move. He preferred to watch Lole coming and going through half-closed eyes.

She'd come out of the bathroom wrapped in a terry towel. She wasn't very big. But she had everything she needed, and in the right places too. And she had gorgeous legs. Then he'd fallen asleep again. His fears had vanished.

It had gotten dark. Lole was wearing a sleeveless black dress. Simple, but it really suited her, hugged her body nicely. He looked at her legs again. This time she felt his eyes on her.

"I'm leaving you the keys. There's coffee heating. I made some more."

She was saying only the most obvious things, avoiding everything else. He sat up, and took out a cigarette, his eyes still on her.

"I'll be back late. Don't wait up for me."

"Are you still a bar girl?"

"Hostess. At the Vamping. I don't want to see you hanging around there."

He remembered the Vamping, overlooking the Catalan beach. Amazing decor, like something out of a Scorsese movie. The singer and the band behind stands full of spangles. Tangos, boleros, cha-chas, mambos, that kind of thing.

"I wasn't planning to."

She shrugged. "I've never been sure what you were planning." Her smile made clear she wasn't expecting a reply. "Are you going to see Fabio?"

He'd thought she'd ask him that. He'd asked himself the same thing. But he'd dismissed the idea. Fabio was a cop. That had drawn a bit of a line under their youth, their friendship. He'd have liked to see Fabio again, though.

"Later. Maybe. How is he?"

"The same. Like us. Like you, like Manu. Lost. None of us have known what to do with our lives. Cop or robber, it makes no difference..."

"You liked him a lot, didn't you?"

"Yes, I liked him a lot."

He felt a pang in his heart. "Have you seen him again?"

"Not in the last three months." She picked up her bag and a white linen jacket. He still hadn't taken his eyes off her.

"Under your pillow," she said at last, and it was clear from her face that his surprise amused her. "The rest is in the sideboard drawer."

And with that, she left. He lifted the pillow. The 9mm was there. He'd sent it to Lole, in an express package, before he left Paris. The subways and railroad stations were swarming with cops. The French Republic had decided it wanted to be whiter than white. Zero immigration. The new French dream. There might be checks, and he didn't want any hassle. Not that kind. Having false papers was bad enough.

The gun. A present from Manu, for his twentieth birthday. Even then, Manu had been a bit crazy. He'd never parted with it, but he'd never used it either. You didn't kill someone like that. Even when you were threatened. That had happened to him a few times, in different places. There was always another solution. That was what he thought. And he was still alive. But today, he needed it. To kill a man.

It was just after eight. The rain had stopped, and the warm air hit him in the face as he left the building. He'd taken a long shower and put on a pair of black cotton pants, a black polo shirt, and a denim jacket. He'd put his mocassins back on, without socks. He turned into Rue du Panier.

This was his neighborhood. He was born here. Rue des Petits-Puits, two streets along from where Pierre Puget was born. His father had lived on Rue de la Charité when he first arrived in France, fleeing poverty and Mussolini. He was twenty, and had two of his brothers in tow. *Nabos*—Neapolitans. Three others had gone to Argentina. They did the jobs the French wouldn't touch. His father was hired as a longshoreman, paid by the centime. "Harbor dogs," they were called—it was meant as an insult. His mother worked packing dates, fourteen hours a day. In the evenings, the *nabos* and the people from the North, the *babis*, met up on the streets. They pulled chairs out in front of their doors, talked through the windows. Just like in Italy. Just like the good old days.

He hadn't recognized his house. That had been redeveloped, too. He'd walked on past. Manu was from Rue Baussenque. A dark, damp building, where his mother, already pregnant with him, moved in with two of her brothers. His father, José Manuel, had been shot by Franco's men. Immigrants, exiles, they all arrived full of hope. By the time Lole appeared on the scene, with her family, Manu and he were already grown up. Sixteen. At least, that's what they told the girls.

Living in the Panier wasn't something you boasted about. Ever since the nineteenth century it had been a neighborhood of sailors and whores. A blight on the city. One big brothel. For the Nazis, who'd dreamed of destroying it, it was a *source of degeneration for the Western world.* His father and mother had lived through the humiliation. Ordered to leave in the middle of the night. January 24th 1943. Twenty thousand people. Finding a wheelbarrow quickly, loading a few possessions. Mistreated by the French gendarmes and mocked by the German soldiers. Pushing the wheelbarrow along the Canebière at daybreak, watched by people on their way to work. At school, the other kids pointed the finger at them. Even working class kids, from Belle de Mai. But not for long. They simply broke their fingers! He and Manu knew their bodies and clothes smelled of mildew. The smell of the neighborhood. The first girl he'd ever kissed had that smell at the back of her throat. But they didn't give a damn. They loved life. They were good looking. And they knew how to fight.

He turned onto Rue du Refuge, to walk back down. Some distance away, six Arab kids, aged between fourteen and seventeen, stood talking, next to a gleaming new moped. They watched him coming, warily. A new face in the neighborhood spelled danger. A cop. An informer. Or the new owner of a renovated building, who'd go to the town hall and complain about the lack of security. The cops would come and check them out. Take them down to the station. Maybe rough them up. Hassle them. When he drew level with the kids, he gave the one who seemed to be the leader a short, sharp look, then walked on. Nobody moved. They'd understood each other.

He crossed Place de Lenche, which was deserted, then walked down toward the harbor. He stopped at the first phone booth. Batisti answered.

"I'm Manu's friend."

"Hi, pal. Come by tomorrow, have a drink. About one, at the Péano. It'll be great to meet. See you, kid."

He hung up. A man of few words, Batisti. No time to tell him he'd rather have gone anywhere but there. Anywhere but the Péano. It was the bar where the painters went. Ambrogiani had showed his first canvases there. Then others had come along, influenced by him. Poor imitations, some of them. But journalists went there, too. From right across the political spectrum. *Le Provençal, La Marseillaise, Agence France Presse, Libération. Pastis* knocked down the barriers between them. At night, they waited till the papers were put to sleep, then went into the back room to listen to jazz. Both Petruccianis had played there, father and son. With Aldo Romano. There'd been so many nights. Nights of trying to figure out what his life was all about. That night, Harry was at the piano.

"All you need to figure out is what you want," Lole said.

"Yeah. And what I want right now is a change of scenery."

Manu had come back with the umpteenth round. After midnight, they stopped counting. Three scotches, doubles. He'd sat down and raised his glass, smiling beneath his moustache.

"Cheers, lovebirds."

"Shut up, you," Lole had said.

He stared at the two of you as if you were strange animals, then turned his back on you and concentrated on the music. Lole was looking at you. You'd emptied your glass. Slowly. Deliberately. Your mind was made up. You were leaving. You stood up and went out, unsteady on your feet. You were leaving. You left. Without saying a word to Manu, the only friend you still had. Without saying a word to Lole, who'd just turned twenty. Who you loved. Who you both loved. Cairo, Djibouti, Aden, Harar. The itinerary of an eternal adolescent. That was before you lost your innocence. From Argentina to Mexico. Ending up in Asia, to get rid of your remaining illusions. And an international arrest warrant on your ass, for trafficking in works of art.

You were back in Marseilles because of Manu. To take out the son of a bitch who'd killed him. He'd been coming out of Chez Félix, a bistrot on Rue Caisserie where he liked to have lunch. Lole was waiting for him in Madrid, at her mother's place. He was about to come into a tidy bit of cash. For a break-in that had gone without a hitch, at a big Marseilles lawyer's, Eric Brunel, on Boulevard Longchamp. They'd decided to go to Seville. To forget Marseilles and the hard times.

You weren't after the guy who'd whacked Manu. A hitman, for sure. Cold and anonymous. Someone from Lyons, or Milan. Someone you wouldn't find. The guy you were after was the scumbag who'd ordered the hit. Who'd wanted Manu killed. You didn't want to know why. You didn't need any reasons. Not a single one. Anyone attacked Manu, it was like they'd attacked you.

The sun woke him. Nine o'clock. He lay there on his back, and smoked his first cigarette. He hadn't slept so deeply in months. He always dreamed that he was sleeping somewhere other than where he was. A brothel in Harar. A Tijuana jail. On the Rome-Paris express. Anywhere. But always somewhere else. During the night, he'd dreamed he was sleeping at Lole's place. And that's where he really was. It was as if he'd come home. He smiled. He'd barely heard her come back and close the door of her bedroom. She was sleeping in her blue sheets, rebuilding her broken dream. There was still a piece missing. Manu. Unless it was him. But he'd long ago rejected that idea. That would have been to put himself in too good a light. Twenty years was a hell of a long time to mourn.

He stood up, made coffee, and took a shower. The water was hot. He felt much better. He closed his eyes, and imagined

Lole coming to join him. Just like before. Clinging to his body. Her pussy against his dick. Her hands gliding over his back, his buttocks. He started to get a hard-on. He turned on the cold water, and screamed.

Lole put on a record. *Pura salsa.* One of Azuquita's first recordings. Her tastes hadn't changed. He attempted a few dance steps, which made her smile. She moved forward to kiss him. As she did so, he caught a glimpse of her breasts. Like pears waiting to be picked. He didn't look away quickly enough. Their eyes met. She froze, pulled the belt of her bathrobe tighter, and went into the kitchen. He felt wretched. An eternity passed. She came back with two cups of coffee.

"A guy asked after you last night. Wanted to know if you were around. A friend of yours. Malabe. Frankie Malabe."

He didn't know any Malabe. A cop? More likely an informer. He didn't like them approaching Lole. But at the same time it reassured him. The Customs cops knew he was back in France, but not where. Not yet. They were angling for leads. He still needed a bit of time. Two days maybe. Everything depended on what Batisti had to sell.

"Why are you here?"

He picked up his jacket. Don't answer, he told himself. Don't get involved in a question and answer session. He wouldn't be able to lie to her, and he wouldn't be able to tell her what he was going to do. Not now. But he had to do it. Just as, one day, he'd had to leave. He'd never been able to answer her questions. There were no answers, only questions. That was the only thing he'd learned in life. It wasn't much, but it was more certain than believing in God.

"Forget I asked." Behind him, she opened the door. "Not asking questions has never gotten me anywhere."

The two-storey parking garage on Cours d'Estienne d'Orves

had finally been demolished, and what had once been the prison canal was now a lovely square. The houses had been restored, the fronts repainted, the ground paved. An Italian style square. The bars and restaurants all had terraces, with white tables and parasols. People wanted to be seen, just like in Italy. The only thing missing was elegance. The Péano also had its terrace, which was already full. Young people mostly. Very clean-cut. The interior had been refurbished. The decor was hip but cold. The paintings had been replaced by crappy reproductions. But he almost preferred it this way. It helped him keep the memories at arm's length.

He sat down at the bar and ordered a *pastis*. In the room, there was a couple who looked to him like a hooker and her pimp. He might be wrong, of course. Although they were talking in low voices, their discussion seemed rather animated. He leaned an elbow on the brand new zinc counter and watched the front door.

The minutes passed. Nobody came in. He ordered another *pastis*. He heard the words "Son of a bitch!" followed by a sharp sound. Eyes turned to the couple. Silence. The woman ran out. The man stood up, left a fifty-franc bill, and went out after her.

On the terrace, a man folded the newspaper he'd been reading. He was in his sixties. A sailor's cap on his head. Blue cotton pants, a white short-sleeved shirt over the pants. Blue espadrilles. He stood up and came toward him. Batisti.

He spent the afternoon staking out the place. Monsieur Charles, as he was known in the underworld, lived in one of the opulent villas overlooking the Corniche. Amazing villas, some with pinnacles, others with columns. Gardens full of palms, oleanders and fig trees. After the Roucas Blanc, the road winds across the little hill, a crisscross of lanes, some of them barely tarred. He had taken the bus, a no. 55, as far as

Place des Pilotes, at the top of the last slope. Then he'd continued on foot.

He could see out over the harbor. The whole sweep of it from L'Estaque to Pointe-Rouge, with the Frioul islands and the Château d'If. Marseilles in Cinemascope. Beautiful. He started on the downward slope, facing the sea. He was only two villas away from Zucca's villa. He looked at his watch. Four fifty-eight. The gates of the villa opened. A black Mercedes appeared, and parked. He walked past the villa, and the Mercedes, and continued as far as Rue des Espérettes, which cuts across the Roucas Blanc. He crossed the street. Another ten paces, and he'd reach the bus stop. According to the schedules, the 55 passed at 5:05. He leaned against the stop, looked at his watch, and waited.

The Mercedes reversed along the curb, and stopped. Two men inside, including the driver. Zucca appeared. He must have been about seventy. Elegantly dressed, like all these old gangsters. He even had a straw hat, and a white poodle on a leash. Preceded by the dog, he walked down as far as the crossing on Rue des Espérettes. He stopped. The bus was coming. Zucca crossed to the shady side of the street, then came down the Roucas Blanc. He passed the bus stop. The Mercedes set off, at a snail's pace.

Batisti's information had been worth the fifty thousand francs he'd paid. It was all there in writing, without a single detail missing. Zucca took the same walk every day, except Sunday, when his family visited with him. At six o'clock, the Mercedes drove him back to the villa. But Batisti didn't know why Zucca had gone after Manu. He'd gotten no farther toward understanding that. There had to be a connection with the break-in at the lawyer's. That was what he was starting to think. But the truth was, he didn't give a damn. All he was interested in was Zucca. Monsieur Charles.

He hated these old gangsters. On intimate terms with the cops and the judges. Never done time. Thought they were better than anyone else. Zucca had a face like Brando in *The Godfather*. They all had faces like that. Here, in Palermo, in Chicago. Everywhere you went. And now he had one of them in his sights. He was going to take one of them out. For friendship's sake. And to give vent to his hatred.

He was looking through Lole's things. The chest, the closets. He'd come back slightly drunk. He wasn't searching for anything in particular, just looking, thinking maybe he'd uncover a secret. About Lole, about Manu. But there was nothing to uncover. Life had slipped through their fingers, faster than money.

In a drawer, he found a whole bunch of photos. That was all they had left. He was disappointed. He almost threw everything in the trashcan. But there were these three photos. The same photo taken three times. Same time, same place. Manu and him. Lole and Manu. Lole and him. It was at the end of the big pier, behind the commercial port. To get there, they'd had to slip past the guards. We were good at that, he thought. Behind them, the city. In the background, the islands. The three of you came out of the water, breathless and happy. You feasted your eyes on boats leaving in the setting sun. Lole read aloud from *Exile* by Saint-John Perse. *The wind's militias in the sands of exile.* On the way back, you took Lole's hand. You dared to do that. Manu never had.

That night, you left Manu at the Bar du Lenche. Everything had turned upside down. No more laughter. None of you had spoken. You'd all drunk *pastis* in embarrassed silence. Desire had distanced you from Manu. The next day, you had to go pick him up from the station house. He'd spent the night there. For starting a fight with two legionnaires. His right eye wouldn't open. He had a cut lip. Bruises everywhere.

"I got two of them! I really did!"

Lole kissed him on the forehead. He hugged her and started sobbing.

"Fuck," he said. "This is hard."

And he fell asleep, just like that, on Lole's lap.

Lole woke him at ten o'clock. He'd slept soundly, but his tongue felt furred. The smell of coffee pervaded the room. Lole sat down on the edge of the bed. Her hand brushed his shoulder. Her lips rested on his forehead, then on his lips. A furtive, tender kiss. If happiness existed, he'd just come close to it.

"I'd forgotten."

"If that's true, get out of here right now!"

She handed him a cup of coffee, and stood up to get hers. She was smiling and happy. As if the sadness hadn't yet reawakened.

"You don't want to sit down. Just like before."

"I prefer—"

"To have your coffee standing up, I know."

She smiled again. He couldn't get enough of her smile, her mouth. He clung to her eyes. They shone the way they had that night. You'd taken off her T-shirt, then your shirt. You'd pressed your bellies together and stayed like that without talking. Just breathing. Her eyes on you all the time.

"Don't ever leave me."

You'd promised.

But you'd left. Manu had stayed. And Lole had waited. But maybe Manu had stayed because someone needed to take care of Lole. And Lole hadn't followed you, because she'd thought it was unfair to abandon Manu. He'd started to think these things, since Manu died. Knowing he had to come back. And here he was. Marseilles had caught in his throat again. With Lole as an aftertaste.

Lole's eyes were shining more brightly. She was holding back the tears. She knew that something was going down. And that whatever it was would change her life. She'd had a premonition after Manu's funeral, during the hours she'd spent with Fabio. She could sense it now. She was good at sensing when something was going to happen. But she wouldn't say anything. It was up to him to speak.

He picked up the brown envelope he'd left beside the bed. "This is a ticket for Paris. The high speed train, 1:54 today. This is a checkroom ticket. The Gare de Lyon. Another one, for the Gare Montparnasse. Two suitcases to be collected. In each one, there's a hundred thousand francs, hidden under a pile of old clothes. This postcard is from a very good restaurant at Port-Mer, near Cancale in Brittany. On the back, Marine's number. Get in touch with her. She can get you anything you want. Whatever she does for you, don't haggle over the price. I've booked a room for you at the Hotel des Marronniers, on Rue Jacob. Five nights, in your name. There'll be a letter for you at the reception desk."

She hadn't moved. She was frozen. Her eyes had gradually emptied of all expression. "Don't I get a word in edgewise?"

"No."

"Is that all you have to say?"

What he had to say would have taken ages, but he could have summed it up in a couple of sentences. I'm sorry. I love you. But they didn't have time for that anymore. Or rather, time had overtaken them. The future was behind them. Ahead, nothing but memories and regrets. He looked up at her, with as much detachment as he could muster.

"Close your bank account. Destroy your credit card. And your checkbook. Change identity as soon as possible. Marine will arrange that for you."

"And you?" she said with difficulty.

"I'll call you tomorrow morning."

He looked at his watch, and stood up. He passed close to her, averting his gaze, and went into the bathroom and locked the door behind him. He didn't want Lole to join him in the shower. He looked at his face in the mirror. He didn't like what he saw. He felt old. He'd forgotten how to smile. Bitter creases had appeared at the corners of his mouth, and they wouldn't go away. He wasn't yet forty-five and today was going to be the worst day of his life.

He heard the first guitar chord of *Entre dos aguas*. Paco de Lucia. Lole had turned the volume up. She was standing in front of the stereo with her arms folded, smoking a cigarette.

"You're getting nostalgic."

"Screw you."

He took the gun, loaded it, put on the safety, and wedged it between his shirt and the back of his pants. She'd turned around and was watching his every movement.

"Hurry up. I wouldn't want you to miss that train."

"What are you going to do?"

"Set the cat among the pigeons. I think."

The moped's engine was idling. It hadn't misfired once. Four fifty-one. Rue des Espérettes, just down the hill from Zucca's villa. It was hot. Sweat ran down his back. He wanted it to be over with.

He'd spent all morning looking for the Arab kids. They constantly changed streets. That was their rule. It probably served no purpose, but he supposed they had their reasons. He'd found them on Rue Fontaine-de-Caylus, which had become a square, with trees and benches. They were the only people there. Nobody from the neighborhood ever sat in the square. They preferred to stay by their front doors. The older kids were sitting on the steps of a house, while the younger ones were standing, the moped beside them. When the leader saw him coming, he'd stood up, and the others had moved aside.

"I need the bike. For the afternoon. Till six o'clock. Two thousand, cash."

He looked anxiously around. He'd counted on there being no one to catch the bus. If someone showed up, he'd let it go. If any passenger wanted to get off the bus, he wouldn't know until it was too late, but that was a risk he was prepared to take. Then he told himself that if he took that risk, he might as well take the other. He started calculating. The bus stops. The door opens. The passenger gets on. The bus starts off again. Four minutes. No, yesterday, it had taken only three minutes. But let's say four. Zucca would have crossed by then. No, he would have seen the moped and let it pass. He emptied his head of all thoughts, counting the minutes over and over. Yes, it was possible. But after that, the shooting would start. Four fifty-nine.

He lowered the visor on his helmet, and gripped the gun firmly. His hands were dry. He moved forward slowly, hugging the curb, his left hand tight on the handlebar. The poodle appeared, followed by Zucca. He felt suddenly cold inside. Zucca saw him coming. He stopped at the edge of the side-walk, holding back the dog. By the time he realized, it was too late. His mouth formed a circle, but no sound emerged. His eyes widened with fear. If he'd crapped in his pants, that would have been enough. He pressed the trigger. Disgusted with himself, with Zucca, with all men, all mankind. He emptied the clip into the guy's chest.

In front of the villa, the Mercedes shot forward. To his right, the bus was coming. It passed the stop, without slowing down. He accelerated, cut across the path of the bus, and went around it. He almost had to mount the sidewalk, but he got through.

The bus came to an abrupt halt, stopping the Mercedes from entering the street. He rode flat out, turning left, then left again, onto Chemin du Souvenir, then Rue des Roses. On Rue des Bois-Sacrés, he threw the gun into a manhole. A few minutes later, he was riding calmly along Rue d'Endoume.

It was only then that he started thinking about Lole. You stood facing each other. You'd both gone beyond words. You wanted her belly against yours. You wanted the taste of her body. The smell. Mint and basil. But there were too many years between you, and too much silence. And Manu. Dead, yet still so alive. You were standing two feet apart. You could have put out your hand and taken her by the waist and drawn her to you. She could have untied the belt of her bathrobe and dazzled you with the beauty of her body. You'd have made love, violently, with unassuaged desire. But what would have happened afterwards? You'd have had to find words. Words that didn't exist. You'd have lost her forever. So you left. Without saying goodbye. Without a kiss. For the second time.

He was shaking. He pulled up outside the first bistro he came to on Boulevard de La Corderie. Like an automaton, he locked the moped and took off his helmet. He had a cognac. He felt the burning sensation spread through him. The cold flowed out of his body. He began to sweat. He rushed to the toilets and threw up. Threw up all he'd done, all he'd thought. Threw up the man that he was. The man who'd abandoned Manu and hadn't had the courage to love Lole. He'd drifted for so long. Too long. He knew that the worst was yet to come. By the second cognac, he'd stopped shaking. He'd recovered.

He parked at Fontaine-de-Caylus. It was 6:20, but the Arab kids weren't there, which surprised him. He took off his helmet and hooked it on the handlebars, but didn't cut the engine. The youngest of the Arabs appeared, kicking a ball. He ran up to him.

"Get out of here, the pigs are coming. They've been watching your girlfriend's house."

He set off, back up the alley. They must be watching all the back streets. Montée des Accoules, Traverse des Repenties. Place de Lenche, of course. He'd forgotten to ask Lole if Frankie Malabe had come back. He might have a chance if he took Rue des Cartiers, right up at the top. He left the moped and ran down the steps. There were two of them, two young plainclothes cops, at the bottom of the steps.

"Police!"

He heard the siren, higher up the street. He was trapped. Car doors slammed. They were here. Behind his back.

"Don't move!"

He did what he had to do. He plunged his hand inside his jacket. He had to get it over with. No more running. He was here. He was home. In his own neighborhood. It might as well be here. Might as well end in Marseilles. He turned toward the two young cops. The ones behind him couldn't see that he was unarmed. The first bullet ripped open his back. His lung exploded. He didn't feel the other two bullets.

1.

IN WHICH EVEN TO LOSE YOU HAVE TO KNOW HOW TO FIGHT

I crouched by the body. Pierre Ugolini. Ugo. I'd only just arrived on the scene. Too late. My colleagues had been playing cowboys. Shoot to kill: that was their basic rule. They followed the General Custer principle that the only good Indian was a dead Indian. And in Marseilles, everyone—or almost everyone—was an Indian.

The Ugolini file had landed on the wrong desk. Captain Auch's desk. In a few years, his team had gained an evil reputation, but it had proved itself. People turned a blind eye to its occasional mistakes. Cracking down on organized crime was a priority in Marseilles. The second priority was maintaining order in the north of the city, where the suburbs were full of immigrants and the housing projects had become no-go areas. That was my job. But I wasn't allowed any mistakes.

Ugo was a childhood friend. Like Manu. He was a friend, even though he and I hadn't talked in twenty years. Ugo dying so soon after Manu cast a shadow over my past. It was something I'd tried to avoid. But I'd gone about it the wrong way.

When I found out that Auch had been given the job of investigating why Ugo was in Marseilles, I'd put one of my informers on the case. Frankie Malabe. I trusted him. If Ugo came to Marseilles, it was obvious he'd go to Lole's, in spite of all the time that had passed. And I'd been sure Ugo would come. Because of Manu, and because of Lole. Friendship has its rules, you can't avoid them. I'd been expecting Ugo for three months. Because I too thought that Manu's death couldn't be left open. There had to be an explanation. There had to be a culprit. Justice had to be done. I wanted to see Ugo, to talk about that. About justice. I was a cop and he was a criminal, but I wanted to stop him doing anything stupid. To protect him from Auch. But to find Ugo, I had to see Lole again, and since Manu's death, I'd lost track of her.

Frankie Malabe had been efficient. He'd hung out at the Vamping, spoken to Lole. But he hadn't passed his information on to me until a day after he'd offered it to Auch. Auch had the power, and he was tough. The informers were scared of him. And being the scumbags they were, they tended to look after their own interests. I should have known that.

My other mistake had been not going to see Lole myself the other evening. I can be a bit of a coward sometimes. I couldn't make up my mind to just show up at the Vamping after three months. Three months from the night following Manu's death. Maybe Lole wouldn't even have spoken to me. Or maybe, seeing me, she'd have gotten the message. And then Ugo would have gotten it, too.

Ugo. He stared up at me with his dead eyes, a smile on his lips. I closed his eyelids. The smile remained. It wouldn't go away now.

I stood up. There was a lot of bustle around me. Orlandi stepped forward to take photos. I looked down at Ugo's body. His hand was open. The Smith and Wesson lay on the step, like an extension of the hand. Orlandi snapped him. What had really happened? Was he getting ready to shoot? Had there been the usual warnings? I'd never know. Or maybe one day in hell, when I met Ugo again. Because the only witnesses would be those chosen by Auch. The people in the neighborhood would keep shtum. Their word wasn't worth anything. I turned away. Auch had just made his appearance. He walked up to me.

"I'm sorry, Fabio. About your friend."

"Go fuck yourself."

I went back up Rue des Cartiers. I passed Morvan, the team's crack shot. A face like Lee Marvin. A killer's face, not a cop's. I put all the hatred I had into the look I gave him. He didn't turn away. For him, I didn't exist. I was a nobody. Just a neighborhood cop.

At the top of the street, a group of Arab kids stood watching the scene.

"Get lost, boys."

They looked at each other, then at the oldest in the gang, then at the moped lying on the ground behind them. The moped abandoned by Ugo. When he was being chased, I'd been on the terrace of the Bar du Refuge, watching Lole's apartment building. I'd finally decided to make a move. Too much time had passed. The risks were getting greater every day. There was no one in the apartment. But I was ready to wait for Lole or Ugo for as long as it took. Ugo had passed just a few yards from me.

"What's your name?"

"Djamel."

"Is that your moped?"

He didn't reply.

"Pick it up and get out of here. While they're still busy."

Nobody moved. Djamel was looking at me, puzzled.

"Clean it, and then hide it for a few days. Do you understand?"

I turned my back on them and walked toward my car. I didn't look back. I lit a cigarette, a Winston, then threw it away. It tasted disgusting. For a month, I'd been trying to change from Gauloises to Virginia cigarettes, to alleviate my cough. In the rear-view mirror, I made sure the moped and the kids were gone. I closed my eyes. I wanted to cry.

Back at the station house, I was told about Zucca. And the killer on the moped. Zucca hadn't been an underworld boss, but he had been a vital linchpin, with all the bosses dead or in prison or on the run. Zucca's death was good news for us, the cops. For Auch, anyhow. I immediately made the connection with Ugo. But I didn't tell anyone. What difference did it make? Manu was dead. Ugo was dead. And Zucca wasn't worth shedding any tears over.

The ferry for Ajaccio was leaving the harbor basin. The *Monte d'Oro*. The only advantage of my shabby office in the station house was that I had a window that looked out on the port of La Joliette. The ferries were almost the only activity left in the port. Ferries for Ajaccio, Bastia, Algiers. A few liners too, doing senior citizen cruises. But there was also still quite a bit of freight. Even now, Marseilles was the third largest port in Europe. Far ahead of its nearest rival, Genoa. The racks of bananas and pineapples from the Ivory Coast piled at the end of the Léon Gousset pier seemed to guarantee Marseilles' future. A last hope.

The harbor had attracted serious interest from property developers. Two hundred hectares to build on, a sizeable fortune. They could easily envisage transferring the port to Fos and building a new Marseilles by the sea. They already had the architects, and the plans were progressing well. But I couldn't imagine Marseilles without its harbor basins, or its old fashioned boathouses without boats. I liked boats. Real boats, big ones. I liked to watch them setting sail. I always felt a twinge of sorrow. The *Ville de Naples* was leaving port, all lit up. I was on the pier, in tears. On board, my cousin Sandra. With her parents and her brothers, they'd stopped off for two days in Marseilles, and now they were leaving again, for Buenos Aires. I was in love with Sandra. I was nine years old. I'd never seen her again. She'd never written me. Fortunately, she wasn't my only cousin.

The ferry had turned into the Grande Joliette basin. It glided behind the cathedral of La Major. The setting sun gave the gray, grime-incrusted stone a degree of warmth. At such times, La Major, with its Byzantine curves, looked almost beautiful. Afterwards, it reverted to being what it had always been: a pompous piece of Second Empire crap. I watched the ferry move slowly past the Sainte-Marie sea wall and head for the open sea. For tourists who'd spent a day, maybe a night, in transit in Marseilles, it was the start of the crossing. By tomorrow morning, they'd be on the Île de Beauté. They'd remember a few things about Marseilles. The Vieux Port. Notre Dame de la Garde, which dominates it. The Corniche, maybe. And the Pharo Palace, which they could see now to their left.

Marseilles isn't a city for tourists. There's nothing to see. Its beauty can't be photographed. It can only be shared. It's a place where you have to take sides, be passionately for or against. Only then can you see what there is to see. And you realize, too late, that you're in the middle of a tragedy. An ancient tragedy in which the hero is death. In Marseilles, even to lose you have to know how to fight.

The ferry was now just a dark patch in the setting sun. I was too much of a cop to take things at face value. There was a lot I couldn't figure out. Who'd put Ugo on to Zucca so quickly? Had Zucca really ordered the hit on Manu? Why? And why hadn't Auch collared Ugo last night? Or this morning? And where was Lole at the time?

Lole. Like Manu and Ugo, I hadn't noticed her growing up, becoming a woman. Then, like them, I'd fallen in love with her. But I had no claims on her. I wasn't from the Panier. I was born there, but when I was two years old, my parents moved to the

Capelette, a wop neighborhood. The most you could hope for—and it was a lot—was to be good friends with Lole. Where I'd really been lucky was in being friends with Manu and Ugo.

At that time, I still had family in the neighborhood, on Rue des Cordelles. Three cousins: two boys and a girl. The girl's name was Angèle. Gélou, we called her. She was grown up. Almost seventeen. She often came to our house. She helped my mother, who was already bedridden most of the time. Afterwards, I had to walk her home. It wasn't really dangerous in those days, but Gélou didn't like to go home on her own. And I liked to walk with her. She was beautiful, and I felt proud when she gave me her arm. The problem started when we reached the Accoules. I didn't like to go into the neighborhood. It was dirty, and it stank. I felt ashamed. Most of all, I was scared stiff. Not when I was with her, but when I walked back alone. Gélou knew that, and it amused her. I didn't dare ask my brothers to walk back with me. I'd set off at a near run, eyes down. There were often boys my age at the corner of Rue du Panier and Rue des Muettes. I'd hear them laughing as I passed. Sometimes they whistled at me, as if I was a girl.

One evening, at the end of summer, Gélou and I were coming up Rue des Petits-Moulins. Arm in arm, like lovers. Her breast brushed the back of my hand. It drove me wild. I was happy. Then I saw them, the two of them. I'd already passed them several times. I guessed we were the same age. Fourteen. They were coming toward us, smiling maliciously. Gélou tightened her grip on my arm, and I felt the warmth of her breast on my hand.

They stepped aside as we passed. The taller one on Gélou's side, the shorter one on my side. He shoved me with his shoulder, and laughed uproariously. I let go of Gélou's arm.

"Hey! Spic!"

He turned in surprise. I punched him in the stomach, and

he bent double. Then I pulled him back up with a left full in the face. An uncle of mine had taught me a bit of boxing, but I was fighting for the first time. The boy was on the ground now, trying to get his breath back. The other one hadn't moved. Neither had Gélou. She was watching, scared, but delighted too, I think.

I walked up to him. "So, spic, had enough?" I said, threateningly.

"You shouldn't call him that," the other one said, behind me.

"What are you? A wop?"

"What's it to you?"

I felt the ground disappear beneath my feet. From where he lay, he'd tripped me up. I found myself on my back. He threw himself on me. I saw that his lip was cut, and he was bleeding. We rolled over. The smell of piss and shit filled my nostrils. I wanted to cry. I wanted to stop fighting and lay my head on Gélou's breasts. Then I felt myself being pulled violently to my feet and slapped on the head. A man was separating us, calling us punks, telling us we'd end up in the joint. I didn't see them again until September, when we found ourselves in the same school, on Rue des Remparts, doing vocational classes. Ugo came up to me and shook my hand, then Manu did the same. We talked about Gélou. They both thought she was the most beautiful girl in the neighborhood.

It was after midnight by the time I got back home. I lived outside Marseilles, at Les Goudes, the last little harbor town but one before the string of rocky inlets known as the *calanques*. You go along the Corniche, as far as the Roucas Blanc beach, then follow the coast. La Vieille Chappelle. La Pointe Rouge. La Campagne Pastrée. La Grotte-Roland. A whole bunch of neighborhoods that were still like villages. Then La

Madrague de Montredon. That, seemingly, is where Marseilles stops. After that, there's a narrow, winding road, cut into the white rock, overlooking the sea. At the end of it, sheltered by arid hills, the harbor of Les Goudes. Less than a mile past there, the road stops. At Callelonge, Impasse des Muets. Beyond that, the *calanques*: Sormiou, Morgiou, Sugitton, En-Vau. Wonders, every one of them. You won't find anything like them anywhere else along the coast. The only way to reach them is on foot, or by boat, which is a good thing. Eventually, you come to the port of Cassis, and the tourists reappear.

Like almost all the houses here, my house is a one-storey cottage, built of bricks, wood and a few tiles. It's on the rocks, overlooking the sea. Two rooms. A small bedroom and a big dining room cum kitchen, simply furnished, with odds and ends. A branch of Emmaus. My boat was moored at the bottom of a flight of eight steps. A fisherman's boat, with a pointed stern, that I'd bought from my neighbor Honorine. I'd inherited the house from my parents. It was their only possession. And I was their only son.

The whole family used to come here on Saturdays. There'd be big plates of pasta in sauce, with headless larks and meatballs cooked in the same sauce. The smells of tomatoes, basil, thyme, and bay filled the rooms. Bottles of rosé wine did the rounds amid much laughter. The meals always finished with songs, songs by Marino Marini and Renato Carosone first, then Neapolitan songs. The last was always *Santa Lucia*, sung by my father.

Afterwards, the men would start playing *belote*. They'd play all night long, until one of them lost his temper and threw down the cards. "Put the leeches on him!" someone would cry. And the laughter would start all over again. There were mattresses on the floor. We shared the beds. We children all slept in the same bed, crosswise. I'd rest my head on Gélou's bur-

geoning breasts and fall asleep happy. Like a child, but with
adult dreams.

My mother's death put an end to the parties. My father never
again set foot in Les Goudes. Even thirty years ago, coming to
Les Goudes was quite an expedition. You had to take the 19, at
Place de la Prefecture, on the corner of Rue Armeny, and travel as far as La Madrague de Montredon. From there, you continued in an old bus whose driver had long since passed retirement age. Manu, Ugo and I started to go there when we were
about sixteen. We never took girls there. It was just for us. Our
hideout. We took all our treasures to the house. Books, record
albums. We were inventing the world. A world in our own
image, to match our own strengths. We'd spend whole days
reading Ulysses' adventures to each other. Then, when night
fell, sitting silent on the rocks, we'd dream of mermaids with
beautiful hair singing 'among the black rocks all streaming with
white foam.' And we cursed those who'd killed the mermaids.

Our taste for books came from Antonin, an old second-hand
bookseller, an anarchist, whose shop was on Cours Julien. We'd
cut classes to go see him. He'd tell us stories of adventurers and
pirates. The Caribbean. The Red Sea. The South Seas...
Sometimes, he's stop, grab a book, and read us a passage. As if
to prove that what he was telling us was true. Then he'd give it
to us as a present. The first one was Conrad's *Lord Jim*.

That was where we also listened to Ray Charles for the first
time. On Gélou's old Teppaz. It was a 45 of the Newport concert. *What'd I Say* and *I Got a Woman*. Fantastic. We played the
record over and over again, at full volume, until Honorine finally cracked.

"My God, you're going to drive us crazy!" she cried from
her terrace, her fists on her fat hips. She threatened to complain to my father. I knew perfectly well she hadn't seen him
since my mother died, but she was so furious, we believed she

was quite capable of doing it. That calmed us down. And anyhow, we liked Honorine. She always worried about us. She'd
come over to see 'if we needed anything.'

"Do your parents know where you are?"

"Of course," I'd reply.

"And didn't they make you a picnic?"

"They're too poor."

We'd burst out laughing. She'd smile, shrug her shoulders,
and leave. She understood us. She was like our mother, and we
were the children she'd never had. Then she'd come back with
a snack. Or fish soup, when we slept over on Saturday night.
The fish was caught by her husband Toinou. Sometimes, he'd
take us out in his boat. Each of us in turn. He was the one who
gave me my taste for fishing. And now, I had his boat, the
Trémolino, beneath my window.

We came regularly to Les Goudes until the army separated
us. We were together at first, during training. At Toulon, then
at Fréjus, in the Colonial Army, among corporals with scars
and medals up to their ears. Survivors of Indochina and
Algeria who were still spoiling for a fight. Manu had stayed in
Fréjus, Ugo left for Nouméa, and I left for Djibouti. After that,
we weren't the same anymore. We'd become men.
Disillusioned and cynical. Slightly bitter too. We had nothing.
We hadn't even learned a trade. No future. Nothing but life.
But a life without a future is worse than no life at all.

We soon got tired of doing shitty little jobs. One morning,
we went to see a Greek guy named Kouros, who owned a con-
struction business in the Huveaune valley, on the road to
Aubagne. We weren't very keen, but this was one of those
times when we had to make up our losses by working. The
night before, we'd blown all our funds in a poker game. We
had to get up early, take a bus, fake our way out of paying,
scrounge smokes from a guy on the street. A real nightmare of

a morning. The Greek offered us 142 francs and 57 centimes a week. Manu went white. It wasn't so much the pitiful wage he couldn't swallow, it was the 57 centimes.

"Are you sure about the 57 centimes, Monsieur Kouros?"

The boss looked at Manu as if he was an idiot, then at Ugo and me. We knew our Manu. It was obvious we'd gotten off to a bad start.

"It isn't 56 or 58, is it? It's really 57? 57 centimes?"

Kouros confirmed that. He really didn't get it. He thought it was a good wage. 142 francs 57 centimes. Manu landed him a well-placed punch. Kouros fell off his chair. The secretary gave a cry, then started screaming. Some guys charged into the office. A brawl. It was a good thing the cops arrived when they did, because the fight wasn't going our way. That was it, we told each other that night, we had to get serious. We had to start working for ourselves. Maybe we could reopen Antonin's shop. But to do that, we needed money. So we made up our minds. We'd hold up an all-night drugstore. Or a tobacco shop. Or a gas station. That was the only way we could put a bit of money together. We'd done plenty of shoplifting. Books from Tacussel on the Canebière, records from Raphaël's on Rue Montgrand, clothes from the Magasin Général or the Dames de France on Rue Saint-Ferréol. It was like a game. But we didn't know anything about holdups. Not yet. We'd soon learn. We spent days working out how to do it, searching for the ideal place.

One evening, we went to Les Goudes for Ugo's twentieth birthday. Miles Davis was playing *Rouge*. Manu took a package out of his bag and put it on the table in front of Ugo.

"Your present."

A 9mm automatic.

"Where did you get it?"

Ugo looked at the gun, but didn't dare touch it. Manu

laughed, then put his hand back inside his bag and took out another gun. A Beretta 7.65.

"Now we're all set." He looked at Ugo, then at me. "I could only get two. But that's no problem. You'll do the driving. When we go in, you stay in the car, be our lookout. There's no risk. The place is deserted after eight o'clock. The guy's an old man. And he's alone."

It was a drugstore on Rue des Trois-Mages, a side street not far from the Canebière. I was at the wheel of a Peugeot 204 that I'd stolen that morning on Rue Saint-Jacques, in the rich part of town. Manu and Ugo had rammed sailor's bonnets down over their ears and had put scarves over their noses. They leaped out of the car, just like they'd seen in the movies. First the old guy put his hands up, then he opened the cash register. Ugo collected the money while Manu was threatening the guy with the Beretta. Half an hour later, we were drinking at the Péano. On us, guys! Drinks all round! We'd bagged one thousand seven hundred francs. Not bad for the period. The equivalent of two months working for Kouros, including the centimes. It was as easy as that.

Soon, our pockets were full. Money was no object, and we blew it on girls, cars and parties. We'd end our nights with the gypsies in L'Estaque, drinking and listening to them play. Relatives of Lole and her sisters, Zina and Kali. Lole often went out with her sisters now. She'd just turned sixteen. She'd stay in a corner, huddled and silent, with a vacant air. Hardly eating, and drinking only milk.

We soon forgot about Antonin's shop. We told each other we'd see about that later, that it was OK to have a good time for a while. And anyway, maybe the shop wasn't such a good idea after all. What kind of money would we make? Not much, seeing how poor Antonin had ended up. Maybe a bar would be better. Or a night club. I went along with it. Gas stations, tobacco shops, drugstores. We covered the region, from Aix to Les Martigues. We once even went as far as Salon-de-Provence. And still I went along with it. But I was becoming less enthusiastic. It was like playing in a rigged poker game.

One evening, we did another drugstore. On the corner of Place Sadi-Carnot and Rue Mery, not far from the Vieux Port. The druggist made a move. An alarm went off. There was a gunshot. From the car, I saw the guy fall to the floor.

Manu got into the back seat. "Step on it," he said.

I drove to Place du Mazeau. I thought I could hear police sirens not far behind us. On the right, the Panier. No streets, just steps. On my left, Rue de la Guirlande, a one-way street. I turned onto Rue Caisserie, then Rue Saint-Laurent.

"Are you crazy or what? It's a rat trap this way."

"You're the one who's crazy! Why did you shoot him?"

I stopped the car on Impasse Belle-Marinière. I pointed to the steps between the new apartment buildings.

"We split that way. On foot." Ugo hadn't yet said anything. "OK, Ugo?"

"There must be five thousand. It's our best job ever."

Manu left via Rue des Martégales, Ugo by Avenue Saint-Jean, me by Rue de la Loge. But I didn't join them at the Péano as usual. I went home, and vomited. Then I began drinking. Drinking and sobbing. Looking at the city from the balcony. I could hear my father snoring. He'd worked hard all his life, and suffered a lot, but I didn't think I'd ever be as happy as he was. Lying on the bed, completely drunk, I swore on my mother, whose picture I had in front of me, that if the guy pulled through I'd become a priest, and if he didn't pull through I'd become a cop. I was talking crap, but it was a vow all the same. The next day, I enlisted in the Colonial Army, for three years. The guy did-n't die but he didn't exactly pull through either: he was paralyzed for life. I asked to go back to Djibouti. That was where I saw Ugo for the last time.

All our treasures were here, in the cottage. All intact. The books, the record albums. And I was the only survivor.

I made you some foccaccia, Honorine had written on a little piece of paper. *Foccaccia* is made with pizza dough, filled with whatever you like, and served hot. Tonight, the filling was cured ham and mozzarella. As she had every day since Toinou died, three years ago, Honorine had made me a meal. She'd just turned seventy and loved to cook. But she could only cook for a man. I was her man, and I loved it. I sat down in the boat, with the *foccaccia* and a bottle of white Cassis—a Clos Boudard 91—next to me. I rowed out, in order not to disturb the neighbors' sleep, then, once past the sea wall, I started the motor and set course for Île Maïre.

That was where I wanted to be. Between the sky and the sea. The whole bay of Marseilles stretched in front of me like a glow-worm. I let the boat drift. My father had put away the oars. He took me by the hands. "Don't be scared," he said, plunging me into the water up to my shoulders. The boat tipped in my direction, and I had his face above mine. He was smiling. "Good, huh?" I nodded, though I was still very nervous. He plunged me back in the water. He was right, it was good. That was my first contact with the sea. I'd just turned five. I remembered the incident as having taken place near Île Maïre, so that was where I went every time I felt sad. The way you always go back to your first image of happiness.

I was certainly sad that evening. Ugo's death was weighing on my mind. I felt suffocated. And alone. More alone than ever. Every year, I ostentatiously crossed out of my address book any friend who'd made a racist remark, neglected those whose only ambition was a new car and a Club Med vacation, and forgot all those who played the Lottery. I loved fishing and silence. Walking in the hills. Drinking cold Cassis, Lagavulin or Oban late into the night. I didn't talk much. Had opinions about everything. Life and death. Good and evil. I was a film buff. Loved music. I'd stopped reading contemporary novels. More than anything, I loathed half-hearted, spineless people.

A fair number of women had found that attractive. I hadn't been able to hold on to any of them. It was always the same story. No sooner had they settled into our new life together than they'd set about trying to change the very things they liked about me. "You'll never change," Rosa had said when she left, six years ago. She'd tried for two years. I'd resisted. Even more than I had with Muriel, Carmen and Alice. And I'd always find myself alone again one night with an empty glass and an ashtray full of cigarette butts.

I drank the wine straight from the bottle. Another one of those nights when I wondered why I was still a cop. Five years ago I'd been assigned to the Neighborhood Surveillance Squad, a unit of untrained cops given the job of keeping order in North Marseilles. I had plenty of experience, and I could keep a cool head. Just the guy to send to the front line when the shit hit the fan. Lahaouri Ben Mohamed, a seventeen-year-old, had been shot dead during a routine identity check. The anti-racist organizations had protested, the left-wing parties had mobilized their members. The usual thing. But he was only an Arab. No reason to care too much about his human rights. In February 1988 on the other hand, when Charles Dovero, the son of a taxi driver, was gunned down, the city was in turmoil. Goddammit, this one was a Frenchman. This time, the police had made a real mistake. Something had to be done. That was where I came in. I took up my post with my head full of illusions. I was going to explain, to persuade. I was going to find answers, preferably good ones. I was going to help. That was the day I'd started down what my colleagues called the slippery slope. The day I'd started to become less of a cop and more of a youth counselor or social worker. Since then, I'd lost the trust of my superiors and made myself a fair number of enemies. True, there hadn't been anymore mistakes, and petty crime hadn't increased, but the tally was nothing to boast about: no spectacular arrests, no big media stunts. Routine, however well managed, was just routine.

The reforms—and there were lots of them—increased my isolation. Nobody new was assigned to the squad. And one day I woke up and realized I'd lost all my power. I'd been disowned by the anti-crime squad, the narcotics squad, the vice squad, the illegal immigration squad. Not to mention the squad waging war on organized crime, led so brilliantly by Auch. I'd become just a neighborhood cop who didn't get any important cases. But, since the Colonial Army, being a cop was the only thing I knew. And nobody had ever challenged me to do anything else. But I knew my colleagues were right, I was on the slippery slope. I wasn't the kind of cop who could shoot a punk in the back to save a colleague's skin, and that meant I was dangerous.

The message machine was flashing. It was late. Everything could wait. I'd just had a shower. I poured myself a glass of Lagavulin, put on a Thelonius Monk album, and went to bed with Conrad's *Between the Tides*. My eyes closed. Monk kept going, solo.

2.

IN WHICH, EVEN WITH NO SOLUTION,
TO WAGER IS TO HOPE

I drew up in the parking lot of La Paternelle. A largely Arab housing project. It wasn't the toughest, but it certainly wasn't the best. It was barely ten o'clock and it was already very hot. The sun had free rein here. No trees, nothing. Just the project, the parking lot, and a patch of waste ground. In the distance, the sea. L'Estaque and its harbor. Like another continent. I remembered a song by Aznavour: Poverty isn't so hard in the sun. I don't suppose he'd ever been here, to this pile of shit and concrete.

It wasn't long after I'd first arrived in the projects that I rubbed shoulders with the three groups who stand out from the crowd and freak people out, not just people downtown, but people in the projects too: the punks, the junkies and the dropouts. The punks are teenagers with a long experience of crime behind them. Holdup men, dealers, racketeers. Some, although barely seventeen, have already done a couple of years in the joint, with several years 'conditional discharge.' They're young, tough and scary, and they'll use a flick knife at the drop of a hat. The junkies, on the other hand, aren't looking for trouble. It's just that sometimes they need cash, and to get it they'd pull any stupid stunt. Whatever they get, they have it coming. Just showing their faces is tantamount to a confession.

The dropouts are cool guys. They don't do anything stupid, and they don't have a police record. They're enrolled in vocational courses, but never attend, which suits everybody just fine: it reduces class numbers and allows the college to hire extra teachers. They spend their afternoons at FNAC or Virgin. Scrounge a smoke here, a hundred francs there. They're resourceful, and clean. Until the day they start dreaming of driving a BMW, because they're pissed off taking the bus. Or they're suddenly 'inspired' by dope and start shooting up.

Then there are all the others, the ones I discovered later. A whole mass of kids who have no story other than that they were born here. And that they're Arabs. Or blacks, or gypsies, or Comorans. High school kids, temporary workers, the unemployed, public nuisances, the sports fans. Their teenage years are spent walking a tightrope. A tightrope from which they're almost all likely to fall. Where will they land? Punk, junkie, dropout? Nobody knows. It's a lottery. They'll find out sooner or later. For me it's always too soon, for them it's too late. In the meantime, they get picked up for trivial offences. Riding a bus without a ticket, a fight on the way out of school, petty shoplifting from a supermarket.

These were the kind of things they discussed on Radio Galère, a talk radio station I listened to regularly in the car. I waited now for the end of the show, with the car door open.

"Our old folks can't help us anymore, dammit! Take me, for instance. I get to eighteen, I need fifty or a hundred francs on a Friday night. It's only natural. There are five of us. Where do you think the old man's going to find five hundred francs? So, then what happens, I don't say me, but... my brother for example, he has to—"

"Pick someone's pocket!"

"That's no joke!"

"Right! And the guy who gets his money stolen sees it's an Arab. And straight away he joins the National Front!"

"Even if he isn't a racist, man!"

"It could have been, I don't know, a Portuguese, a Frenchman, a gypsy."

"Or a Swiss guy! Shit, man! There are thieves everywhere."

"Just your luck that in Marseille, it's more likely to be an Arab than a Swiss guy."

Since the neighborhood had become my beat, I'd collared a few real gangsters, and a reasonable number of dealers and holdup men. Caught them red-handed, chased them through the projects or out along the beltway. Next stop Les Baumettes, Marseilles' biggest jail. I had no pity for them, no hate either. But I did have my doubts. Whoever the guy is, he goes into the joint at eighteen, his life is screwed up. When I was doing holdups with Manu and Ugo, we didn't think about the risks. We knew the rules. You play the game. If you win, fine. If you lose, too bad. If you don't like it, you might as well stay at home.

The rules were still the same now. But the risks were a hundred times greater. And the prisons were overflowing with minors. Six minors for every one adult. A figure I found really depressing.

About ten kids were chasing each other, throwing stones as big as fists. "As long as they're doing that, they aren't doing something stupid," one of the mothers had told me. What she meant by 'something stupid' was something you called in the police for. This was just the junior version of the OK Corral. In front of Block C12, six Arab kids, aged from twelve to seventeen, stood talking. In the few feet of shade offered by the building. They saw me coming toward them. Especially the oldest of them, Rachid. He started shaking his head and making blowing noises, convinced that just my being there meant the hassles were starting. I had no intention of disappointing him. "Open air classes today?" I said, to no one in particular.

"It's teachers' day, monsieur," the youngest of them said. "They have classes for each other."

"Yeah, to see if they're good enough to stuff our heads with their shit," another kid said.

"Great. So I guess this is kind of like your practical work right now?"

"What do you mean?" Rachid said. "We ain't doin' nothin' wrong."

For him, school was long over. Expelled from vocational college, after threatening a teacher who called him a moron. A good kid, all the same. He was hoping for an apprenticeship. Like a lot of kids in the projects. That was the future, waiting to go on some kind of course, whatever it was. It was better than waiting for nothing at all.

"I didn't say you were, I was just asking." He was wearing a blue and white tracksuit: the colors of OM, the Marseilles soccer team. I felt the material. "Mmm. Brand new."

"It's paid for. My mother bought it for me."

I put my arm around his shoulders and pulled him away from the group. His friends looked at me as if I'd broken the law. They were ready to scream.

"Look, Rachid, I'm going over there to B7. You see? Fifth floor. To Mouloud's apartment. Mouloud Laarbi. Do you know him?"

"Yeah. What about it?"

"I'll be there... oh, maybe an hour."

"What's it to me?"

I walked him a few more steps, toward my car. "Now, this is my car. Nothing amazing, I can hear you say. I agree. But I like it. I wouldn't want anything to happen to it. I wouldn't even want it to get scratched. So I'd like you to keep an eye on it. And if you have to go take a leak, get one of your buddies to take over. OK?"

"I'm not the super."

"Get in some practice. There may be a job for you there." I

squeezed his shoulder a bit harder. "Remember, Rachid, not a scratch, or else..."

"Else what? I'm not doin' nothin'. You can't accuse me of nothin'."

"I can do anything I like. I'm a cop. Don't forget that." I ran my hand down his back. "If I put my hand here, on your ass, what'll I find in your back pocket?"

He freed himself quickly. He was on edge. I knew he didn't have anything. I just wanted to be sure.

"I don't have nothin'. I don't touch that shit."

"I know. You're just a poor little Arab being harassed by a stupid cop, right?"

"Didn't say that."

"You think it, though. Keep an eye on my car, Rachid."

B7 was no different than the other blocks. The lobby was filthy, and stank of piss. Someone had thrown a stone at the light bulb and smashed it. And the elevator didn't work. Five floors. Climbing them certainly wasn't taking a stairway to Paradise. Mouloud had called last night and left a message. Surprised at first by the recorded voice, he'd said 'Hello' a few times, then left a silence, and then spoken his message. "Please, Monsieur Montale, you must come. It's about Leila."

Leila was the eldest of his three children. The others were Kader and Driss. He might have had more, if his wife, Fatima, hadn't died giving birth to Driss. Mouloud was the immigrant dream personified. He'd been one of the first to be hired for the Fos-sur-Mer site, at the end of 1970.

Fos had been like Eldorado. There was enough work for centuries. They were building a port that would welcome enormous methane gas tankers, factories to produce steel for the whole of Europe. Mouloud was proud of taking part in this adventure. That's what he liked, building, constructing. He'd molded his whole life, and his family, in that image. He'd never forced his children to cut themselves off from other people, to keep clear of the French. All he'd asked is that they avoid bad company. Keep their self-respect. Acquire decent manners. And aim as high as possible. Become integrated in society without denying either their race or their past.

"When we were little," Leila told me one day, "he made us recite after him: *Allah akbar, la ilah illa Allah, Mohamed rasas Allah, Ayya illa Salat, Ayya illa el Fallah*. We didn't understand a word. But it was nice to hear. It reminded us of all the things he'd told us about Algeria." It had been a happy time for Mouloud. He'd settled with his family in Port-de-Bouc, between Les Martigues and Fos. They'd been 'kind to him' at the town hall and he'd soon obtained a nice public housing unit on Avenue Maurice Thorez. The work was hard, and the more Arabs there were, the better it was. That was what the veterans of the naval shipyards, who'd all been taken on at Fos, thought. Italians, mostly Sardinians, Greeks, Portuguese, a few Spaniards.

Mouloud joined the CGT. He was a worker, and he needed to find a family of workers, to understand him, help him, defend him. "This is the biggest," Gutierrez, the union organizer, had told him. "When the building work's finished," he'd added, "you can go on a course, learn to handle steel. Stick with us, and you've got a job in the factory for sure."

Mouloud liked that. He believed it, with a kind of blind faith. Gutierrez believed it too. The CGT believed it. Marseilles believed it. All the surrounding towns believed it, and built one housing project after the other, along with schools and roads, to welcome all the workers expected in this Eldorado. The whole of France believed it. By the time the first ingot of iron was cast, Fos was already nothing more than a mirage. The last great dream of the Seventies. The cruelest of disappointments. Thousands of men out of a job. Mouloud was one of them. But he wasn't discouraged.

He went on strike with the CGT, occupied the site, fought the riot police who came to dislodge them. They'd lost, of course. You can never win against the arbitrary decisions of the men in suits. Driss had just been born. Fatima was dead. And Mouloud had a police record now as an agitator, and couldn't get any real work. Just little jobs. Right now, he was a packer at Carrefour. Minimum wage, after all these years. But, as he said, 'it was an opportunity.' Mouloud was like that, he believed in France.

Mouloud had told me his life story in my office at the station house one evening. He told it proudly. He wanted me to understand. Leila was with him. That was two years ago. I'd taken Driss and Kader in for questioning. A few hours before, Mouloud had bought some batteries for the transistor his children had given him. The batteries didn't work. Kader went down to the drugstore on the boulevard to change them. Driss went with him.

"You don't know how to use them, that's all."

"Yes I do," Kader replied. "It isn't the first time."

"You Arabs always think you know everything."

"It's not very polite of you to say that, madame."

"I'm polite when I want to be. But not to filthy Arabs like you. You're wasting my time. Take your batteries. They're old ones, anyhow, and you didn't buy them here."

"My dad bought them here earlier."

Her husband came out of the back of the store with a hunting rifle. "Tell your lying father to come here, and I'll make him swallow his batteries." He threw the batteries on the floor. "Get out of here, you sons of bitches!"

Kader pushed Driss out of the store. After that, things happened very fast. Driss, who hadn't said a word so far, picked up a big stone and threw it at the window. He ran off, followed by Kader. The guy came out of the store and fired at them, but missed. Ten minutes later, a hundred kids were besieging the drugstore. It took more than two hours, and a van of riot police, to restore calm. Nobody dead, nobody injured. But I was furious. Part of my mission was to avoid calling in the riot police. No riots, no provocation, and above all no mistakes.

I'd listened to the druggist.

"Too many Arabs. That's the problem."

"They're here. You didn't bring them. Neither did I. But they're here, and we have to live with them."

"Are you on their side?"

"Don't be a pain in the ass, Varounian. They're Arabs. You're an Armenian."

"And proud of it. You have something against Armenians?"

"No. Nothing against Arabs either."

"Yeah, and what's the result? Have you been downtown lately? I have. It's like Algiers or Oran. Stinks just the same." I let him talk. "Before, you bumped into an Arab on the street, he'd say sorry. Now he wants you to say sorry. They're arrogant, that's what they are! Shit, they think this is their home!"

I didn't want to listen anymore, or even argue. It sickened me. I'd heard it all before. The local far-right newspaper *Le Méridional* printed hateful crap like that every day. *Sooner or later*, they'd written once, *the riot police and their dogs will have to be called in to destroy the casbahs of Marseilles...* One thing was sure: if nothing was done, all hell was going to break loose. I didn't have any solutions. Neither did anyone else. We just had to wait and not resign ourselves. Wager on Marseilles surviving this latest racial mix and being reborn. Marseilles had seen it all before.

I'd sent them all on their different ways, with fines for 'public disorder' preceded by a little moral tirade. Varounian was the first to leave.

"We'll get you and cops like you," he said as he opened the door. "Soon. When we're in power."

"Goodbye, Monsieur Varounian," Leila replied, disdainfully.

He gave her a filthy look. I wasn't sure, but I thought I heard him mutter the word 'bitch' under his breath. I smiled at Leila. A few days later, she called me at the precinct house to thank me and to invite me to have tea with them on Sunday. I accepted. I liked Mouloud.

Now, Driss was an apprentice in a garage on Rue Roger Salengro. Kader was in Paris, working in his uncle's grocery store on Rue de Charonne. Leila was at college, in Aix-en-Provence, and was just completing a master's in French language and literature. Mouloud was happy again. His children were settling down. He was proud of them, especially his daughter. I understood how he felt. Leila was intelligent, confident and beautiful. The image of her mother, Mouloud had told me. And he'd showed me a photo of Fatima, Fatima and him in the Vieux Port. Their first day together in years. He'd gone to Algeria to fetch her, to bring her over to Paradise.

Mouloud opened the door. His eyes were red.

"She's disappeared. Leila's disappeared."

Mouloud made tea. He hadn't heard from Leila in three days. That wasn't like her, I knew. Leila respected her father. He didn't like her to wear jeans or smoke or drink aperitifs, and told her so. They'd argue about it, shout at each other, but he never imposed his ideas on her. He trusted her. That was why he'd allowed her to take a room at the university residence in Aix. To be independent. She phoned every two days and came to see him on Sundays. Often, she slept over. Driss left her the couch in the living room and slept with his father.

The thing that made Leila's silence worrying was that she

hadn't even called to tell him if she'd gained her master's or not.

"Maybe she failed, and she feels ashamed... She's in her room, crying. She doesn't dare come back."

"Maybe."

"You should go find her, Monsieur Montale. Tell her it doesn't matter."

He didn't believe a word he was saying. Neither did I. If she'd failed her master's, she'd have cried, sure. But hiding away in her room, no, I couldn't believe that. Plus, I was convinced she'd gained her master's. *Poetry and the Need for Identity*, her thesis was called. I'd read it two weeks earlier. I'd thought it was a remarkable piece of work. But I wasn't one of the judges, and Leila was an Arab.

She'd taken her inspiration from a Lebanese writer named Salah Stetie and had developed some of his ideas. Her concern was to build bridges between East and West, across the Mediterranean. She pointed out, for example, that Sinbad the Sailor in the *Arabian Nights* recalled certain elements of Ulysses in the *Odyssey*, especially his ingenuity and his mischievousness.

What I liked most was her conclusion. As a child of the East, she considered that the French language was becoming a place where the migrant could draw together strands from all the lands through which he had passed and finally feel at home. The language of Rimbaud, Valéry and René Char would crossbreed, she asserted. It was the dream of a generation of North African immigrants. You already heard a strange kind of French spoken in Marseilles, a mixture of Provençal, Italian, Spanish and Arabic, with bits of slang thrown in. Speaking it, the kids understood each other perfectly well. At least on the streets. At school and at home, it was another story.

The first time I went to see her at college, I found the walls covered with racist graffiti. Insulting, obscene graffiti. I'd stopped in front of the most laconic: *Arabs and blacks out!* I'd assumed the law faculty, some five hundred yards from there, was the fascist stronghold, but clearly, human stupidity had reached French language and literature now! In case anyone hadn't gotten the point, someone had added: *Jews too.*

"It can't be a pleasant atmosphere to work in," I said to her.

"I don't see them anymore."

"Yes, but they're in your head, aren't they?"

She shrugged, lit a Camel, then took me by the arm and led me out of there.

"One day we'll get people to take our rights seriously. I vote, and that's the reason why. And I'm not the only one anymore."

"Your rights, maybe. But you'll still have the same face."

She turned to look at me, with a smile on her lips and a gleam in her dark eyes. "Oh, yeah? What's wrong with my face? Don't you like it?"

"It's a very nice face," I stammered.

She looked like Maria Schneider in *Last Tango in Paris.* Same round face, same long, curly hair, only hers was black. Like her eyes, which were looking deep into mine. I went red.

I'd seen a lot of Leila these last few years. I knew more about her than her father did. We got into the habit of having lunch together once a week. She talked to me about her mother, who she'd barely known. She missed her. Time didn't help. In fact, it only made it worse. Every year, when Driss's birthday came around, all four of them had to find a way of getting through it.

"I think that's why Driss has become, not bad exactly, but aggressive. Because of that curse. He has hatred in him. One day, my father said to me, 'If I'd had a choice, I'd have chosen your mother.' He said it to me, because I was the only one who could understand."

"You know, my father said that too. But my mother pulled through. And here I am. An only child. It can be lonely."

"Death is a lonely business." She smiled. "It's the title of a novel. Have you read it?"

I shook my head.

"It's by Ray Bradbury. A detective story. I'll lend it to you. You ought to read more contemporary novels."

"They don't interest me. They lack style."

"This is Bradbury, Fabio!"

"OK, maybe Bradbury."

And we'd launch into long discussions about literature. The future teacher and the self-taught cop. The only books I'd read were those we'd been given by old Antonin. Adventure stories, travel books. Poetry, too. Long forgotten Marseilles poets like Émile Sicard, Toursky, Gérald Neveu, Gabriel Audisio, and my favorite, Louis Brauquier.

The weekly lunch wasn't enough anymore, and we started meeting one or two evenings a week. Whenever I wasn't on duty, or she wasn't baby-sitting. I'd go to fetch her in Aix, and we'd take in a movie, then go have dinner somewhere.

We launched on a major survey of foreign cuisines. Considering the number of restaurants between Aix and Marseilles, it was likely to take us many months. We gave stars to those we liked, black marks to those we didn't. Top of our list was the Mille et une nuits, on Boulevard d'Athenes. You sat on pouffes and ate from a big brass platter, listening to raï. Moroccan cuisine. The most refined in North Africa. They served the best pigeon *pastilla* I've ever tasted.

That evening, I'd suggested Les Tamaris, a little Greek restaurant in a *calanque* called Samena, not far from my house. It was hot, with a thick, dry heat, typical of late August. We ordered simple things: cucumber salad with yoghurt, stuffed vine leaves, taramasalata, spicy kebabs grilled on vine shoots

with a drizzle of olive oil, goat's cheese. All washed down with
a white Retsina.

We walked on the little shingly beach, then sat down on the
rocks. It was a glorious night. In the distance, the Planier light-
house revealed the cape. Leila laid her head on my shoulder.
Her hair smelled of honey and spices. She slipped her arm
beneath mine and took my hand. I shivered at the contact. I
wasn't quick enough to free myself from her grip. She began
reciting a poem by Brauquier, in Arabic.

> The shadows and the mystery are gone,
> The spirit fled, and we are poor again;
> And only sin can give us back the earth,
> That makes our bodies move and sigh and strain.

"I translated it for you. I wanted you to hear it in my language."

Part of that language was her voice. A voice as sweet as
halva. I was moved. I turned my face to her, slowly, so that her
head stayed on my shoulder and I could get drunk on her
smell. I saw a glimmer in her dark eyes, the reflection of the
moon on the water. I wanted to take her in my arms and hold
her close and kiss her.

I was well aware, and so was she, that our increasingly fre-
quent encounters had been leading up to this moment, and it
was a moment I dreaded. I knew my own desires only too well.
I knew how it would all end. In bed, then in tears. I'd never
known anything but failures, one after the other. I was looking
for a woman, and I had to find her, if she existed. But Leila was-
n't her. She was so young, and what I felt for her was only
desire. I had no right to play with her. With her feelings. She
was too good for that. I kissed her on the forehead. I felt her
hand caress my thigh.

"Will you take me home with you?"

"I'll take you back to Aix. I think that's best for both of us. I'm just an old fool."

"I like old fools."

"Let it go, Leila. Find someone who isn't a fool. Someone younger."

On the drive back, I kept my eyes on the road. We didn't look at each other once. Leila was smoking. I'd put on a Calvin Russel tape that I liked a lot. It was good to drive to. If I could, I'd have crossed the whole of Europe rather than take the turnoff that led to Aix. Russel was singing *Rockin' the Republicans*. Leila, still without speaking, stopped the tape before *Baby I Love You*.

She put in another tape that I didn't know. Arab music. An oud solo. The music she had dreamed of for this night with me. The sound of the oud spread through the car like an aroma. The peaceful aroma of an oasis. Dates, dried figs, almonds. I risked a look at her. Her skirt had ridden up her thighs. She was beautiful, beautiful for me. Yes, I desired her.

"You shouldn't have done it," she said just before she got out.

"Shouldn't have done what?"

"Let me fall in love with you."

She slammed the car door. Not violently. But there was sadness in the action, and the anger that goes with sadness. That was a year ago. We hadn't seen each other since. She hadn't called. I'd brooded over her absence. Two weeks ago, I'd received her master's thesis in the mail, and a card with just four words: "For you. So long."

"I'm going to find her, Mouloud. Don't worry."

I gave him my nicest smile. The smile of the good cop you can trust. I remembered something Leila had said, talking about her brothers. "When it's late, and one of them hasn't come home, we get worried. Anything can happen in this place." Now it was my turn to be worried.

Rachid was alone in front of Block C12, sitting on a skate-board. He stood up when he saw me come out of the building, picked up his skateboard, and vanished into the lobby. I sup-posed he was telling me to go fuck myself and my mother. But I didn't care. When I got to my car in the parking lot, I saw it didn't have a single new scratch.

3.

IN WHICH THE MOST HONORABLE THING
A SURVIVOR CAN DO IS SURVIVE

A heat haze enveloped Marseilles. I was driving along the highway, with the windows down. I'd put on a B. B. King tape. Full volume. Nothing but the music. I didn't want to think. Not yet. All I wanted was to empty my head, to dispel the thoughts that were flooding in. I was on my way back from Aix and my worst fears had been confirmed. Leila really had disappeared.

I'd wandered through the empty faculty looking for the administration offices. I needed to know if Leila had gained her master's before I went to the residence. The answer was yes. With distinction. It was after that that she'd disappeared. Her old red Fiat Panda was still in the parking lot. I'd glanced inside, but nothing had been left lying around. Either it had broken down—which I hadn't checked—and she'd taken the bus, or someone had come to pick her up.

The super, a pudgy little man, his cap pulled down tight on his head, opened the door to Leila's room for me. He remembered seeing her come in, but not go out again. He himself had left around six in the evening.

"She hasn't done anything wrong, has she?"

"No, no. She's disappeared."

"Shit," he said, scratching his head. "She's a nice girl. Polite. Not like some of the French girls."

"She is French."

"That's not what I meant, monsieur."

He fell silent. I'd upset him. He stood by the door while I

checked out the room. I wasn't looking for anything in particular. I just wanted to make sure Leila hadn't suddenly decided to fly off to Acapulco for a change of scenery. The bed had been made. Above the sink, a toothbrush, toothpaste, beauty products. In the closet, her things, neatly arranged. A bag of dirty washing. On a table, sheets of paper, notepads, and books.

The book I was looking for was here. *Harbor Bar* by Louis Brauquier. A first edition, from 1926, on pure laid Lafuma, published by the review *Le Feu*. Numbered 36. I'd given it to her as a present.

It was the first time I'd parted with one of the books I had in my house. They belonged to Manu and Ugo as much as to me. They were the great treasure of our teenage years. I'd often dreamed that one day they would bring the three of us back together. The day Manu and Ugo finally forgave me for being a cop. The day I admitted that it was easier to be a cop than a criminal and I could embrace them like long-lost brothers, with tears in my eyes. When that day came, I knew I'd read the poem by Brauquier that ended with these words:

> For a long time I searched for you
> Night of the lost night.

We'd discovered Brauquier's poems in Antonin's second-hand bookstore. *Fresh Water for Ships, Beyond Suez, Freedom of the Seas.* We were seventeen. Antonin was recovering from a heart attack. We stopped blowing our money on the pinball machines, and took it in turn to mind the store. It was a chance to indulge our grand passion, old books. The novels, travel books and poems I read had a particular smell. The smell of cellars. An almost spicy smell, a mixture of dust and grease. Verdigris. Books today don't have a smell. They don't even smell of print.

I'd found the original edition of *Harbor Bar* one morning, emptying some boxes Antonin had never opened, and taken it home with me. I leafed through the book, with its yellowed pages, closed it, and put it in my pocket. I looked at the super.

"I'm sorry for what I said earlier. I'm a bit on edge."

He shrugged. He was the kind of guy who must be used to other people putting him down.

"Did you know her?"

I didn't answer, but gave him my card. Just in case.

I'd opened the window and lowered the blind. I was exhausted. I was longing for a cold beer. But, before anything else, I had to do a report on Leila's disappearance and pass it on to the missing persons bureau. Then Mouloud would need to sign a request for a search. I'd called him. I could hear the hopelessness in his voice, the sense of misery that grabs hold of you and won't let you go. "We'll find her." That was all I could say. Behind the words, a chasm opened up. I imagined him sitting at his table, not moving, eyes staring into the distance.

Mouloud's image gave way to Honorine's, this morning, in her kitchen. I'd gone there at seven, to tell her about Ugo. I didn't want her to find out from the newspapers. Auch's squad had been very discreet. There was only a short paragraph on the inside pages. A dangerous criminal, wanted by the police of several countries, had been shot dead yesterday as he was getting ready to open fire on the police. There were a few details about his life, but no mention of why Ugo was considered dangerous, or what crimes he'd committed.

Zucca's death had made the headlines. The journalists all kept to the same version. Zucca wasn't a famous gangster like Mémé Guérini or, more recently, Gaëtan Zampa, Jacky Le Mat or Francis the Belgian. It wasn't even certain he'd ever killed anyone, or maybe just one or two people, to prove himself. He was the son of a lawyer, and a lawyer himself. Basically, he was a manager. Since Zampa had killed himself in prison, he'd been running the Marseilles mafia's empire. Steering well clear of family feuds or battles for territory.

His execution had gotten everyone nervous. Was it the start of a gang war? Marseilles really didn't need this right now. The city's economic downturn was already a heavy enough burden to bear. SNCM, the company that ran the ferry service to Corsica, was threatening to take its business elsewhere, Toulon for instance, or La Ciotat, a former naval shipyard 25 miles from Marseilles. For months, there'd been a dispute between the company and the longshoremen over their status. The longshoremen had had a monopoly of hiring and firing on the waterfront since 1947, but all that was in the balance now.

It was a trial of strength, and the city was holding its breath for the outcome. In all the other ports, they'd surrendered. Even if the city had to die, for the Marseilles longshoremen it was a question of honor. Honor was central to Marseilles life. "You have no honor," was the worst insult you could say to someone. You could kill a man for the sake of honor. Your wife's lover, the guy who'd insulted your mother, or wronged your sister.

That was why Ugo had come back. For the sake of honor. Manu's honor. Lole's honor. The honor of our youth, our shared friendship. Our memories.

"He shouldn't have come back."

Honorine had looked up from her coffee cup. I could see it in her eyes: that wasn't the thing that was tormenting her. It was the trap I was walking into. Did I have honor? I was the last of the three. The one who inherited all the memories. Could a cop take the law into his own hands? Make sure justice was done? Did anyone even care about justice when it was just criminals killing criminals? That was what I saw in

Honorine's eyes. She was answering her own questions: yes, yes, yes again, and finally no. She could already see me lying in the gutter. With five bullets in my back, like Manu. Or three, like Ugo. Three or five, the number didn't matter. Just one was enough to end up face down in the gutter. And that was something Honorine didn't want. I was the last, the sole survivor. The most honorable thing a survivor could do was survive. If you stayed on your feet, stayed alive, you were the winner.

I'd left her sitting over her coffee. I'd looked at her. She looked the way my mother might have looked. She had the ravaged face of a woman who'd already lost two of her sons in a war that didn't concern her. She turned away to look at the sea.

"He should have come to see me," she'd said.

Since it opened, I'd only used Line 1 of the subway about ten times. Castellane to La Rose. From the hip neighborhoods—the new downtown—with their bars, restaurants and cinemas, to North Marseilles, which was a place you didn't hang out in if you didn't have to.

For the last few days, a group of Arab kids had been causing trouble on the line. Subway security was inclined to favor strong arm tactics. That was something all Arabs understood. The same old song. Except that it had never worked. Not on the subway, and not on the main line railroad. Every time heads were cracked, there'd been reprisals. A blockade on the Marseilles-Aix line, after the Septèmes-les-Vallons station, a year ago. Stones thrown at the train at the Frais-Vallon subway station, six months ago.

So I'd suggested the other method. Talking to the gang. In my own way. The subway cowboys had laughed. But for once, the management ignored them and gave me a free hand.

Pérol and Cerutti came with me. It was six in the evening.

The ride was about to start. An hour before, I'd dropped by the garage where Driss worked. I wanted to talk to him about Leila.

He was just finishing for the day. While I waited for him, I talked to his boss. A firm believer in contracts for apprentices. Especially when the apprentices did as much work as the regular staff. And Driss pulled out all the stops when it came to work. He mainlined on axle grease. By evening he'd overdosed. It wasn't as bad for you as crack or heroin. At least that's what they said, and I believed it. But it screwed with your head all the same. Driss still had to prove himself. And don't forget to say yes sir, no sir. And keep your mouth permanently shut, because, what the hell, he was only a dirty Arab, after all. For the moment, he was holding out.

I'd taken him to the bar on the corner. The Disque bleu. The bar was filthy, like its owner. You could see from his face that this was a place where Arabs were allowed to play the lottery and the tote and drink standing up. Even though I tried to give myself a vaguely Gary Cooper look, I almost had to show him my police badge in order to have two beers at a table. I was still too tanned for some people.

"Have you stopped training?" I said, coming back with the beers.

On my advice, he'd enrolled in a boxing gym in Saint-Louis, run by an old friend of mine named Georges Mavros. Georges had been a young hopeful, who, after winning a few fights, had had to choose between boxing and the woman he loved. He got married, and became a truck driver. By the time he found out that his wife was sleeping around whenever he was on the road, it was too late to be a champion. He dumped his wife and his job, sold what he had, and opened a gym.

Driss had all the qualities needed to be a good boxer. He had intelligence and passion. He could be as good as his idols, Stéphane Haccoun and Akim Tafer. Mavros would make him a champion. I truly believed that. But in that too he'd have to hold out.

"Too much work. The hours are too long. And the boss is like a sponge. He's always on my back."

"You didn't phone. Mavros was expecting you."

"Do you have any news about Leila?"

"That's why I came to see you. Do you know if she has a boyfriend?"

He looked at me as if I was putting him on. "Aren't you her guy?"

"I'm her friend. Just like I'm your friend."

"I thought you were humping her."

I almost hit him. There are certain expressions that make me throw up. That one in particular. Pleasure involves respect, and respect starts with words. That's something I've always thought.

"I don't hump women. I love them... Try to, anyhow..."

"And Leila?"

"What do you think?"

"I like you."

"Then let it go. Young guys like you are a dime a dozen."

"What does that mean?"

"It means I don't know where she is, Driss. Shit, just because I never slept with her doesn't mean I don't love her."

"We'll find her."

"That's what I told your father. And that's why I'm talking to you now."

"She doesn't have a boyfriend. Just us. Me, Kader, Dad. College. Her girlfriends. And you. She never stops talking about you. Find her. That's your job!"

Before he left, he gave me the telephone numbers of two of Leila's girlfriends, Jasmine and Karine, whom I'd met once, and Kader in Paris. But we couldn't see why she would have gone to Paris without telling him. Even if Kader had problems, she'd have said something. Anyhow, Kader was clean. He was the one who kept the grocery store going.

There were eight of them. Sixteen, seventeen years of age. They got on at Vieux-Port. We were waiting for them at Saint Charles mainline station. They'd gathered at the front end of a carriage, and were standing on the seats, using the walls and windows as tomtoms, beating on them in time to the music from a ghetto blaster. Rap, of course. I knew it. IAM, one of the best Marseilles bands. They were often played on Radio Grenouille, the equivalent of Nova in Paris. It played all the rap and ragga bands in Marseilles and the south. IAM, Fabulous Trobadors, Bouducon, Hypnotik, Black Lions. And Massilia Sound System, which had sprung up in the middle of neo-Nazi territory, just south of the soccer stadium. The band had given the supporters of OM a taste for ragga and hip hop that had then spread to the whole city.

Marseilles was a place where people liked to talk a lot. Rap was just talk, and lots of it. Our Jamaican cousins had brothers here. The rappers talked the way people talked in bars. About Paris, the centralized State, the decaying suburbs, the night buses. Their lives, their problems. The world, seen from Marseilles.

You hear that rhythm, that's the rhythm of rap,
We hit it hard 'cause we don't take no crap.
All they think about in Paris is power and money,
But us kids down here don't think that's funny.
I'm 22 years old and I'm better than those mothers,
'Cause never in my life would I betray my brothers.
I have to go now, but make no mistake,
I ain't working like a slave for no fuckin' State.

And they were certainly hitting hard in the carriage. Tomtoms from Africa, the Bronx, the planet Mars. Rap wasn't my kind of music, but I had to admit that IAM really did hit their target. A bull's eye every time. They were pretty funky too. You had only to see the two young kids dancing in front of me to know that.

The travelers had surged to the rear of the carriage. They had their heads down, pretending not to see or hear anything, keeping their thoughts to themselves. What was the point of opening your mouth if you ended up with a knife in your belly? At the next station, people hesitated before getting on. They pressed together at the rear, sighing and grumbling, dreaming of what they might do to these kids if they had the chance.

Cerutti slipped in among them. He was keeping radio contact with HQ. In case things turned ugly. I went and sat down in the middle of the gang, and opened a newspaper.

"Couldn't you make a little less noise?"

There was a moment's hesitation. "Don't jerk us around, man!" one of them said, dropping onto a seat.

"We bothering you, is that it?" another said, sitting down next to me.

"Yeah, that's it. How did you guess?"

I looked my neighbor in the eye. The others stopped beating on the walls. This was serious now. They pressed around me.

"What are you talking about, man? What is it you don't like? Rap? Our faces?"

"I don't like you breaking my balls."

"You seen how many of us there are? Go to hell, man."

"Yeah, I seen. Eight of you together, you're pretty impressive. Alone, you don't have the balls."

"And you have the balls, do you?"

"If I wasn't here, you wouldn't need to ask me that."

Behind me, people were raising their heads. Hey, he's right. We're not going to be dictated to. The courage of words. At Réformés-Canebière, the carriage filled some more. I could sense people behind me. Cerutti and Pérol must have come closer.

The kids were a bit confused. I guessed they didn't have a leader. They were just fooling around. Trying to annoy people, to provoke them. For the hell of it. But it might cost them their lives. A bullet could so easily go astray. I opened the paper again. The one with the ghetto blaster started up again. Another started knocking on the window, but not so loudly this time. Testing the water. The others were watching, winking, smiling knowingly, nudging each other with their elbows. Just kids.

The one opposite me almost put his sneakers on my newspaper. "Where you getting off?"

"What's it to you?"

"Well, I'd feel better if you wasn't here."

Behind my back, I imagined hundreds of eyes staring at us. I felt like a camp counselor with a class of teenagers. The stations followed one another. Cinq-Avenues-Longchamp. Les Chartreux. Saint-Just. The kids kept shtum. They were watching and waiting. The carriage was starting to empty. Malpasse. Emptiness behind me.

"If we smash your face, no one will lift a finger," one of them said, standing up.

"There are less than ten people. A chick and two old guys."

"But you won't do anything."

"Oh, yeah? What makes you say that?"

"You're all mouth."

Frais-Vallon. Housing projects, no horizon.

"Let's go!" one of them cried.

They ran out of the compartment. I leaped up and caught the last one by the arm and twisted it behind his back, not violently but firmly. He struggled. The passengers were hurrying to leave the platform.

"You're on your own now."

"Shit, man, let go of me!" He appealed to Cerutti and Pérol, who were slowly walking away. "This guy's crazy. He wants to smash my face."

Cerutti and Pérol ignored him. The platform was deserted. I could feel the kid's anger. His fear, too.

"No one's going to defend you. You're an Arab. I could take you out if I wanted, right here, on the platform, and nobody would lift a finger. Do you understand? So you and your pals had better stop fooling around. If you don't, one day you're going to run into guys who won't miss. Do you understand?"

"Yes, OK! Shit, man, you're hurting my arm!"

"Pass the message on. If I see you again, I won't just hurt your arm, I'll break it!"

By the time I resurfaced, it was already night. Almost ten o'clock. I was exhausted. Too drained to go home. I needed to hang out. To see people. To feel the heartbeat of something that resembled life.

I went into O'Stop, an all-night restaurant, on Place de l'Opéra. A place where music lovers and prostitutes rubbed shoulders amicably. I knew who I wanted to see. And there she was, Marie-Lou, a young West Indian hooker. She'd arrived in the neighborhood three months ago. A real looker. Like Diana Ross at the age of twenty-two. Tonight, she was wearing a pair of black jeans and a low-cut sleeveless top. Her hair was pulled back and tied with a black ribbon. There was nothing vulgar about her, not even the way she sat. She was almost imperious. Not many men dared approach her without her having agreed to it with a look.

Marie-Lou didn't hustle. She worked on Minitel. Being selective, she fixed her appointments here, so that she could check out the client's looks. Marie-Lou really turned me on. I'd been with her a few times since that first appointment. We liked seeing each other. For her, I was an ideal client. For me, it was easier than being in love. And at the moment it suited me just fine.

O'Stop was packed, as usual. A lot of hookers, taking a break: scotch or Coke and a leak. Some, the older ones, knew their Verdi, especially their Pavarotti. I winked and smiled at some of them, and sat down on a stool at the bar, next to Marie-Lou. She was staring into her empty glass, lost in thought.

"How's business?"

"Oh, hi. Buy me a drink?"

A margarita for her, a whisky for me. The night was off to a good start.

"I was going to do something tonight. But I wasn't too keen on it."

"And what did this 'something' involve?"

"A cop!" She burst out laughing, then kissed me on the cheek. I immediately felt the electricity, not just on my cheek, but in my pants too.

We were on our third round when I saw Molines. We'd talked a bit, about nothing very important. We'd concentrated on our drinking, which suited me fine. Molines was one of Auch's team. He was standing on the sidewalk outside O'Stop. He seemed to be bored stiff. I ordered another round and got down off my stool.

When he saw me, he jumped like a jack in the box. Clearly, my presence didn't send him into raptures.

"What are you doing here?"

"One, drinking. Two, drinking. Three, drinking. Four, eating. From five on, I haven't decided. How about you?"

"Duty."

A real cowboy. The strong, silent type. He started to walk away from me. Obviously I wasn't worthy of his company. As I watched him go, I saw them. The rest of the team, on different street corners. Besquet and Paoli on the corner of Rue Saint-Saëns and Rue Molière. Sandoz and Mériel, now joined by Molines, on Rue Beauvau. Cayrol pacing up and down in front of the Opéra. The others I couldn't see. I guessed they were in cars parked around the square.

A metal-gray Jaguar turned onto Rue Saint-Saëns from Rue Paradis. Besquet lifted his walkie-talkie to his mouth. He and Paoli left their post, crossed the square, taking no notice of Cayrol, and slowly walked up Rue Corneille.

The door of one of the cars opened, and Morvan climbed out. He crossed the square, then Rue Corneille, as if he was headed for the Commanderie, a night club where journalists, cops, lawyers and gangsters rubbed shoulders. He passed a taxi that was double-parked directly in front of the Commanderie. A white Renault 21. Its indicator light was on 'busy.' As he passed, Morvan casually knocked on the door. Then he continued on his way, stopped outside a sex shop, and lit a cigarette. Something was going down. I didn't know what it was, but I was the only one to see it.

The Jaguar turned, and parked behind the taxi. I saw Sandoz and Mériel approach. Followed by Cayrol. They were closing in. A man got out of the Jaguar. A muscular Arab, wearing a suit and tie, his jacket unbuttoned. A bodyguard. He looked right and left, then opened the rear door of the car. A man got out. Shit! Al Dakhil. Known as the Immigrant. The head of the Arab underworld. I'd only ever seen him once before, when he was being held in custody. Auch hadn't been able to pin anything on him. His bodyguard closed the car door and walked to the door of the Commanderie.

Al Dakhil buttoned his jacket and leaned over to say something to the driver. Two men got out of the taxi. The first was a short guy, about twenty, wearing jeans and a linen jacket. The other was of medium height, not much older, with close-cropped hair. Black cotton jacket and pants. Instinctively, I made a mental note of the taxi's license number as it drove away: 675 JLT 13. Then the shooting started. The shorter guy opened fire first, on the bodyguard. Then he swiveled and shot the driver as he was getting out of the car. The other guy emptied his magazine into Al Dakhil.

Before the guy with close-cropped hair could turn around, Morvan shot him. No warning had been given. The other one ducked, and dodged between two cars, with his gun still in his hand. He glanced quickly—too quickly—behind him, and started walking backwards. Sandoz and Meriel fired at the same time. I heard shouts. People appeared as if from nowhere. Auch's men, and onlookers too.

I heard police sirens. The taxi had disappeared along Rue Francis Davso, to the left of the Opéra. Auch came out of the Commanderie, with his hands in the pockets of his jacket. Behind my back, I felt Marie-Lou's warm breasts.

"What's going on?"

"Something not very nice."

That was putting it mildly. The war had started. But it was Ugo who'd taken Zucca out. And what I'd just seen left me speechless. Everything seemed to have been staged. Down to the last detail.

"A settling of scores."

"Shit! That won't be good for business!"

I really needed a pick-me-up. I didn't want to lose myself in conjecture. Not now. I needed to empty myself. To forget about everything. The cops, the gangsters. Manu, Ugo, Lole. Leila. And above all, myself. I wanted to melt into the night, if that was possible. Alcohol and Marie-Lou were what I needed. And fast.

"Set your meter to 'busy.' Let me buy you dinner."

4.

IN WHICH A COGNAC IS NOT
WHAT HURTS YOU THE MOST

I was jolted awake by a muted noise. Then I heard a child crying, somewhere upstairs. For a moment, I had no idea where I was. My tongue was furred, my head heavy. I was lying on a bed, fully clothed. Lole's bed. I remembered now. I'd left Marie-Lou in the early hours of the morning, and come here. I'd even forced open the door.

We'd had no reason to stick around Place de l'Opéra. The neighborhood was cordoned off. The cops would soon be all over it. Too many people I preferred not to see. I'd taken Marie-Lou by the arm and led her to the other side of Cours Jean Ballard. Chez Mario, on Place Thiars. Mozzarella and tomatoes, with capers, anchovies and black olives, for starters. Spaghetti with clams as a main dish. Tiramisu for dessert. To drink, a Bandol, from the Pibarnon vineyards.

We talked about this and that. She talked more than I did. Languidly, separating her words as if she was peeling a peach. I listened to her, but only with my eyes, letting myself be transported by her smile, the shape of her lips, the dimples in her cheeks, the astonishing mobility of her face. Looking at her, and feeling her knee against mine, gave me a chance not to think.

"What concert?" I finally said.

"Which planet are you on? The Massilia concert. At la Friche."

La Friche was the former tobacco factory behind the Saint-Charles railroad station. A hundred and twenty thousand square meters, housing workshops, rehearsal studios, a news-paper, *Taktik*, Radio Grenouille, a restaurant, and a concert hall. It was something like the artists' squats in Berlin, or P.S.1 in New York.

"Five thousand of us! Fantastic! Those guys really get you fired up."

"So I guess you understand Provençal?"

Half Massilia's songs were in dialect. Maritime Provençal. What the Parisians call Marseilles French. *Parlam de realitat dei cavas dau quotidian*, as Massilia sang.

"It doesn't matter whether you understand or not. We're slaves, not idiots. That's all you have to understand."

She looked at me, curiously. Maybe I was an idiot. I was more and more disconnected from reality. I moved through Marseilles, but I'd stopped seeing anything except the violence and racism simmering just under the surface. I was starting to forget that life was more than that. That this was a city where, despite everything, people liked to live, to have a good time. That happiness was a new idea every day, even if the night ended with some strong-arm guy checking your identity.

We'd finished eating, emptied the bottle of Bandol, and had two coffees.

"Let's see what we can see."

That was the established formula. Seeing what we could see meant doing something exciting for the night. I'd let her lead me. We'd started at the Trolleybus on Quai de Rive-Neuve, a huge club I hadn't even known existed. Marie-Lou found that amusing.

"But how do you spend your nights?"

"Fishing for bream."

She laughed. In Marseilles, 'bream' is also a slang word for a pretty girl. The Trolleybus was housed in what had once been the arsenal of the penal colony. You went along a corridor of

TV screens, and at the end, beneath the vaults, were separate rooms for rap, techno, rock and reggae. Tequila to start, and reggae to quench your thirst. How long was it since I'd last been out dancing? A hundred years, or a thousand years? As the night wore on, we went from club to club, from bar to bar. The Passeport, the Maybe Blues, the Pell Mell. Always moving on, like the Spaniards.

We'd ended up at the Pourquoi, a West Indian club on Rue Fortia. We were already pretty merry by the time we arrived. All the more reason to continue. Tequila. And salsa! Our bodies soon moved in harmony. Pressed tightly together.

It was Zina who taught me to dance salsa. She was my girlfriend for six months before I went into the army. Then I saw her again in Paris, where I had my first police posting. Some nights we'd go to the Chapelle on Rue des Lombards and other nights to the Escale on Rue Monsieur-le-Prince. I liked spending time with Zina. She didn't give a damn that I was a cop. We were old friends. She regularly gave me news from 'down there,' news about Manu and Lole. Sometimes about Ugo, when they heard from him.

Marie-Lou felt increasingly light in my arms. Her sweat released her body's spices. Musk, cinnamon, pepper. Basil, too, like Lole. I loved bodies that smelled of spice. The bigger my hard-on, the more I felt her firm belly rubbing against me. We knew we'd end up in bed, and we wanted to delay it as long possible. Until the desire became unbearable. Because afterwards, reality would catch up with us. I'd be a cop again and she'd be a hooker.

I'd woken up about six o'clock. Marie-Lou's bronzed back reminded me of Lole. I drank half a bottle of Badoit, dressed, and left. It wasn't till I got out on the street that it hit me. That same maddening sense of dissatisfaction I'd been feeling ever since Rosa had left. I'd loved all the women I'd lived with. I'd loved them passionately. And they'd loved me too. But probably with a greater degree of honesty. They'd given me time out of their lives. Time is an essential thing in a woman's life. To women, time is real, whereas for men it's relative. Yes, they'd given me a lot. And what had I given them in return? Affection. Pleasure. Short-term happiness. I was quite good at those things. But after that?

With me, it was after the love that everything fell apart, that I stopped giving and didn't know how to take. After the love, I went back on the other side of my border. Back to the territory where I have my own rules, my own laws, my own code, and my own stupid obsessions. The territory where I lose my way, and where I lost the women who ventured onto it.

I could have taken Leila there, into that desert. But all she'd have found at the end of the road would have been sadness, anger, tears and loathing. She wouldn't have found me, because I'm a coward, a runaway, afraid to go back over the border and see how things are on the other side. Maybe, as Rosa had said one night, I didn't like life.

Having slept with Marie-Lou, having paid for sex, had at least taught me one thing. When it came to love, I was all at sea. Each of the women I'd loved, from the first to the last, could have been the love of my life. But I hadn't wanted it. This was why I was so pissed. At Marie-Lou, at myself, at women, and at the whole world.

Marie-Lou lived in a little studio apartment at the top of Rue Aubagne, just above the little metal bridge that goes over Cours Lieutaud and leads to Cours Julien, one of Marseilles' hip new neighborhoods. That was where we'd staggered into another rai-ragga-reggae club, called the Degust'Mars C'et Ye, for a final drink. Marie-Lou told me that Bra, the owner, was an ex-junkie, who'd done time. The club was his dream. *We're at home here* was written in big letters, surrounded by a mass of graffiti. The Degust' claimed to be a place 'where life flows by.' What flowed was tequila. A final drink, one for the road, before making love. Looking deep in each other's eyes, our bodies charged with electricity.

Walking down Rue d'Aubagne at any hour of the day was like going on a journey. The stores and restaurants were ports of call. Italy, Greece, Turkey, Lebanon, Madagascar, Reunion, Thailand, Vietnam, Africa, Morocco, Tunisia, Algeria. Most important of all, Arax, which sells the best *loukoum* in Marseilles.

I didn't feel up to going to the station house, picking up my car and heading home. I didn't even want to go fishing. On Rue Longue-des-Capucins, the market was in full swing. Smells of coriander, cumin, curry, mint. The East. I turned right, through the Halle Delacroix, went into a bistro and ordered a double espresso and a few slices of bread and butter.

The newspapers led with the shootout at the Opéra. According to the journalists, the police had had Al Dakhil under surveillance ever since the Zucca slaying. Everyone had been expecting the score to be evened up. Obviously, it couldn't stay at 1-0. Last night, acting quickly and coolly, Captain Auch's squad had prevented the Place de l'Opéra from being transformed into a battlefield. No passers-by wounded, not even a broken pane of glass. Five gangsters dead. A good tally. Now everyone was waiting for the sequel.

I remembered Morvan crossing the square, and knocking with the flat of his hand on the parked taxi. I remembered Auch coming out of the Commanderie, with a smile on his face. Well, certainly with his hands in his pockets, I may have invented the smile. I wasn't sure anymore.

The two gangsters who'd opened fire, Jean-Luc Trani and Pierre Bogho, were both wanted by the Paris police. But they were small fry. A bit of pimping, a bit of burglary. A few holdups, but nothing to put them in the top ten of the underworld hierarchy. Why should they hit a big shot like Al Dakhil? Someone must have ordered it, but who? That was the real question. But Auch was making no comment. That was his style: to say as little as possible.

After a second double espresso, I didn't feel any better. I was really and truly hungover. But I forced myself to keep moving. I crossed the Canebière, and walked up Cours Belzunce, then Rue Colbert. On Avenue de la République, I took Montée des Folies-Bergère, in order to cut across the Panier. Rue de Lorette, Rue du Panier, Rue des Pistoles. A few moments later, I was rooting about in the lock of Lole's apartment with my skeleton key. It was a bad lock, and didn't resist for long. Neither did I. I went straight to the bedroom and collapsed on the bed. I was exhausted, my head full of dark thoughts. I didn't want to think. I just wanted to sleep.

I'd fallen asleep again. When I woke, I was bathed in sweat. Behind the shutters, I could feel the heavy, dense heat. Two-twenty already. It was Saturday. Pérol was on duty until tomorrow evening. I only did one weekend a month. With Pérol there, I could sleep easy. He was the kind of cop who kept a cool head. And if anything went down, he could find me anywhere in Marseilles. I was more anxious when Cerutti replaced me. He was young and spoiling for a fight. He still had a lot to learn. I really needed to make a move. Tomorrow, like every Sunday, when I wasn't on duty, Honorine was coming for a meal. I always made fish, and the rule was that the fish had to be freshly caught.

I took a cold shower, but it didn't make me feel any better. I wandered naked through the apartment. Lole's apartment. I still didn't know why I'd come here. Lole had been like a magnet to Ugo, Manu and me. Not only for her beauty. She didn't become beautiful until later. As a teenager, she was skinny, not much of a figure. Not like Zina or Kali, whose sex appeal was obvious.

It was our desire that made Lole beautiful. The desire she'd seen in us. It was what she had behind her eyes that had attracted us. That sense of some distant, unknown country from where she'd come and toward which she seemed to want to return. She was a gypsy, a traveler. She moved through space, and time seemed to have no effect on her. It was she who gave. The lovers she'd had, between Ugo and Manu, were chosen by her, as if she was the man. That was what made her inaccessible. Reaching out to her was like trying to embrace a ghost. All you were left with was the dust of eternity, the dust on a road that never ended. I knew that. Because our paths had crossed, just once. Almost by accident.

Zina had given me Lole's number in Madrid, and I'd called her. To tell her about Manu, and to get her to come back. Even if we'd avoided seeing each other when Manu was around, there are some ties that can't be broken. Ties of friendship, which are stronger and more real than family ties. It was up to me to tell Lole that Manu was dead. I wouldn't have let anyone else do it. Especially not a cop.

I'd gone to meet her at the airport, then driven her to the morgue. To see him, one last time. We were the only ones to accompany him on his last journey. The only ones to love him. Three of his brothers came to the cemetery. Without their wives or children. Manu's death was a relief to them. They were ashamed. We didn't speak to each other.

After they left, Lole and I stayed by the grave. Dry-eyed, but with lumps in our throats. Manu was gone, and, with him, part of our youth. We left the cemetery and went to have a drink. A cognac. Then a second, and a third. We didn't say a word. Surrounded by cigarette smoke.

"Do you want to eat something?"

I was trying to break the silence. She shrugged her shoulders and signaled to the waiter to serve us again.

"After that, we'll go back," she said, looking for approval in my eyes.

It was dark. After the rain of the last few days, an icy mistral was blowing. I went back with her to the little house Manu had rented in L'Estaque. I'd only been there once before. Almost three years ago, when Manu and I had had a violent quarrel. He was involved in smuggling stolen cars to Algeria. The net was closing in on the gang, and he'd be caught in the trap. I'd come to warn him. To tell him to get out while he could. We drank *pastis* in the little garden. He'd laughed.

"Fuck you, Fabio! Don't meddle in this."

"I took the trouble to come here, Manu."

Lole watched us without saying a word. She was sipping her drink, and puffing slowly on her cigarette.

"Finish your drink, and get out. I've listened to enough of your bullshit, OK?"

I finished my drink, and stood up. He had that cynical smile of his. The one I remembered from the botched drugstore holdup and had never forgotten. And, behind his eyes, that despair that was uniquely his. Like a madness that would explain everything. An Artaud look. He looked increasingly like Artaud since he'd shaved off his moustache.

"A long time ago, I called you a spic. That was the wrong word. What you are is a loser."

Before he could react, I punched him in the face. He fell flat on his face in a scruffy rose bush. I walked up to him, calmly, coldly.

"Get up, loser."

As soon as he was on his feet, I smashed my left fist into his stomach and followed it with a right to the chin. He fell back again into the roses. Lole had put out her cigarette. She came toward me.

"Get out of here! And never come back."

I hadn't forgotten those words. Now, outside her door, I'd left the engine running. Lole looked at me, then, without a word, got out of the car. I followed her. She went straight to the bathroom. I heard the water running. I poured myself a glass of whisky then lit a fire. She came back dressed in a yellow bathrobe. She picked up a glass and the whisky bottle, then dragged a foam mattress in front of the fireplace and sat down by the fire.

"You ought to take a shower," she said without turning around. "Wash off the smell of death."

We spent hours drinking. In the dark. Without talking. Putting more wood on the fire, playing records. Paco de Lucia. Sabicas. Django. Then Billie Holiday, the complete edition. Lole had huddled up against me. Her body felt hot. She was shaking.

We reached the end of night. The hour when demons dance. The fire was crackling. I'd spent years dreaming of Lole's body. Pleasure at my fingertips. Her cries made my blood freeze. Thousands of knives stabbing my body. I turned to the fire. I lit two cigarettes and handed her one.

"How do you feel?" she asked.

"Like hell. How about you?"

I stood up and put my pants on. I felt her eyes on me while I dressed. For a moment, I saw her smile. It was a weary smile, but not a sad one.

"The whole thing stinks," I said.

She stood up and walked toward me. Naked and unashamed. Tenderly, she placed her hand on my chest. Her fingers were burning hot. I felt as if she was branding me. For life.

"What are you going to do now?"

I didn't have an answer to her question. I didn't have *the* answer to her question.

"The things a cop can do."

"Is that all?"

"It's all I can do."

"You can do more, if you want. Like fuck me."

"Is that why you did this?"

I didn't see the slap coming. She'd put her heart and soul in it.

"I don't barter or exchange. I don't blackmail, and I don't haggle. You can take me or leave me. Yes, go ahead, say it, the whole thing stinks."

She opened the door, her eyes still fixed on mine. I felt like an idiot. I was really ashamed of myself. I had a last vision of her body, her beauty. I knew how much I was going to lose as soon as the door slammed behind me.

"Get out of here!"

It was the second time she'd chased me away.

I was on the bed, leafing through a book I'd found on top of a pile of books and brochures under the bed. *Grand Suitcase Hotel* by Christian Dotremont, an author I didn't know.

Lole had highlighted a few phrases and a few poems in yellow:

At your window sometimes I do not knock
to your voice I do not reply
to your gesture I do not respond
  in order to deal only
with the immovable sea.

I suddenly felt like an intruder. I put the book away, timidly. I had to go. I took a last look at the bedroom, then the living room. I couldn't figure it out. Everything was tidy. The ashtrays were clean, the kitchen things had been put away. It was as if Lole was coming back any minute now. Or as if she'd left forever, free at last of the burden of nostalgia cluttering her life: books, photos, ornaments, record albums. But where was she? Since I had no answer to that, I watered the basil and the mint. I did it tenderly. Because I loved the way they smelled. And because I loved Lole.

There were three keys hanging from a nail. I tried them. The keys to the door, and the letter box, I supposed. I closed the door and put the keys in my pocket.

I passed Pierre Puget's unfinished masterpiece, the Vieille Charité. In the nineteenth century it had sheltered plague victims, at the beginning of the twentieth the destitute, and then, after the Germans ordered the area to be destroyed, all the people who'd been thrown out of their homes. It had seen a lot of misery. Now it was brand new, and looked magnificent, its lines accentuated by the pink stone. The buildings housed several museums, and the big chapel had become an exhibition space. There was a library, and even a tea room and restaurant. Every intellectual and artist Marseilles could muster put in an appearance there, almost as regularly as I went fishing.

There was a show of work by César, the Marseilles genius who'd made a fortune out of compressing pieces of scrap. Most people in Marseilles thought that was funny, but I just wanted to throw up. Tourists were flooding in, by the busload. Italians, Spanish, English, Germans. And Japanese, of course. So much bad taste in a place with such a painful history seemed to me a symbol of the end of the century.

Parisian bullshit had reached Marseilles. The city dreamed of being a capital. The capital of the South. Forgetting that what made it a capital was the fact that it was a port. A place where every race on earth mixed, and had done for centuries, ever since Protis had set foot on the shore and married the beautiful Ligurian princess Gyptis.

Djamel was coming along Rue Rodillat. He froze when he saw me, a look of surprise on his face. But he couldn't do anything except continue in my direction. Desperately hoping, I suppose, that I wouldn't recognize him.

"How are things, Djamel?"

"Fine, monsieur," he said, half-heartedly.

He looked around. I knew that, for him, just to be seen talking to a cop was shame enough. I took his arm. "Come on, I'll buy you a drink."

With my chin, I indicated the Bar des Treize-Coins, a bit farther along. The place I hung out. The police station was just over five hundred yards away, at the bottom of Passage des Treize-Coins, on the other side of Rue Sainte-Françoise. I was the only cop to come here. The others had their regular haunts farther down, either on Rue de l'Evêché or on Place des Trois-Cantons.

Despite the heat, we sat down inside, so as not to be seen. Ange, the owner, brought us two draft beers.

"So, what about the moped? Did you put it in a safe place?"

"Yes, monsieur. Just like you said." He drank some of his beer, then gave me a sidelong look. "Listen, monsieur. They already asked me a whole lotta questions. Do I have to start all over again?"

It was my turn to be surprised. "Who did?"

"You're a cop, ain't you?"

"Did I ask you any questions?"

"The others."

"What others?"

"The others. You know. The ones who gunned him down. They really put the heat on me. They told me they could take me in as an accessory to murder. Because of the moped. Did he really whack a guy?"

I felt a hot flash. So they knew. I drank, with my eyes closed.

I didn't want Djamel to see how agitated I was. The sweat streamed over my forehead and cheeks and down my neck. They knew. Just the thought of it gave me the shivers.

"Who was the guy?"

I opened my eyes. I ordered another beer. My mouth felt dry. I wanted to tell Djamel the whole story. Manu, Ugo and me. The story of three buddies. But whatever way I told him the story, he'd only remember Manu and Ugo. Not the cop. The cop represented everything that made him throw up. Injustice personified.

I piss on you and your police machine
Brainless sons of whores
Upholders of the laws

That was a lyric by NTM, a rap band from Saint-Denis. A big hit in the suburbs, among fifteen- to eighteen-year-olds, despite being boycotted by most radio stations. Hatred of the cops was the one thing that united the kids. True, we didn't help them have a very exalted image of us. I should know. And the words 'friendly cop' weren't written on my forehead. Anyhow, I wasn't a friendly cop. I believed in justice, the law, things like that. Things that no one respected, because we were the first to ignore them.

"A gangster," I said.

Dajamel didn't give a fuck about my answer. It was the only kind of answer a cop could give. He hadn't expected me to say, "He was a good guy, and besides, he was my buddy." But maybe that's what I should have said. Maybe. But I'd stopped knowing what to answer kids like him, kids like the ones I met in the projects. Sons of immigrants, without jobs, without futures, without hope.

They had only to switch on the TV news to realize that their fathers had been fucked over and that they themselves were going to fucked over even worse. Driss had told me about a friend of his named Hassan who'd gone straight to the bank, overjoyed, the day he'd received his first wages. He finally felt respectable, even on a minimum wage. "I'd like a loan of 30,000 francs, monsieur. To buy a car." The bank people had laughed in his face. That day, he'd understood it all. Djamel already knew it. And in his eyes, it was Manu, Ugo and me that I saw. Thirty years before.

"Can I take the moped out again?"

"If you want my advice, you should get rid of it. "

"The others told me it was no problem." He gave me another surreptitious look. "I didn't tell them you'd asked me to do the same."

"The same what?"

"You know. To hide it."

The telephone rang. From the counter, Ange signaled to me. "Pérol, for you."

I took the receiver. "How did you know I was here?"

"Never mind, Fabio. We found the girl."

I felt the earth vanish beneath my feet. I saw Djamel stand up and leave the bar without turning around. I was holding myself at the bar, like someone gripping a lifebelt. Ange was looking at me anxiously. I gestured to him to serve me a cognac. Just one. I drank it straight down. It wasn't a cognac that could hurt me the most.

5

IN WHICH, AT MOMENTS OF MISFORTUNE, YOU REMEMBER YOU'RE AN EXILE

I'd seen a lot of ugly things in my life, but nothing to compare with this. Leila was lying face down and naked in a country lane. Her clothes were bunched together under her left arm and there were three bullets in her back. One of them had perforated her heart. Columns of big black ants were scurrying around the bullet holes and the scratches that streaked her back. Now the flies were attacking too, fighting the ants for their share of dried blood.

Leila's body was covered in insect bites. But it didn't seem to have been bitten by a hungry dog or a field mouse. Small comfort, I told myself. There were long yellowish streaks between her buttocks and on her thighs. Dried shit. Her bowels must have loosened with the fear. Or when the first bullet struck.

After raping her, they must have let her think she was free. It must have excited them to see her running naked. Racing to the end of the lane, to the main road, hoping to see the lights of a car. Retrieving the power of speech. Help! Someone help me! Forgetting her fear, forgetting the terrible thing that had happened to her. Hoping a car would stop and humanity would come to the rescue, at last.

Leila must have kept on running after the first bullet. As if she'd felt nothing. As if that burning sensation in her back that took her breath away didn't even exist. She was already running away from this world, to a place where there was nothing but shit, piss and tears. And the dust she'd be eating forever. A place far from her father, her brothers, her occasional lovers, the love she'd longed for with all her heart, the family she'd never have, the children she'd never give birth to.

She must have screamed when the second bullet hit her. Because, whatever happens, the body just can't keep silent. It cries out. Not because of the pain now, intense as that is. It's gone beyond that. The mind summons all its energy and searches for a way out. Search, keep searching. Forget that what you'd like more than anything is to lie down in the grass and go to sleep. Shout, cry, but run. Run. They'll leave you alone now. The third bullet had put an end to all her dreams. The sadists.

With the back of my hand, I angrily brushed aside the ants and flies. I took a last look at the body, the body I'd once desired. The hot, heady scent of wild thyme rose from the ground. I'd have liked to make love to you here, Leila, on a summer evening. Yes, I'd have liked that. We'd have had as much pleasure and happiness as we wanted. Of course, every new caress would only have taken us closer to the inevitable: break-ups, tears, disillusionment, sadness, anguish, loathing. It wouldn't have made the slightest difference to the mess that human beings make of this world. I knew that. But at least it would have existed, that coming together in a passion that would have challenged the mess. Yes, Leila, I should have loved you. Old fool that I am. Forgive me.

I covered Leila's body again with the white sheet the gendarmes had thrown over her. I hesitated when I reached her face. The burn mark on her neck, the torn left ear where she'd lost an earring, the mouth biting the ground. I felt my stomach heave. I pulled the sheet angrily over her face and stood up. There was silence all around. Nobody was speaking. Only the cicadas continued their whine, indifferent to human tragedies.

As I stood up, I noticed that the sky was blue. An absolutely pure blue, made all the more luminous by the dark green of the pines. Like a picture postcard. Fucking sky. Fucking cicadas. Fucking country. Not that I was any better. I staggered away, drunk with hate and grief.

I walked back down the lane, with the cicadas singing all around me. We weren't far from the village of Vauvenargues, a few kilometers from Aix-en-Provence. Leila's body had been found by a couple of hikers. The lane was one of those that lead to Sainte-Victoire, the mountain that was such an inspiration to Cézanne. How many times had he come this way? Maybe he'd even stopped here and set up his easel and tried once more to capture its light.

I folded my arms on the hood of the car and laid my forehead on them and closed my eyes. Leila's smile. I couldn't feel the heat anymore. The blood was running cold in my veins. My heart had dried up. So much violence. If God existed, I'd have strangled him on the spot. Without batting an eyelid. And with all the fury of the damned. I felt an almost timid hand on my shoulder, followed by Pérol's voice:

"Do you want to stick around?"

"There's nothing to stick around for. Nobody needs us. Here or anywhere. You know that, Pérol, don't you? We're just worthless cops. We don't exist. Come on, let's get out of here."

He sat down at the wheel. I wedged myself into the seat, lit a cigarette, and closed my eyes. "Who's on the case?"

"Loubet. He was on duty. I think that's good."

"Yeah, he's a good cop."

Pérol took the Saint-Antoine turnoff from the highway. Being the conscientious cop he was, he'd switched on the police radio frequency. Its crackling filled the silence. Neither of us had said another word. But he didn't need to ask any questions, he'd already guessed what I wanted to do: see Mouloud before the others got to him. I knew Loubet would be tactful, but to me, Leila was like family. Pérol had understood that, and I was touched. I'd never confided in him. I'd gradually gotten to know him since he joined the squad. We respected each other, but that was as far as it went. We could have a drink together, but we were both too cautious to go beyond that and become friends. One thing was for sure: like me, he had no future as a cop.

He was thinking about what he'd seen. He felt the same pain and the same hatred as I did. And I knew why.

"How old is your daughter?"

"Twenty."

"And... is everything OK?"

"She listens to the Doors, the Stones, and Dylan. It could have been worse." He smiled. "I mean, I'd have preferred her to be a teacher or a doctor. Anything. Instead of which, she's a cashier at FNAC, and I can't say I'm crazy about it."

"And you think she's crazy about it? You know, there are hundreds of cashiers out there who may be all kinds of things one day. Kids don't have much of a future these days, so they grab whatever they can, when they can."

"Have you ever wanted to have children?"

"I've thought about it."

"Did you love the girl?" he asked, and immediately bit his tongue for daring to be so direct. But I knew he'd asked as a friend, and again, I was touched. All the same, I didn't want to answer. I don't like answering private questions. The answers are often ambiguous and can be interpreted in different ways. Even when the other person is close to you. He sensed that.

"You don't have to talk about it."

"You know, Leila had the kind of opportunities only one

immigrant's child in a thousand has. It must have been too much. Life took it all away from her again. I should have married her, Pérol."

"That's doesn't stop shit from happening."

"Sometimes, all it takes is one gesture, one word, to change the course of someone's life. Even if you know it won't last forever. Did you think about your daughter?"

"I think about her every time she goes out. But you don't find scumbags like these on every street corner."

"True. But right now, they're out there somewhere."

Pérol suggested he wait for me in the car. I told Mouloud everything. Apart from the ants and the flies. I told him that other cops would come see him, and that he'd have to identify the body and fill out a lot of papers. And that if he needed me, of course I'd be there.

He'd sat down and listened to me without flinching. Looking me right in the eyes. The tears weren't ready to flow yet. Like mine, his heart had turned to ice. Forever. He started to shake, without even realizing it. He'd stopped listening. He was ageing right there in front of my eyes. The years were suddenly moving faster, catching up with him. Even the happy years had a bitter taste now. It's at moments of misfortune that we remember we're all exiles. My father had told me that.

Mouloud had just lost the second great love of his life. His pride and joy. The one who'd have made all his sacrifices, even the latest ones, worthwhile. The one who'd finally have proved to him that he'd done the right thing in uprooting himself. Algeria wasn't his country anymore. And now France had rejected him once and for all. Now he was nothing but a poor Arab, and no one would care what happened to him.

He'd wait for death, here in this shitty housing project. He'd never go back to Algeria. He'd gone back once, after

Fos. With Leila, Driss and Kader. To see how things were 'down there.' They'd stayed twenty days. He'd soon realized that Algeria wasn't his story anymore. It was a story that didn't interest him. The empty, neglected shops. The land, parceled out to former mujaheddin and left uncultivated. The deserted villages, turned in on their own misery. He couldn't start over again, make his dreams come true, in a place like that. He hadn't rediscovered his youth on the streets of Oran. Everything was on 'the other side.' And he'd started to miss Marseilles.

The evening they'd moved to this little two-room apartment, Mouloud, instead of offering up a prayer, spoke to his children. "We're going to live here, in this country, France. With the French. It isn't a good thing, but it isn't the worst that could happen. It's fate. We have to adapt, but we mustn't forget who we are."

I called Kader, in Paris. I told him to come right away, and to plan on spending some time here. Mouloud would need him, and Driss too. Mouloud then said a few words to him in Arabic. Finally, I phoned Mavros at the gym. It was Saturday afternoon, which meant that Driss was there, training. But it was Mavros I wanted. I told him about Leila.

"Give him a fight, Georges. Soon. And make him work. Every evening."

"Shit, man, if I put the boy in a fight now, or even in two months, he'll be killed. He'll be a good boxer one day, but he isn't ready yet."

"I'd rather he was killed in the ring than did something stupid. Georges, do this for me. Take care of him. Personally."

"OK, OK. Shall I pass him to you?"

"No. His father will tell him later. When he gets home."

Mouloud nodded. He was the father. It was up to him to tell him the news. I hung up.

Mouloud got up from the armchair, moving like an old man. "You should go now, monsieur. I'd like to be alone."

He was already alone. Alone and lost.

The sun had just set, and I was out at sea. I'd been out more than an hour. I'd brought bread, sausage and a few beers with me. But I couldn't fish. To fish, your mind has to be clear. It's like billiards. You look at the ball. You concentrate on it, and the trajectory you want it to move along, then, confidently and decisively, you transmit the required force to the cue. In fishing, you cast the rod, then concentrate on the float. You don't cast the rod just any old how. You can recognize an angler by the way he casts. Casting is part of the art of angling. Once you've attached the bait to the hook, you have to let yourself be imbued by the sea and the play of light on it. It isn't enough to know that the fish is there, under the surface. The hook has to touch the water as lightly as a fly. You have to anticipate the bite, to strike the fish at the very moment it bites.

My casting lacked conviction. I had a lump in the pit of my stomach, and the beer did nothing to dissolve it. A lump of nerves and tears. It would have done me good to cry. But nothing came out. I'd live with that horrible image of Leila, and that pain, as long as those bastards were still at large. I was reassured by the fact that Loubet was on the case. He was really thorough. He wouldn't overlook any clues. If there was one chance in a thousand that he'd track down the bastards, he'd find it. He'd proved himself. As a detective, he was a whole lot better than most, a whole lot better than me.

I felt bad, though, about not leading the investigation. Not because I wanted to make it a personal affair, but because I couldn't bear the thought that these bastards were at large. No, it wasn't really that. I knew what was tormenting me. It was hate. I wanted to kill them.

I wasn't catching anything today. But I couldn't resign myself to long-line fishing. You catch a lot of fish that way. Pandora, sea bream, gurnard, goby. But I don't enjoy it. You attach hooks every six feet along the line, and let it trail on the water. I still had a long line in the boat, just in case. For days when I didn't want to get home empty-handed. But to me, fishing meant a rod and line.

Thinking about Leila had reminded me of Lole, and Lole had brought me back to Ugo and Manu. It all made a hell of a noise in my head. Too many questions, and no answers. But there was one question that stood out, a question I didn't want to answer. What was I going to do? I hadn't done anything when Manu died. Although I hadn't wanted to admit it to myself, I'd been sure Manu would end up like that. Shot down on the street. By a cop, or, more likely, by some small time gangster working for someone else. That was the nature of things on the streets. For Ugo to die in the same way wasn't so predictable. He didn't have that hatred of the world that Manu carried deep inside him, and which had continued growing as the years went by.

I didn't think Ugo had changed that much. I couldn't believe he was capable of taking out a gun and shooting a cop. He knew what life was about. That was why he'd broken with Marseilles, and Manu. And given up Lole. I was sure someone capable of doing that wouldn't have put his life on the line. If he'd been cornered, he'd have let himself be arrested. The joint is just an interlude. You get out eventually. Alive. If there was one thing I had to do for Ugo, it was that: understand what had happened.

I was thinking again about my conversation with Djamel when I felt the bite, and didn't strike quickly enough. I pulled in the line and attached another bait. If I wanted to understand, I had to follow that lead. Had Auch identified Ugo from the testimony of Zucca's bodyguards? Or had he had him tailed as soon as he left Lole's? Had he let Ugo kill Zucca? It was possible, but I couldn't accept it. I didn't like Auch, but I didn't think he was that Machiavellian. I went back to another question: how had Ugo found out about Zucca so quickly? Who'd told him? Another lead to be followed up. I didn't yet know how to go about it, but I had to try. Without getting in Auch's way.

I finished the beers and actually managed to catch a bass. About four and a half pounds. For such a bad day, it was better than nothing. Honorine was waiting for me when I got back. Sitting on her terrace, watching TV through the window.

"Poor man!" she said, when she saw my bass. "You'd never have made your fortune as a fisherman!"

"I never set out to make my fortune."

"But a bass like that..." She looked at it regretfully. "How are you going to cook it?"

I shrugged.

"It mightn't be too bad with a *Belle Hélène* sauce."

"I'd need a crab for that, and I don't have one."

"Oh, no, you've got that look in your eyes. I guess I'd better not do anything to annoy you! Hey, I have some cod tongues. They've been marinating since yesterday. How about I bring them tomorrow?"

"I've never tried them. Where did you get them?"

"A niece of mine brought them from Sète. I haven't eaten them since my poor Toinou passed on. Anyhow, I've left you some vegetable soup. It's still warm. You need a rest, you're not looking so good."

Babette didn't hesitate for a moment.

"Batisti," she said.

Batisti. Shit! Why hadn't I thought of him earlier? It was so obvious, it hadn't even entered my mind. Batisti had been a henchman of Mémé Guérini, the Marseilles boss in the Forties. He'd dropped out about twenty years ago, after the massacre at the Tanagra, a bar in the Vieux-Port, in which four rivals, all associates of Zampa's, had been slain. As Batisti was a friend of Zampa's, had he felt threatened himself? Babette didn't know.

He'd started a little import-export company and led a quiet life, respected by every gangster in Marseilles. He'd never taken sides in the gang wars, had appeared indifferent to power and money. He advised, served as a go-between, put guys together. For the Spaggiari heist in Nice, he was the one who organized the team that had gotten into the safes of the Société Générale in the dead of night, using blowtorches. When the time came to share out the loot, he refused to take any commission. He'd simply done a good turn. He became even more respected. And in the underworld, respect is the best life insurance.

One day, Manu showed up on his doorstep. It was something you had to do, if you didn't want to remain a small time holdup man all your life. Manu had hesitated for a long time. Since Ugo's departure, he'd become a loner. He didn't trust anyone. But holdups were more dangerous than they used to be. Plus, there was more competition now. For a lot of young Arabs, it had become a favorite sport. A few successful jobs and you could get together the money you needed to become a dealer and have control of a patch, maybe a whole housing project. Gaëtan Zampa, the man who'd rebuilt the Marseilles underworld, had just hanged himself in his cell. Le Mat and The Belgian were trying to avoid things fragmenting even more. New recruits were needed.

Manu started doing occasional jobs for The Belgian. Batisti and Manu had liked each other from the start. For Manu,

Batisti was the father he'd never had. An ideal father, someone who was just like him, and never lectured him. For me, that was the worst kind of father. I didn't like Batisti. But I'd had a real father, and hadn't had anything to complain about.

"Batisti," Babette repeated. "Obvious, sweetheart, when you think about it."

She was very pleased with herself. She poured herself another *marc* from the Garlaban. "Chin-chin," she said, raising her glass and smiling. After coffee, Honorine had gone back to her house to take a little nap. We were sitting in deckchairs under a parasol on the terrace, in our bathing costumes. The heat clung to our skins. I'd called Babette the night before, and had been lucky to find her in.

"So, handsome, have you finally decided to marry me?"

"No, just to invite you, gorgeous. Lunch at my place, tomorrow."

"You want to ask me for something. Same old bastard! How long has it been? Huh? I bet you don't even know."

"Er... about three months?"

"Eight, asshole! You must have been putting it about all over town."

"Only with hookers."

"Shame on you! And here was I sitting at home, moping." She sighed. "OK, what's on the menu?"

"Cod tongues, grilled bass, and freshly made lasagne with fennel."

"Are you dumb or something? I meant, what do you want to talk about? Just so's I can revise."

"I want you to explain what's going on in the underworld at the moment."

"Is this in connection with your buddies? I read about Ugo. I'm sorry."

"Maybe."

"Hey, what was that you said? Cod tongues? Are they good?"

"Never tried them, gorgeous. It'll be a first, for both of us."

"Hmm. How about a first course right now? I'll bring my little nightdress, and I'll supply the rubbers. I have blue ones, to match my eyes!"

"The thing is, it's almost midnight, the sheets are dirty, and the clean ones haven't been ironed."

"Bastard!" She'd laughed and hung up.

I'd known Babette for nearly twenty-five years. I'd met her one night at the Péano. She'd just been hired as a proofreader on *La Marseillaise*. We'd had an affair, the kind people had in those days. It might last a night, or a week. Never more than that.

We'd met again at the press conference where the reorganization of the Neighborhood Surveillance Squads was announced. With me as the guest star. She'd become a journalist, specializing in local news, then had left the paper to go freelance. She worked regularly for *Le Canard enchaîné*, and often did investigative pieces for both daily and weekly papers. She knew a lot more about crime, the underworld and the politics of law and order than I did. She was a walking encyclopedia. Cute, too. Good enough to eat. There was a touch of the Botticelli Madonnas about her. But you had only to look in her eyes to see it wasn't God that inspired her, but life. And all the pleasures that went with it.

We had another affair, as brief as the first one. But we continued seeing each other from time to time. We'd have dinner, and spend the night together. Sometimes a whole weekend. She didn't expect anything, and I didn't ask for anything. We got on with our lives, until the next time. Until the day there wasn't a next time. And the last time, we'd both known it was the last time.

I'd started cooking early in the morning, listening to old

blues songs by Lightnin' Hopkins. After washing the bass, I'd filled it with fennel, then drizzled olive oil over it. Then I made the lasagne sauce. The rest of the fennel had simmered gently in salt water, with a touch of butter. In a well-oiled pan, I gently fried slivers of onion, garlic and finely chopped pepper. A spoonful of vinegar soup, then I added tomatoes that I'd cut into little cubes and plunged in boiling water. When the water evaporated, I added the fennel.

I was finally calming down. Cooking had that effect on me. My mind could escape the twisted labyrinth of thought and concentrate on smells and tastes. And pleasure.

Babette arrived just as *Last Night Blues* was playing and I was pouring myself a third *pastis*. She was wearing very tight-fitting black jeans, a polo shirt—blue to match her eyes—and a white cotton cap on her long, curly hair. We were more or less the same age, but she never seemed to get any older. The tiny wrinkles around her eyes or at the corners of her lips merely added to her seductive power. She knew it and made skillful use of it. It always had the same effect on me. She went straight over to the frying pan and sniffed, then offered me her lips.

"Hi, sailor," she said. "Hmm, I could use a *pastis*."

I'd started the barbecue on the terrace. Honorine brought the cod tongues. They were marinating in a pot with oil, chopped parsley and pepper. I'd followed her instructions and made fritters, using two stiffly beaten egg whites for the pastry.

"Go and drink your *pastis* in peace, you two. I'll take care of the rest."

Cod tongues, she told us when we sat down to eat, were a refined dish. They could be made with grated cheese, with a clam or *Provençale* sauce, in foil parcels, or even cooked in white wine with a few strips of truffles and mushrooms. But, in her opinion, they were best in fritters. In fact, they were so delicious, Babette and I couldn't wait to try the other recipes.

"Now do I get my stick of barley sugar?" Babette asked, licking her lips.

"Don't you think we're too old for that?"

"You're never too old to have a little treat, sweetheart!"

I needed to think over all the things she'd told me about the underworld. It had been quite a lesson. I was dying to go see Batisti. But it could wait till tomorrow. Today was Sunday, and Sunday was a special day for me.

Babette must have read my thoughts. "Cool it, Fabio. Let it go, it's Sunday." She stood up and took my hand. "Shall we go for a swim? That'll calm you down!"

We swam until our lungs were bursting. I liked it like that, and so did she. She'd wanted me to take the boat out and head for the sea off the Baie des Singes. I'd had to resist. It was a rule that I never allowed anyone else on the boat. My boat was my island. She'd yelled at me, called me an asshole and a loser, then dived into the water. It was as cool as anyone could wish. When we were breathless and our arms ached, we floated on our backs.

"What do you plan to do about Ugo?"

"Understand first. Then I'll see."

For the first time I realized that understanding mightn't be enough. Understanding is like opening a door without knowing what's behind it.

"Be careful what you're getting into."

She dived again and swam toward my house.

It was late. Babette had stayed. We'd gone to get a cuttlefish pizza from Louisette's and ate it on the terrace, drinking a Côtes de Provence rosé from Mas Negrel, chilled just right. We knocked back the whole bottle. Then, slowly, in between cigarettes, searching for the right words, I started talking about Leila. The rape, and everything else. By the time I finished, it was dark. I fell silent. I was drained. Silence enveloped us. No music, nothing. Nothing but the sound of the water against the rocks. And whispers in the distance.

On the sea wall, families were having dinner by the dim light of kerosene lamps, their fishing rods wedged into the rock. Occasionally, we heard laughter, followed by a 'shhh.' As if laughing might frighten away the fish. We were in a distant place, a long way from the all the shit of the world. There was a feeling of happiness. The waves. The voices in the distance. The salt smell. Even Babette beside me.

She ran her hand through my hair and gently drew my head down onto her shoulder. She smelled of the sea. Tenderly, she stroked my cheek, then my neck, then moved her hand up again to the back of my head. It felt soft. At last, I started to cry.

6.

IN WHICH DAWN IS MERELY AN ILLUSION THAT THE WORLD IS BEAUTIFUL

The aroma of coffee woke me. That was something that hadn't happened in years. Since long before Rosa. Getting her out of bed in the morning was no easy matter. Seeing her get up to make coffee was little short of a miracle. Carmen maybe? I couldn't remember. I smelled toast, and decided to get up. Babette hadn't gone home. She'd lain down next to me. I'd rested my head on her shoulder. She'd put her arm around me. I'd fallen asleep, without another word. I'd said everything there was to say. My despair, my hates, my solitude.

On the terrace, breakfast was ready. Bob Marley was singing *Stir It Up*. It suited the day. Blue sky, glassy sea, sun already up. Babette had put on my bathrobe. She had a cigarette in her mouth, and was buttering bread, her body moving almost imperceptibly to the rhythm of the music. For a fraction of a second, happiness existed.

"I should have married you!" I said.

"Don't talk bullshit!"

And instead of giving me her lips to kiss, she offered me her cheek. She was establishing a new relationship between us. We'd moved into a world where lies had ceased to exist. I liked Babette. I told her so.

"You're nuts, Fabio, you know that? You're crazy for love. I'm crazy for sex. No common ground." She looked at me as if she was seeing me for the first time. "And ultimately, I prefer it that way. Because I like you too."

The coffee she'd made was delicious. She told me she was going to propose an investigation into Marseilles for *Libération*. The economic downturn, the Mafia, soccer. It would be a way of getting paid for the information she'd be bringing me. When she left, she promised to call me in two or three days.

I sat there smoking and looking at the sea. Babette had painted me a precise picture of the situation. The Marseilles underworld was finished. Inter-gang rivalry had weakened it, and there was nobody around these days who had the caliber to be a boss. Marseilles was just a market now, coveted by the Neapolitan Camorra, whose activities centered on the heroin and cocaine traffic. In 1991, a Milan weekly called *Il Mondo* had estimated the turnover of the Camorra bosses Carmine Alfieri and Lorenzo Novoletta at seven billion and six billion dollars respectively. For the past ten years, two organizations had been fighting it out for control of Marseilles: the New Camorra, run by Raffaele Cutolo, and the New Family, controlled by the Volgro and Guiliano families.

Zucca had chosen sides. *La Nuova famiglia.* He'd pulled out of prostitution, night clubs and gambling, leaving part of it to the Arab mafia and the other part to the Marseilles gangs who'd taken over from the Corsicans. He ran things for them, but his real business was with the Camorra boss Michele Zaza, known as O Pazzo, the Madman, who operated the Naples-Marseilles-Sint Marteens route, Sint Marteens being the Dutch part of the island of Saint-Martin in the West Indies. For Zaza, Zucca recycled drug profits into supermarkets, restaurants and apartment buildings. They practically owned Boulevard Longchamp, one of the ritziest streets in the city.

Zaza had been busted a month earlier at Villeneuve-Loubet, near Nice, in a *Mare verde* operation. But that made no difference to anything. With a skill that amounted almost to genius, Zucca had developed strong financial connections with

Switzerland and Germany. Zucca was protected by the Neapolitans. Everyone knew that. Taking him out was an act of total insanity.

I'd told Babette it was Ugo who killed Zucca, in revenge for Manu. And that I couldn't see who might have put an idea like that in his head, or why. I rang Batisti.

"Fabio Montale. Name mean anything to you?"

"The cop," he replied, after a short silence.

"Manu's friend, and Ugo's."

He gave a short, ironic laugh.

"I want to see you."

"I'm really busy right now."

"I'm not. I'm even free at noon. Why don't you invite me somewhere nice? We need to talk."

"And if I don't?"

"I can make things difficult for you."

"So can I."

"But from what I hear, you don't like too much publicity."

I was feeling great when I got back to the station. My head was clear, and I was determined to see this through to the end, for Ugo's sake. The Leila case I'd leave to the official investigation for the moment. I went down to the squad room for the weekly ritual of putting the teams together.

Fifty uniformed cops. Ten cars. Two vans. Night teams, day teams. Allocated by neighborhoods, housing projects, supermarkets, service stations, banks, post offices, schools. Routine. Some of the guys I hardly knew, some not at all. They were rarely the same. Not quite the mission I'd originally been given. Young and old. Family men and young married men. Quiet family men and young guys spoiling for a fight. Not racists, or only toward Arabs. And blacks, and gypsies. That was none of my business. All I had to do was put the teams together. I did the roll call, and chose the team members according to the guys' faces, which didn't always give the best results.

Among the guys was a West Indian. He was the first one they'd sent me. Tall, well built, with close-cropped hair. I didn't like that. Guys like that think they're more French than a peasant from the Auvergne. They weren't crazy about Arabs. Or gypsies.

I'd rubbed shoulders with them in Paris, at the Belleville precinct. They really took it out on anyone who wasn't a peasant from the Auvergne. "You don't see any Arabs where I come from," one of them had said to me. "Well, they've chosen which side they're on!" I didn't feel like I was on any particular side. I was simply serving the law. But events were proving him right. I preferred to see guys like that working for the Post Office, or the electricity company. The West Indian answered to his name. Luc Reiver. I put him together with three older guys. I was interested to see what would happen.

Days are only beautiful early in the morning. I should have remembered that. Dawn is merely an illusion that the world is beautiful. When the world opens its eyes, reality reasserts itself, and you're back with the same old shit. That's what I told myself when Loubet came into my office. I knew what it was about, because he remained standing, with his hands in his pockets.

"The girl was killed around two o'clock on Saturday morning. With the heat, and the field mice... well, it could have been even more disgusting than it was. What happened before that, we don't know. According to the lab, she was gang-raped. Thursday, Friday. But not where she was found... From behind and in front, if you really want to know."

"You can spare me the details."

From the right pocket of his jacket, he took a little plastic bag. One by one, he placed three bullets on the table.

"These were taken from the girl's body."

I looked at him, and waited. He took another small bag from his left pocket, and put down two bullets, parallel with the others.

"And these we took from Al Dakhil and his bodyguards."

They were identical. They'd come from the same weapons. The two killers and the rapists were the same. My throat went dry. "Shit!" I managed to say.

"The case is closed, Fabio."

"There's one missing." I pointed to the third bullet. An Astra special.

He looked straight back at me. "They didn't use it on Saturday night."

"There were only two of them. There's a third man still out there."

"A third man? Where did you get that idea?"

I had a theory about rapes. A rape could only be committed by one man or three, never two. With two, there has to be one who doesn't mind waiting his turn. One man alone was the classic. With three, it became a perverted game. But I'd only just constructed this theory. It was a pure hunch. And it came out of anger. I couldn't accept that the case was closed. There had to be another man, because I had to find him.

Loubet looked at me regretfully. He collected the bullets and put them back in their bags. "I'm open to suggestion, but... I do have four other cases on my hands."

He was holding the bullet from the Astra special between his fingers.

"Is this the one that perforated her heart?" I asked.

He looked surprised. "I have no idea. Why?"

"I'd like to know."

An hour later, he called to confirm. That was indeed the bullet that had perforated Leila's heart. Of course, that didn't get me anywhere. It just endowed that particular bullet with its own mystery, a mystery I was determined to solve. From Loubet's tone, I guessed he didn't consider the case completely closed.

I met Batisti at the Bar de la Marine. The place he hung out. It had become a meeting place for skippers. Louis Audibert's painting of the card game from *Marius* and the photo of Pagnol and his wife on the waterfront were both still on the wall. At a table behind us, Marcel, the owner, was explaining to two Italian tourists that, yes, the movie really had been filmed here. The dish of the day was fried cuttlefish and aubergine in grated cheese. With a nice Le Rousset rosé, from the owner's reserve stock.

I'd come on foot. For the pleasure of strolling around the harbor, eating salted peanuts. I loved that walk. Quai du Port, Quai des Belges, Quai de Rive-Neuve. I loved the smell of the harbor. Sea and oil.

The fishwives were as loud as ever. They were selling the day's catch. Bream, sardine, bass and pandora. In front of an African's stall, a group of Germans were haggling over some little ebony elephants. The African would get the better of them. He'd add a fake silver bracelet, with a fake hallmark, agree to a hundred francs for the lot, and still come out on top. I smiled. It was as if I'd always known these things. My father let go of my hand, and I ran toward the elephants and crouched to see them better. I didn't dare touch them. The African was looking at me and rolling his eyes. It was my father's first present to me. I was four years old.

"Why did you point Ugo in Zucca's direction?" I asked Batisti. "That's all I want to know. And who stands to gain by it?"

Bastisti was a sly old fox. He chewed his food slowly, and finished his glass of wine. "How much do you know?"

"I know a lot of things I shouldn't know."

He looked straight at me, trying to figure out if I was bluffing. I didn't bat an eyelid. "My informants were positive."

"Stop right there, Batisti! I don't give a damn about your informants, because they don't exist! You'd been told what to say, and you said it. You sent Ugo to do what nobody else had the balls to do, because it was too risky. Zucca was being protected. And then Ugo got himself whacked. By cops. Cops who knew what he'd done. It was a trap."

I felt as if I was long-line fishing. Setting out a lot of hooks, and waiting for a bite. He finished his coffee. I had the feeling I'd used up my credit.

"Listen, Montale. There's an official version. Why don't you stick to it? You're just a neighborhood cop, you should stay that way. You have a nice little house, try to keep it." He stood up. "The advice is free. I'll pick up the tab."

"And how about Manu? Know nothing about that either? You don't give a damn, do you?"

It was a dumb thing to say, but it was anger that had made me say it. I'd come out with the theories I'd fabricated for myself, none of them solid. All I'd gotten in return was a barely veiled threat. The only reason Batisti had come here was to find out how much I knew.

"What holds true for Ugo holds true for Manu too."

"But you liked Manu, didn't you?"

He gave me a nasty look. I'd hit home. But he didn't reply. He stood up and headed for the counter, the check in his hand. I followed him.

"Let me tell you this, Batisti. You've been jerking me around, I know that. But don't think I'm going to drop this. Ugo came to see you for information. All he wanted was to avenge Manu, and you fucked him over real good. So I'm not going to let go of you." He picked up his change. I put my hand on his arm and moved my face close to his ear. "One more thing," I whispered.

"You're so scared of dying you'd do anything. You're crapping yourself with fear. You're a man without honor, Batisti. When I find out the truth about Ugo, I won't forget you. You can take my word for that."

He freed his arm, and looked at me pityingly. "You'll be whacked first."

"You'd better hope I am."

He went out without turning back. I stood for a moment and watched him go. Then I ordered another coffee. The two Italian tourists stood up and left in a profusion of *Ciao, ciaos*.

If Ugo still had any relatives in Marseilles, they probably didn't read the newspapers. Nobody had come forward after he was killed, or after the appearance of the death notice, which I'd passed on to the three morning dailies. The burial certificate had been issued on Friday. I'd had to make a decision. I didn't want to see him buried in a communal grave, like a dog. I'd broken into my reserves and agreed to cover the funeral expenses. I wouldn't take a vacation this year. What the hell, I never took a vacation anyway.

The guys opened the vault. It was my parents'. There was still a place for me in it, but I'd decided to take my time. I didn't think my parents would mind too much about having a visitor. The heat was hellish. I looked at the dark, damp hole. Ugo wasn't going to like it. Neither would anybody. Neither would Leila. Her funeral was set for tomorrow. I hadn't yet decided if I was going or not. To Mouloud and his children, I was just a stranger now. And a cop. A cop who hadn't been able to stop it from happening.

Things were falling apart. I'd spent the last few years in a state of calm indifference, as if I'd said goodbye to the world. Nothing really touched me. The old friends who'd stopped calling. The women who'd left me. I'd put my dreams and my anger on hold. I was getting older and I'd lost all desire, all passion. I fucked hookers. Happiness was at the end of a fishing line.

Manu's death had shaken all that. But I don't suppose it had registered that much on my personal Richter scale. Ugo's death, on the other hand, was like a slap in the face. It startled me out of an uneasy sleep, and when I woke up, I saw I was still alive, and how stupid I'd been. What I thought of Manu and Ugo made no difference. They'd lived. I'd have liked to talk to Ugo. I'd have liked him to tell me about his travels. Sitting on the rocks at night, at les Goudes, that had been our big dream: to just up sticks and leave.

"Why the hell do they want to go so far?" Toinou had screamed, appealing to Honorine. "What do these boys want to see what they can't see here? Tell me that! You can find every country in the world in Marseilles. People from every race, every latitude."

Honorine had placed a plate of fish soup on the table in front of us.

"Our fathers all arrived in this town from somewhere else. Whatever they were looking for, they found it here. Even if they didn't find it, they stayed." He'd paused for breath, then looked at us angrily. "Taste that!" he'd cried. "It's a cure for every stupid notion you can think of!"

"We're dying here," Ugo had dared to say.

"We die in other places too, my boy! And that's worse!"

Ugo had come back, and he'd died. That was the end of his journey. I nodded, and the coffin was swallowed up by the dark, damp hole. I choked back my tears. A taste of blood stayed in my mouth.

I stopped off at the head office of Radio Taxis, on the corner of Boulevard de Plombière and Boulevard de la Glacière. I wanted to follow the trail of the taxi. It might not lead anywhere, but it was the only thing connecting the two killers on Place de l'Opéra with Leila.

The guy in the office was leafing wearily through a porn mag. A typical *mia*. Ray-bans shielding his eyes, long hair down the back of his neck, a horrible blow-dry, a flowery shirt opened to reveal a chest covered in black hair, a big gold chain with a figure of Jesus at the end of it, with diamonds for eyes. The expression *mia* came from Italy. Lancia had launched a car called the Mia, with an opening in the window, which allowed you to put your elbow outside without lowering the window. That was too much for the wits of Marseilles!

The bars were full of *mias*. Vulgar, narrow-minded posers and wheeler-dealers. They spent their days propping up the bar, drinking Ricard. They sometimes did a bit of work, if they had to.

This one probably drove a Renault 12 covered with headlights, with the names Dédé and Valérie displayed in the front, a couple of soft toys dangling from the roof, and the steering wheel covered in moquette. He turned a page. His eyes rested on the crotch of a buxom blonde. At last he deigned to look up at me.

"What can I do for you?" he said, with a strong Corsican accent.

I showed him my badge. He barely looked at it, as if he knew it by heart.

"Can you read?" I said.

He pushed his glasses down his nose, and looked at me indifferently. Talking seemed to exhaust him. I told him I wanted to know who'd been driving a Renault 21, registration number 625 JLT 13, on Saturday night. Something about a red light passed on Avenue des Aygalades.

"So they send you out for things like that now, do they?"

"They send us out for all kinds of things. If we don't look into them, people write to the minister. There's been a complaint."

"A complaint? For running a red light?" It was as if the sky had fallen in! What kind of world were we living in?

"There are a lot of crazy pedestrians out there," I said.

This time, he took off his Ray-bans and gave me the once-over. Just in case I was putting him on. I shrugged my shoulders, wearily.

"Yeah," he said, "and we're the ones who pay for it! You'd be better off wasting less time on shit like this and keeping the streets safe instead."

"Pedestrian crossings need to be kept safe, too," I replied. He was starting to break my balls. "I want the name, address and telephone number of the driver."

"I'll tell him you want to see him at the station house."

"Not good enough. I have to make out a written summons."

"Which precinct are you from?"

"Central."

"Can I see your badge again?"

He took it and noted my name on a piece of paper. I knew I was crossing a line, but it was too late. He gave me back the badge, with a look of distaste.

"Montale. Italian, isn't it?" I nodded. He seemed lost in thought for a bit, then he looked at me again. "I'm sure we can come to some arrangement over the red light. We do you a lot of good turns, don't we?"

Five more minutes of this banter, and I'd have strangled him with his gold chain, or made him eat his Jesus figure. He leafed through a register, stopped at a page, and ran his finger down a list.

"Pascal Sanchez. Can you remember that, or do you want me to write it down for you?"

Pérol reviewed the day for me. 11:30: a minor caught shoplifting, at Carrefour. A trivial offence, but the parents had to be sent for and a file started. 1:13: a fight in a bar called the Balto, on Chemin du Merlan, between three gypsies with a girl in the middle. They'd all been brought in, then immediately released, because no one pressed charges. 2:18: A radio call. A mother arrived at her local station house with her son, who had a severely bruised face. According to him, he'd been beaten up outside his school, the Lycée Marcel Pagnol. The alleged perpetrators and their parents had been sent for and confronted with the boy. The case had taken up the whole afternoon. There were apparently no drugs involved, no extortion. There'd be a follow-up, all the same. The parents had been given a sermon, in the hope that it might serve some purpose. Pure routine.

But the good news was that we'd finally found a way to collar Nacer Mourrabed, a young dealer who operated out of the Bassens housing project. He'd gotten into a fight last night coming out of a bar in L'Estaque called the Miramar. The guy had registered a complaint. He'd even pressed charges and had showed up at the station house to make a statement. A lot of people chickened out, and decided to keep shtum, even in the case of a straight robbery, without violence. They were afraid, and they didn't trust the cops.

Mourrabed. I knew his sheet by heart. Twenty-two years old. He'd been in police custody seven times, the first time when he was fifteen. A good score. But he was clever. We'd never been able to pin anything on him. Maybe this time.

He'd been dealing on a big scale for months, but always kept his hands clean. He had eight or ten kids, no older than fifteen or sixteen, doing the dirty work for him. One would carry the junk, the other would take the money. He'd stay in his car and watch. He'd collect later. In a bar, in the subway or on a bus, in a supermarket. Somewhere different every time. Nobody had ever tried to double-cross him. Except once. The kid had been found with a gash on his cheek. Naturally, he hadn't fingered Mourrabed. If he had, he might have gotten something worse than a gash on the cheek.

We'd gone after the kids several times. But it was pointless. They'd rather spend time in the joint than give up Mourrabed. Whenever we collared the one who had the junk, we'd take his picture, start a file, and let him go. The quantities were always too small to make the charge stick. We'd tried, and it had been thrown out by the judge.

Pérol suggested we collar Mourrabed when he woke up tomorrow morning, while he was still in bed. That was fine by me. Before he left, early for once, Pérol said, "How was the funeral? Not too hard?"

I shrugged, but didn't reply.

"It'd be nice if you could come over for a meal one day."

He left without waiting for an answer. That was the way Pérol was: direct and unassuming. I took over for the night, with Cerruti.

The phone rang. It was Pascal Sanchez. I'd left a message with his wife.

"Hey, I've never run a red light. Especially not in the place you say. I never touch that part of town. Too many Arabs."

I didn't pick him up on that. I wanted to bring Sanchez around gently. "I know, Monsieur Sanchez, I know. But there's a witness. He took down your number. It's his word against yours."

"What time was it you said?" he asked, after a silence.

"10:38 p.m."

"Impossible," he replied, without hesitation. "I was on a break at the time. I went for a drink at the Bar de l'Hôtel de Ville. Hey, I even bought some smokes. People saw me. I'm not lying to you. I have at least forty witnesses."

"I don't need as many as that. Come by my office tomorrow, about eleven. I'll take your statement. And the names, addresses and telephone numbers of two witnesses. It should be easy to clear this up."

I had an hour to kill before Cerutti arrived. I decided to go have a drink at the Treize-Coins.

"The boy's been looking for you," Ange said. "You know, the one you brought here on Saturday."

I downed a beer, and set off to find Djamel. I'd never spent so much time in the neighborhood since being posted to Marseilles. The first time had been the other day, when I was trying to find Ugo. All these years I'd stayed on the outside. Place de Lenche, Rue Baussenque and Rue Sainte-Françoise, Rue Francois-Moisson, Boulevard des Dames, Grand-Rue, Rue Caisserie. The farthest in I went was Passage des Treize-Coins and Ange's bar.

What struck me now was that there was something unfinished about the way the neighborhood was being redeveloped. There were plenty of art galleries, boutiques and other new businesses, but I wondered if they attracted customers. And if so, where did the customers come from? Not Marseilles, I was sure. My parents had never come back to the neighborhood after being expelled by the Germans. The metal shutters were down. The streets deserted. The restaurants empty, or nearly empty. Except for Étienne's, on Rue de Lorette. But Étienne Cassaro had been there for twenty-three years. And he did make the best pizza in Marseilles. *Prices and opening times depend on the owner's mood*, I'd read in a report on Marseilles in *Géo*. Thanks to Étienne's mood, Manu, Ugo and I had often eaten there for free. Even if he did yell at us that we were idlers and good for nothings.

I walked back down Rue du Panier. My memories echoed louder than the footsteps of the people on the street. The neighborhood wasn't Montmartre yet. It still had a bad reputation. And a bad smell. And Djamel was nowhere to be found.

7.

IN WHICH IT'S BEST TO SAY WHAT'S ON YOUR MIND

They were waiting for me outside my house. My mind was on other things, and I was exhausted. I was dying for a glass of Lagavulin. They emerged from the shadows, as silent as cats. By the time I realized they were there, it was too late.

They pulled a thick plastic bag down over my head, and two arms slid under my armpits and around my chest and lifted me off the ground. The arms were like steel. I was pinned against the guy's body. I struggled.

A powerful blow hit me in the stomach. I opened my mouth and swallowed all the oxygen that was still in the bag. Shit! What was the guy hitting me with? A second blow. Same strength. A boxing glove. Fuck! A boxing glove! There was no more oxygen in the bag. Shit! I kicked out with my legs, and hit nothing but air. On my chest, the vice-like grip grew tighter.

A blow landed on my jaw. I opened my mouth, and another blow followed in my stomach. I was going to suffocate. I was sweating gallons. I wanted to bend double, to protect my stomach. The guy with steel arms must have felt it. For a fraction of a second, he let me slide down. Then he pulled me up again, still pinned to him. I could feel his cock against my buttocks. The bastard was getting a hard-on! Two more blows. Left, right. In the stomach again. With my mouth wide open, I moved my head in every direction. I tried to cry out, but no sound emerged, except a slight moan.

My head seemed to be floating in a kettle, with no safety valve. The vice on my chest did not relax. I was nothing but a punching bag now. I lost all sense of time, didn't even feel the blows anymore. My muscles had stopped reacting. I wanted oxygen. That was all. Air! A little air! Just a little! Then my knees hit the ground, hard. Instinctively, I rolled up into a ball. A breath of air had just entered beneath the plastic bag.

"This was a warning, asshole! Next time, you're dead!"

A kick landed in my back. I groaned. I heard a motorcycle engine. I tore off the plastic bag and breathed in all the air I could.

The motorcycle rode off. I stayed there without moving, trying to get my breathing back to normal. A shiver went through me, then I began to shake all over. Move, I told myself. But my body refused to obey. It wouldn't do it. If I moved, the pain would start all over again. Lying there in a ball, I felt nothing. But I couldn't stay like this.

Tears were running down my cheeks. I felt the salty taste of them on my lips. I must have started to cry when I was hit and hadn't stopped.

I licked my tears. The taste was almost good. How about going in and pouring yourself a glass of scotch, huh, Fabio? You just have to get up and go inside. No, don't stand up straight. You can't. Take it easy. Get down on all fours and crawl to your door. There it is, you can see it. Good. Now sit down with your back to the wall. Breathe. Go on, find your keys. Good, lean on the wall, get up slowly, put all your weight against the door. Now open it. The top lock first. Then the middle one. Shit, you forgot to lock that one!

The door opened, and I fell into Marie-Lou's arms. The

impact made her lose her balance. I saw the two of us tumble to the floor. Marie-Lou. I must be hallucinating. Then everything went black.

I had a glove soaked in cold water on my forehead. I felt the same cold sensation on my eyes and cheeks, then on my neck and chest. A few drops of water slid down over my shoulder blades. I shivered, and opened my eyes. Marie-Lou smiled at me. I was on my bed, naked.

"Are you all right?"

I nodded, and closed my eyes. Despite the dim light, I found it hard to keep my eyes open. She took the glove off my forehead. Then put it back. It was cold again. It felt good.

"What time is it?" I asked.

"Twenty after three."

"Got any cigarettes?"

She lit one for me and put it between my lips. I sucked on it, then lifted my left hand to take it out of my mouth. It was a small movement, but it gave me an excruciating pain in my stomach. I opened my eyes.

"What are you doing here?"

"I had to see you. I mean, I had to see someone, and I thought of you."

"How did you get my address?"

"Minitel."

Minitel. Shit! Fifty million people could show up here uninvited, thanks to Minitel. Stupid fucking invention. I closed my eyes again.

"I was sitting outside the door. The woman next door, Honorine, suggested I wait in her house. We talked. I told her I was a friend. Then she opened this door for me. It was getting late, and she thought it was better for me to wait here. She said you'd understand."

"Understand what?"

"What happened to you?"

I told her. As succinctly as I could. Before she could ask me why, I rolled over on my side and sat up. "Help me. I need a shower."

I put my right arm around her shoulders. I weighed only a hundred and fifty pounds, but it took all the strength of Hercules to lift myself from the bed. I was still bent over. I was afraid of reawakening the pain that still lurked in my stomach.

"Lean on the wall."

I put my back against the wall. She turned on the faucets.

"Lukewarm," I said.

She took off her T-shirt and jeans and helped me into the shower. I felt weak. The water immediately did me good. I was standing against Marie-Lou, my arms around her neck. I closed my eyes. The effect didn't take long to make itself felt.

"Well, I'll be damned!" she cried, becoming aware of my hard-on. "So you're not dead yet!"

I smiled, despite myself. All the same, I was feeling increasingly unsteady on my legs, and I was shaking.

"Shall I make it hotter?"

"No. I want it cold. Get out." I placed my hands on the tiles. Marie-Lou got out of the shower. "Go on!"

She turned the faucet full on. I screamed. She stopped the water, grabbed a towel, and rubbed me. I went to the bathroom sink. I needed to see my face. I switched on the light. What I saw didn't thrill me. My own face was intact, but behind me, I could see Marie-Lou's face. Her left eye was swollen, and almost blue. I turned slowly, holding onto the sink.

"Who did that?"

"My pimp."

I drew her to me. She had two bruises on her shoulder and a red mark on her neck. She huddled against me and began to cry, softly. Her belly was against mine. It felt hot. That made me feel a whole lot better. I stroked her hair.

"We both look like hell. Tell me all about it."

I freed myself from her, opened the medicine cabinet, and took out a bottle of Dolipran. The pain was intense.

"Get two glasses from the kitchen. And there's a bottle of Lagavulin around in there somewhere."

I went back to the bedroom, still bent over. I collapsed on the bed, then set the alarm for seven.

Marie-Lou came back. She had a wonderful body. She wasn't a hooker anymore, and I wasn't a cop. We were two of life's walking wounded. I took two Dolipran with a little scotch. I offered her one. She refused.

"There's nothing to tell. He beat me up because I was with you."

"With me?"

"You're a cop."

"How does he know?"

"Everyone knows everything at the O'Stop."

I looked at the time. I emptied my glass. "Stay here. Until I get back. Don't move. And..."

I don't think I even finished the sentence.

They picked up Mourrabed as planned. He was in bed, his eyes swollen with sleep, his hair a mess. There was a girl with him, just a kid, not yet eighteen. He was wearing a pair of flowered shorts and a T-shirt with the word 'Again' on it. We hadn't told anyone in advance. The Narcs would have told us to drop the idea. They didn't like us collaring the middlemen. It threw the big boys in a panic, they said, and jeopardized their operations. And the local station would have quickly spread the word all over the projects, just to frustrate us. That was happening more and more frequently.

We took in Mourrabed like a common criminal. For assault. And now, corrupting a minor. But he was no ordinary criminal. We grabbed him just as he was, didn't even let him get dressed. We were humiliating him, quite gratuitously. He started yelling, calling us fascists, Nazis, telling us to go fuck ourselves and our mothers and sisters. We just laughed. Doors opened on the landings, and everyone could see him with handcuffs on his wrists, wearing nothing but his shorts and T-shirt.

Outside, we even took time to have a smoke before we put him in the van. Just to give everyone a chance to gawp at him from their windows. The news would spread through the projects. Mourrabed in shorts: it was an image that would amuse people, and would stay in their minds. It was a whole lot different than getting arrested after a car chase through the projects.

We took him to the station house in L'Estaque. They didn't know we were coming, and they weren't thrilled. They could already see themselves being besieged by hundreds of kids armed to the teeth. They wanted to send us back where we came from. To our local station house.

"The complaint was registered here," Perol said. "So it seemed sensible to deal with it here." He pushed Mourrabed ahead of him. "We're expecting another customer. An under-age girl we picked up with him. She's just getting dressed."

We'd left Cerutti at the scene with a dozen men. I wanted them to take an initial statement from the girl. And to go through the apartment, and Mourrabed's car, with a fine-tooth comb. Then they'd inform the girl's parents and bring her here.

"There are going to be a lot of people here," I said.

Mourrabed had sat down, and was listening to us. He seemed to be finding it funny. I went up to him, grabbed him by the neck, and pulled him to his feet without letting go.

"Why are you here? Do you have any idea?"

"Yeah. I hit a guy the other night. I was drunk."

"Just hit him, right? What did you have in your hands? Razor blades?"

Then my strength failed me. I went pale. My legs started to shake. I was going to fall, and I felt like throwing up. I didn't know which to do first.

"Fabio!" Perol said.

"Take me to the toilet."

Since the morning I'd taken six Dolipran, three Guronsan and gallons of coffee. I wasn't feeling great, but I was still standing. When the alarm had rung, Marie-Lou had moaned and turned over. I made her take a Lexomil, so she could sleep in peace. My shoulders and back ached. And the pain wouldn't go away. As soon as I put my feet on the ground, I got these stabbing pains, as if I had a sewing machine in my stomach. That filled me with hate.

"Batisti," I said as soon as he picked up the phone. "Those buddies of yours should have finished me off. But you're nothing but a low-down scumbag piece of shit. You're going to sweat like you've never sweated in your rotten life."

"Montale!" he screamed into the receiver.

"Yeah, I'm listening."

"What the fuck are you talking about?"

"I was run over by a steamroller, you piece of shit. If I gave you the details, would it give you a hard-on?"

"Montale, I had nothing to do with this, I swear."

"Don't swear, scumbag! Just explain."

"I had nothing to do with it."

"You're repeating yourself."

"I don't know anything about it."

"Listen, Batisti, to me you're just a prize bastard. But I'd like to believe you. I'll give you twenty-four hours to find out what happened. I'll call you tomorrow and tell you where to meet me. You'd better come up with something good."

Pérol had seen that I wasn't feeling myself as soon as I'd met him, and had been throwing me worried looks. I'd reassured him, telling him it was an old ulcer.

"Yeah, I see," he'd said.

He saw it only too well. But I didn't want to tell him about the beating I'd received. Or the rest of it. Manu, Ugo. I'd scored a bull's eye, somewhere. I couldn't make head or tail of any of it, but I'd gotten myself involved in something that could easily cost me my life. But there was only me, Fabio Montale. I didn't have a wife or kids. No one would weep over me. I didn't want to drag Pérol into my business. I knew him. I knew that, for friendship's sake, he'd be ready to dive head-long into anything, however shitty. And it was obvious that wherever I was heading stank really badly. Worse than the toi-let in this station house.

The smell of urine seemed to impregnate the walls. I spat. Coffee-colored phlegm. My stomach went from high to low tide in thirty seconds. With a cyclone in between. I opened my mouth even wider. It would have been a relief to throw up everything. But I hadn't put anything in my stomach since noon yesterday.

"Coffee," Pérol said, behind me.

"It won't go down."

"Try."

He was holding a plastic cup in one hand. I rinsed my face with cold water, grabbed a paper towel, and wiped myself. I was feeling a bit better. I took the cup, and swallowed a mouth-ful of coffee. It went down without too many problems. I imme-diately broke out in a sweat. I could feel my shirt sticking to my skin. I was sure I had a fever.

"It's OK," I said.

Then I retched again. It felt as if I was taking the punches one more time. Behind me, Pérol was waiting for me to explain. He wouldn't budge until I did.

"OK, let's deal with the asshole, and then I'll tell you all about it."

"That's fine with me. But let me handle Mourrabed."

All I had to do now was find a story that was more convincing than the one about the ulcer.

Mourrabed watched me coming, with a sardonic smile. Pérol slapped him, then sat down opposite him, astride the chair.

Mourrabed turned to me. "What do you want, man?"

"To send you down," I said.

"That's cool. I can play soccer inside." He shrugged. "All I did was hit a guy. The judge is gonna take some convincing. My lawyer will eat you for breakfast."

"We have a closet with ten bodies in it," Pérol said. "I'm sure we can stick one of them on you. And see what your crap lawyer makes of that."

"Hey, I never killed a guy."

"You almost killed him. In my book, that makes you a kind of murderer."

"I told you, I was plastered. Shit, I only punched the guy."

"Tell me about it."

"OK. I'm coming out of the bar, and I see this guy. Looks like a girl from a distance, with his long hair. I ask him for a smoke. Guy says he doesn't have any. He's jerking me around, you know. So I say to him, If you don't have any, suck my dick! And you know what he does, he starts laughing! So I punch him. That's all I did, man. That's the truth. He takes off like a rabbit. He was just a fag."

"Except you weren't alone," Pérol said. "You had your buddies with you. You all ran after him. Stop me if I'm getting this wrong. He ran into the Miramar. You dragged him out. And you really made a mess of him. Might have killed him, if we hadn't gotten there. And you're really out of luck, because in L'Estaque you're a star, and everyone knows your face."

"That fag is going to withdraw his fucking complaint."

"Doesn't look like it." Pérol looked at Mourrabed, letting his gaze linger on his shorts. "Nice shorts. The kind a fag would wear, don't you think?"

"Hey, I'm no fag. I got a girlfriend."

"Let's talk about that. Was she the one we found in bed with you?"

I'd stopped listening. Pérol knew what he was doing. He was just as disgusted by Mourrabed as I was. Mourrabed was beyond hope. He was on a downward spiral. He'd stop at nothing, not even murder. Perfect fodder for gangsters. In two or three years, he'd be taken out by someone tougher than he was. Maybe the best thing that could happen to him would be to go inside for twenty years. But I knew that wasn't the answer. The fact was, for someone like Mourrabed, there was no answer.

The telephone made me jump. I must have dozed off.

"Can you take it?"

It was Cerutti. "We couldn't find a thing. Nothing. Not even a gram of marijuana."

"How about the girl?"

"A runaway. Saint-Denis, Paris region. Her father wants to send her back to Algeria to get married, and..."

"I get the picture. Bring her here. We'll take her statement. You stay there with two guys and check if it's Mourrabed who rents the apartment. If he doesn't, find out who does. I need to know as soon as possible." I hung up.

Mourrabed watched us coming back. "Anything wrong?" he said, smiling.

Pérol slapped him again, more violently than the first time. Mourrabed rubbed his cheek.

"My lawyer won't like it when I tell him about this."

"So is she your girlfriend?" Pérol asked, as if he hadn't heard.

I put on my jacket. I had to go. I had an appointment with Sanchez, the taxi driver, and I didn't want to miss him. If the strong-arm men last night hadn't been sent by Batisti, maybe they were connected to the taxi driver. And to Leila. That was a whole other story. But could I believe Batisti?

"I'll see you at the station."

"Wait," Pérol said. He turned to Mourrabed. "About your girlfriend. You have a choice. Say yes, and I'll introduce you to her father and brothers. In a closed cell. Seeing as how you weren't part of their plans, you may have a hard time convincing them. Say no, and you're looking at corruption of a minor. Think it over. I'll be back."

The sky was filling with heavy black clouds. It wasn't ten o'clock yet, but the air was humid and sticky. Pérol joined me outside.

"Don't do anything stupid, Fabio."

"Don't worry. I have an appointment. I'm hoping for a tip-off. About Leila. The third man."

He shook his head. Then he pointed at my stomach. "And that?"

"A fight, last night. Over a girl. I'm out of training, so I didn't do too well." I smiled at him with that seductive smile of mine, the one that women like.

"Fabio, we know each other pretty well by now. So give it a rest." He looked at me, waiting for me to react but I didn't. "I know you have your own troubles. I'm starting to get an idea what they are. But you don't owe me anything. You can keep it all to yourself. Stick it up your ass if you want, that's your business. But if you want to talk about it, I'm here for you. OK?"

It was the most he'd ever spoken. I was touched by his sincerity. If there was anyone I could still count on in this town, it was Pérol, even though I didn't know anything about him. I couldn't imagine him as a family man. I couldn't even imagine what his wife was like. It had never bothered me. I'd never even wondered if he was happy or not. We were partners, but strangers. We trusted and respected each other. That was all that mattered. To both of us. Why was it so difficult to make new friends once you were past forty? Was it because we didn't have dreams anymore, only regrets?

"That's just it. I don't want to talk about it." He turned his back on me. I caught him by the arm, before he could step away. "I've been thinking it over. It might be better if you and your wife came to my place for lunch on Sunday. I'll cook."

We looked at each other. I walked to my car. The first raindrops started falling. I saw him go back into the station, looking determined. Mourrabed would have to behave himself. I sat down, put in a Ruben Blades tape, and started the car.

I drove through the centre of L'Estaque on the way back. L'Estaque was trying to stay faithful to its old image. A little harbor town, a village really. It was only a few minutes from Marseilles, but people said: I live in L'Estaque. Not Marseilles. But the little harbor was surrounded and dominated by housing projects full of immigrants who'd been chased out of downtown Marseilles.

It's always best to say what's on your mind. Of course it is. But although I was a good listener, I'd never been very good at confiding in anyone. At the last moment, I always clammed up. I was always ready to lie, rather than talk about what was wrong. I guess my life could have been different. I'd never dared tell my father about the things I got up to with Manu and Ugo. I'd had a really rough time in the Colonial Army, but I hadn't learned my lesson. With women, there was an even worse lack of communication, and then I suffered when they left me. Muriel, Carmen, Rosa. By the time I reached out my hand, by the time I finally opened my mouth to explain myself, it was too late.

It wasn't that I didn't have the courage. I just didn't trust anyone. Not enough, anyhow, to put my life and my feelings in another person's hands. And I knocked myself out trying to solve everything on my own. The vanity of a loser. I had to face it, I'd lost everything in my life. Manu and Ugo for starters.

I'd often told myself I shouldn't have run away that night, after that botched holdup. I should have confronted them, told them what I'd been thinking for months: that what we were doing was getting us nowhere, that we could do something better with our lives. And it was true, we had our lives ahead of us. The world was waiting to be discovered. It would have been great, to go around the world together. I was convinced of that. Maybe we'd have quarreled. Maybe they'd have carried on without me. Maybe. But maybe they'd also be here today. Alive.

I took the coast road past the harbor and the sea wall. My favorite route into Marseilles, with a glimpse of the various basins. Bassin Mirabeau, Bassin de la Pinède, Bassin National, Bassin d'Arenc. The future of Marseilles was here. I still wanted to believe it.

Ruben Blades' voice and the rhythm of the music, full of Caribbean sunshine, were starting to have an effect on my head, dispelling my anxieties and soothing my pains. The sky was low and gray, but full of an intense light. The sea was turning a metallic blue. I liked it when Marseilles clothed itself in the colors of Lisbon.

Sanchez was already there, waiting for me. I was surprised. I'd been expecting some kind of loudmouthed *mia*, but he was short and pudgy, and from the way he greeted me—limp hand-shake, lowered eyes—I could see he wasn't a very self-confident kind of guy. More the kind who always says yes, even when he's thinking no.

He was scared. "I'm a family man, you know," he said, as he followed me into my office.

"Take a seat."

"I've got three children. My cab's my livelihood. I can't afford to make mistakes. Red lights, speed limits..."

He handed me a sheet of paper. Names, addresses, phone numbers. Four people. I looked at him.

"They can confirm it. At the time you say, I was with them. Until half after eleven. After that, I went back to work."

I put the paper down on my desk, lit a cigarette, and looked him straight in the eyes. Little piggy eyes, bloodshot. He lowered them very quickly. He kept wringing his hands. There were beads of sweat on his forehead.

"What a pity, Monsieur Sanchez." He looked up. "If I send for your friends, they'll be forced to make false statements. You're going to get them into trouble."

He looked at me with his red eyes. I opened a drawer, took out a file at random, a thick one, put it down in front of me and started leafing through it.

"I'm sure you realize we'd never have asked you to come in here for something as trivial as a red light." His eyes widened. Now he was really sweating. "It's more serious than that. Much more serious, Monsieur Sanchez. Your friends will be sorry they trusted you. And you—"

"But I was there! From nine to eleven!"

Fear had made him raise his voice. But he seemed sincere, and that surprised me. I decided to quit fooling around.

"No, monsieur," I replied, firmly. "I have eight witnesses, and they're as good as all your witnesses. Eight police officers, all on duty at the time." He opened his mouth, but no sound came out. In his eyes, I could see his worst nightmares coming true. "At ten fifteen, your taxi was on Rue Corneille, in front of the Commanderie. I could charge you as an accessory to murder."

"It wasn't me," he said, in a weak voice. "It wasn't me. I can explain."

8

IN WHICH NOT SLEEPING DOESN'T
SOLVE A THING

S anchez was bathed in sweat. Big drops were running down his forehead. He wiped himself with the back of his hand. The sweat was all over his neck too. After a moment he took out a handkerchief and mopped himself. I started to smell his sweat. He couldn't keep still on his chair. He must be desperate to take a leak. Maybe he'd already wet his underpants.

I didn't like this guy Sanchez but I couldn't bring myself to hate him. He was probably a good father and husband. He worked hard, every night. He went to sleep at the same time his children went to school. When they came home, he went back to work. He probably never saw them. Except on the rare Saturdays and Sundays when he took a day off. Once a month, I guessed. At the beginning, he'd fucked his wife when he came home, waking her up, which she didn't like. After a while, he'd given up, and now he made do with a hooker a few times a week. Either before going to work, or after finishing. With his wife, it was probably only once a month now, when his day off fell on a Saturday.

My father had led the same kind of life. He was a typesetter on the daily paper *La Marseillaise*. He'd leave for the paper about five o'clock in the afternoon. I'd grown up during his absences. When he got home at night, he'd come in and kiss me, smelling of lead, ink and cigarettes. It didn't wake me up. It was just part of my sleep. Whenever he forgot, which sometimes happened, I had bad dreams. I imagined him abandoning my mother and me. When I was about twelve or thirteen, I often dreamed that he had another woman in his life. She looked like Gélou. He'd be feeling her up. Then, instead of my father, it'd be Gélou who came in and kissed me, which would give me a hard-on. I'd hold on to Gélou and caress her. She'd come into my bed. Then my father would appear, and make an angry scene. And my mother would join in, in tears. I never found out if my father had had other women. He'd loved my mother, I was sure of that, but their lives remained a mystery for me.

Sanchez moved around on his chair. My silence worried him.

"How old are your children?"

"The boys, fourteen and sixteen. The girl, ten. Laure. Laure, like my mother."

He took out a wallet, opened it, and handed me a photo of the family. I didn't like what I was doing, but I wanted to put him at his ease, in order to get as much from him as I could. I looked at his kids. They all had flabby faces and shifty eyes, without a spark of rebellion. They'd been born bitter. They'd never hate anyone except those poorer than themselves. Anyone they thought might take bread off their tables. Arabs, blacks, Orientals. Never the rich. It was already clear they'd never amount to much. Best case scenario, the boys would be taxi drivers, like their dad. And the girl a trainee hairdresser. Or an assistant at Prisunic. Ordinary French people. Citizens of fear.

"Nice kids," I said, hypocritically. "So tell me. Who was driving your taxi?"

"Let me explain. I have a friend, Toni, well, not exactly a friend. We're not really close. He's got this thing going with Charlie, the bellhop from the Frantel. They find groups of suckers. Businessmen, executive types, you know what I mean?

Toni lets them use the cab for the night. Takes them to the hottest new restaurants, clubs where they won't have any problems. To finish off the evening, he fixes them up with hookers. High class ones, of course! The kind who have little studio apartments..."

I offered him a cigarette. He felt more at ease. He'd stopped sweating.

"I guess they go gambling too. Play for high stakes. Am I right?"

"Yeah. There are some really top class places. Like the hookers. Know what they like, these guys? Exotic women. Arabs, blacks, Vietnamese. But clean ones, you know what I mean? Sometimes they even make a cocktail."

He was unstoppable now. It made him feel important to tell me all this. Plus, it excited him. I guessed he sometimes got paid in hookers.

"And you lend him your taxi."

"That's right. He pays me, and I hang out. Play *belote* with the guys. Go to see OM if they're playing. I just declare what's on the meter. All profit. And this isn't peanuts we're talking. Toni gets a cut of everything. The suckers, the restaurants, the clubs, the hookers. The whole caboodle."

"And how often does this happen?"

"Two or three times a month."

"Including Friday night."

He nodded, and retreated back into his shell like a snail. We were back in a place he didn't like. He was scared again. He knew he was saying too much, and that he hadn't yet said enough.

"Yeah. He asked me."

"What I don't get, Sanchez, is this. Your pal wasn't carrying suckers, that night. He was carrying two killers."

I lit another cigarette, without offering him one this time. I stood up. I could feel the shooting pains coming back. Hurry it up, I told myself. I looked out the window at the harbor and the sea. The clouds were lifting. The light was incredible. Hearing him talk about hookers made me think of Marie-Lou. The blows she'd received. Her pimp. Her clients. Was she included in these round trips? Sent to take part in orgies with a bunch of rich pigs? "With or without pillows?" they asked when you made a reservation in some hotels that specialized in conferences and seminars.

The sea was silvery. What was Marie-Lou doing in my house right now? I couldn't imagine it. I couldn't imagine a woman in my house anymore. A sailing ship was heading out to sea. I'd have liked to go fishing. Anything not to be here. I needed silence. I'd been hearing these crummy stories ever since morning, and I was sick of it. Mourrabed. Sanchez and his pal Toni. The same old human corruption.

"So, Sanchez," I said, walking up to him. "How do you explain it?"

My change of tone made him jump. He guessed the second half was starting.

"I can't explain it. There's never been any trouble."

"Listen," I said, sitting down again. "You have a family. Great kids. A nice wife, I guess. You love them. You care about them. You want to bring in a little more money. I understand that. We're all the same. But you've gotten yourself mixed up in something ugly. Your back's against the wall, and your choices are strictly limited. You have to cough it up. The name and address of your pal Toni."

He knew we'd get to this point. He was sweating again, and that turned my stomach. Big patches had appeared around his armpits. He started to beg. I'd lost all sympathy for him. He disgusted me. I couldn't even stand the thought of slapping him.

"But I don't know it. Can I smoke?"

I didn't reply. I opened the door of the office and signaled to the duty cop to come in. "Favier, book this guy."

"I swear to you. I don't know where he lives."

"Sanchez, if you want me to believe this Toni of yours exists, tell me where to find him. Otherwise what am I supposed to think? Huh? I'll tell you what I think. I think you're jerking me around."

"I don't know. I never see him. I don't even have his telephone number. I work for him, not the other way around. When he wants me, he calls me."

"Just like a hooker."

He didn't pick up on that. He knew he was in real trouble, and his little brain was searching for a way out.

"He leaves messages for me. At the Bar de l'Hotel de Ville. Call Charlie, at the Frantel. You can ask him. Maybe he knows."

"We'll see about Charlie later. Book him," I said to Favier.

Favier grabbed him forcefully under his arm and pulled him to his feet.

Sanchez started to blubber. "Wait. I know where you could find him. Chez Francis, on the Canebière. He often goes there for an aperitif. And sometimes, he has dinner at Le Mas."

I signaled to Favier, and he let go of his arm. Sanchez slumped on the chair, like the piece of shit that he was.

"That's good, Sanchez. At last we understand each other. What are you doing this evening?"

"Well, I'm driving my taxi. And—"

"Go to Chez Francis, about seven. Sit down. Grab a beer. Eye up the women. And when your buddy arrives, say hello to him. I'll be there. Don't try any tricks. I know where to find you. Favier will see you out."

"Thanks," he whined.

He stood up, sniffing, and headed for the door.

"Sanchez!"

He froze, and lowered his head.

"Let me tell you what I think. Last Friday night was the first time this Toni of yours drove your cab. Am I right or am I wrong?"

"Well..."

"Come on, Sanchez. You're a fucking liar. You'd better not have been jerking me around about Toni, or you can say goodbye to your taxi."

"I'm sorry. I didn't mean—"

"What? To tell me you get a cut from dealing with criminals? How much did they pay you for Friday?"

"Five. Five thousand."

"Considering what they used your cab for, they really screwed you over, if you ask me."

I walked around my desk, opened a drawer, and took out a small tape recorder. I pressed one of the buttons at random and showed it to him.

"It's all here. So don't forget, tonight."

"I'll be there."

"One more thing. You can tell everyone, your boss, your wife, your friends, that we've dropped the red light business. Out of the kindness of our hearts."

Favier pushed him out of the office and closed the door behind him, with a wink at me. I had a lead. Or at least something to think about.

I was lying down. On Lole's bed. It was an instinctive thing. I'd gone there again, just like I had on Saturday morning. I wanted to be in her apartment, in her bed. Just like I wanted to be in her arms. And I hadn't hesitated. For a moment, I imagined Lole opening the door for me and letting me in. She'd make me a coffee. We'd talk about Manu and Ugo. The old times. The present. Us, maybe.

The apartment was shrouded in shadow. It was cool, and the smell of mint and basil was still strong. The two plants needed watering, so I watered them. That was the first thing I did. Then I undressed and took an almost cold shower. Then I set the alarm for two o'clock and lay down between the blue sheets, exhausted. With Lole's eyes on me. The way her eyes were when her body moved above mine. They were black as anthracite, and thousands of years of wandering shone in them. She was as light as the dust of the open road. Follow the wind, her eyes said, and you'll find the dust.

I didn't sleep long, no more than fifteen minutes. There were too many things on my mind. I'd held a little meeting with Pérol and Cerruti in my office. The window was wide open, but there was no air. The sky had become overcast again. A storm would have been welcome. Pérol had brought beer and sandwiches. Tomatoes, anchovies and tuna. Not so easy to eat, but better than the usual revolting ham sandwiches.

"We took Mourrabed's statement, then brought him here," Pérol said. "This afternoon, we'll confront him with the guy he beat up. We'll keep him for forty-eight hours. Maybe we can find something on him that'll stick."

"How about the girl?"

"She's here, too. Her family's been notified. Her elder brother's coming to get her. He's taking the high speed train at 1:30. Bad news for her. She'll be back in Algeria in no time."

"You could have let her go."

"Yeah," Cerutti said. "And in a month or two we'd have found her dead in a cellar."

These kids' lives had barely started and already they'd reached a dead end. Other people had made the choice for them, and it was always between the lesser of two evils. Cerutti was looking at me out of the corner of his eye. He was surprised by the way I was hounding Mourrabed. He'd been in the team a year and had never seen me like this. Mourrabed didn't deserve any pity. He was ready to do anything. You could see it in his eyes. Plus, he felt protected by his suppliers. Yes, I wanted him to go down. And I wanted it to be here and now. Maybe it was a way of convincing myself that I was still capable of leading an investigation, and seeing it through to the end. That way, I'd feel more confident about seeing Ugo's case through to the end too. Maybe even Leila's.

There was something else. I needed to believe in myself as a cop again. I needed boundaries, rules, codes. Something to hold on to. Every step I was about to take would move me farther away from the law. I was aware of that. I knew that when it came to Ugo and Leila, I wasn't thinking like a cop. I was being swept along by my lost youth. All my dreams belonged to that part of my life. If I still had a future, that was the way I had to return.

I was like any man staggering toward his fifties. Wondering if life had lived up to my hopes. I wanted to answer yes, and I didn't want that yes to be a lie, but I was running out of time. Unlike most men, I couldn't have another kid with a woman I didn't love anymore, as a way of keeping the lie at bay and allaying suspicion. I knew that was common enough. I was alone, and I was forced to look the truth in the face. No mirror would tell me I was a good father, a good husband. Or a good cop.

The bedroom seemed less cool now. Behind the shutters, I could sense a storm was still brewing. The air was getting heavier all the time. I closed my eyes, thinking maybe I could go back to sleep. Ugo was lying on the other bed. We'd pushed the two beds together under the fan. It was mid-afternoon. The slightest movement, and we'd sweat gallons. He'd rented a little room on Place Ménélik. He'd arrived in Djibouti three weeks earlier, without warning. I'd taken two weeks' leave and we'd hotfooted it to Harar to pay homage to Rimbaud and the deposed princesses of Ethiopia.

"So, Sergeant Montale, what about it?"

Djibouti was a free port. You could do a whole lot of business there. You could buy a boat, a yacht, at a third of the usual price, take one as far as Tunisia and sell it for twice what you paid. Better still, you could fill it with cameras and tape recorders, and sell them to tourists.

"I still have three months to serve, then I'm going home."

"And after that?"

"Hell, I don't know!"

"You'll see, it's even worse than it used to be. If I hadn't left, I'd have killed someone, one day or another. Just to eat. To live. I don't want the happiness they have in store for us. I don't believe in that kind of happiness. It stinks. The best thing is not to go back. I'm never going back." He took a thoughtful drag on his Nationale. "I left, and I'm never going back. You felt the same."

"I didn't feel the same, Ugo. It's just that I was ashamed. Of me. Of us. Of what we were doing. I just found a way to burn my bridges. I don't want to go back to that."

"So what are you going to do?"

I shrugged.

"Don't tell me you're going to re-enlist with these dickheads."

"No. I've given them enough."

"So?"

"I really don't know, Ugo. I don't want to fuck up again like we did before."

"Then go get a job in the Renault factory!"

He stood up angrily and went to take a shower. Ugo and Manu loved each other like brothers. I'd never been able to compete with their friendship. But Manu was consumed by his hatred of the world. He couldn't see beyond that. Even the sea meant nothing to him anymore, though it was still the place where our adolescent dreams set sail. That was too much for Ugo, and he'd turned to me. Over the years, we'd gotten really close. Despite our differences, we had the same fantasies.

Ugo knew why I'd 'escaped.' He'd understood it later, after another holdup that had turned violent. He'd left Marseilles, given up Lole. He was sure I'd follow him. To revive our dreams, all the things we'd read about. The wine-dark sea: that, for us, was the only true starting point for every adventure. That was why Ugo had come all the way here. But I didn't want to follow where he wanted to go. I had neither the inclination nor the courage for that kind of adventure.

I'd come back here. Ugo had left for Aden, without a word of goodbye. Manu wasn't too pleased to see me again. Lole wasn't very enthusiastic either. Manu was mixed up in some ugly stuff. Lole waited tables at a bar in the Vieux Port called the Cintra. They were dying to see Ugo again. They each had affairs, which made them strangers to each other. Manu loved out of despair. Every new woman took him farther from Lole. Lole loved the way other people breathed. She moved to Madrid for two years, then came back to Marseilles, then left again and went to live with some cousins of hers in Ariège. Each time she came back, Ugo still wasn't there.

Three years ago, Manu and Lole had started living together in L'Estaque. For Manu, it had come too late. Bitterness must have driven him to it. Or fear of Lole leaving again, fear of being alone. Alone with his lost dreams and his hatred. As for me, I'd worked hard for months. Ugo was right. You had to make up your mind. Go away, or stay and kill someone. But I wasn't a killer, so I'd become a cop. Shit! I said to myself, furious at not being able to sleep.

I got up, made coffee, and took another shower. I drank my

coffee still naked. I put on a Paolo Conte album, and sat down in the armchair.

Guardate dai treni in corsa...

OK, so I had a lead. Toni. The third man. Maybe. How had these guys cornered Leila? Where? When? Why? What was the point of asking myself these questions? They'd raped her, then killed her. That was the answer. She was dead. Why ask questions? To understand. I always had to understand. Manu, Ugo, Leila. And Lole. And all the others. But was there anything still to understand? Weren't we all beating our heads against a brick wall? The answers didn't exist. And the questions led nowhere.

Come di come di
La comédie d'un jour, la comédie d'la vie

Where would Batisti lead me? Deeper into trouble. That much was sure. Was there a connection between Manu's death and Ugo's? A connection other than Ugo wanting to avenge Manu? Who stood to gain from Zucca's death? One of the Marseilles families. I couldn't see beyond that. But which one? And how much did Batisti know? Whose side was he on? He'd never taken sides before. Why now? What was the meaning of that show the other night? The slaying of Al Dakhil, and then the two killers being taken out by Auch's men. Was Toni involved in it? Was he being covered by the cops? Did Auch know about his tricks and have some kind of hold over him? And how had the three guys lifted Leila? Back to square one.

Ecco quello che io ti darò,
E la sensualità delle vite disperate...

The sensuality of desperate lives. Only poets talk like that. But poetry has never had an answer for anything. All it does is bear witness. To despair. And desperate lives. And who the hell had beaten me up?

Of course, I was late for Leila's funeral. I'd lost my way in the cemetery looking for the Muslim section. It was in the new annex, a long way from the old cemetery. I didn't know if more people died in Marseilles than anywhere else, but death extended as far as the eye could see. All this part was treeless. Paths hastily tarred. Side paths of beaten earth. Rows of graves. The cemetery followed the geography of the city. This section was like North Marseilles. The same desolation.

I was surprised how many people were there. Mouloud's family. Neighbors. And a lot of young people. About fifty of them. Mostly Arabs. I recognized some of them. I'd seen them in the projects. Two or three of them had even been brought into the station house for trivial offences. Two blacks. Eight whites, also young, boys and girls. Next to Driss and Kader, I recognized Leila's two girlfriends, Yasmine and Karine. Why hadn't I called them? I'd put my head down and charged straight ahead, and hadn't even questioned her closest friends. I wasn't thinking straight. But then I never had.

Mavros was standing a few steps behind Driss. He was a good man. He'd see things through with Driss. Not only as a boxing coach, but as a friend. Boxing isn't just about hitting. The most important thing is learning to take the blows. To roll with the punches. To make sure the blows caused the least possible harm. Life was nothing but a series of rounds. Roll with the punches. Hold steady, don't flinch. And land punches in the right place, at the right time. Mavros would teach Driss all that. He rated him highly, even thought he was the best fighter in the gym. He'd pass on everything he knew. He'd treat

Driss like a son, even if there were sometimes conflicts. Driss could become what he hadn't been able to.

I was reassured by that, because I knew Mouloud wouldn't have the strength or the courage to do it anymore. If Driss did anything stupid, he'd give up. Most parents of the kids I had dealings with had given up. Life had kicked them around so much, they refused to confront what was happening. They turned a blind eye to everything. Bad company, bad behavior at school, fights, shoplifting, drugs. A million times a day, a slap might have done the trick, but never came!

I remembered going the previous winter to collar a boy in the Busserine project. The youngest of four children, and the only one who hadn't so far either been arrested or spent time in prison. He'd been identified as being involved in some minor holdups. A thousand francs maximum. His mother opened the door to us. All she said was, "I've been expecting you," then she burst into tears. For more than a year he'd been extorting money from her to buy drugs. By way of persuasion, he'd beaten her. She'd started hustling tricks around the project to keep her husband out of it. He knew everything, but preferred to keep his mouth shut.

The sky was leaden. Not a breath of air. The asphalt was burning hot. Nobody could keep still. It was impossible to stay here much longer. Someone must have realized that, because from that point the ceremony picked up speed. A woman started crying. She was the only one. For the second time, Driss avoided my eyes. But I knew he was watching me. There wasn't any hatred in his eyes, but a hell of a lot of contempt. He'd stopped respecting me. I hadn't been equal to the task. As a man, I should have loved his sister. And as a cop, I should have protected her.

When my turn came to embrace Mouloud, I felt out of place. Mouloud had two big red holes where his eyes should have been. I hugged him. But I meant nothing to him anymore. Just a bad memory. The man who'd told him to hope. Who'd made his heart beat faster. On the way out, Driss hung back with Karine, Jasmine and Mavros just to avoid me. I'd said a few words to Mavros, but my heart wasn't in it. I found myself alone again.

Kader put his arm around my shoulders. "Dad's stopped talking. Don't be angry. He's like that with us too. You have to understand him. It'll take Driss a long time as well." He squeezed my shoulder. "Leila loved you."

I didn't answer. I didn't want to get into a discussion about Leila. Or about love. We walked side by side, in silence.

"How did she let herself get picked up by those guys?" he said.

The same question again. When you're a girl, an Arab, and you've lived in the suburbs, you don't just get in any old car. Not unless you were crazy. But Leila had her feet on the ground. The Panda was in working order. Kader had brought it back from the university residence, with Leila's things. So someone had come to pick her up. She'd left with him. Someone she knew. Who? I had no idea. I had the beginning and the end. Three rapists, according to my theory. Two were dead. Was the third one Toni? Or someone else? Was he the one Leila knew? The one who'd come to pick her up? And why? But I couldn't tell Kader what I was thinking. The case was closed. Officially.

"Luck," I said. "Bad luck."

"Do you believe in luck?"

I shrugged. "I don't have any other answers. No one does. The guys are dead and—"

"What would you have preferred? To see them in jail?"

"They got what they deserved. But I still wish I could have had them in front of me, alive."

"I've never understood how you can be a cop."

"Neither do I. It just happened."

"It's a pity it did."

Yasmine joined us. She slipped her arm into Kader's, and snuggled up to him. Kader smiled at her. A loving smile.

"How much longer are you staying?" I asked Kader.

"I don't know. Five, six days. Maybe less. I don't know. There's the store. Uncle can't manage it anymore. He wants to leave it to me."

"That's good."

"I also have to see Yasmine's father. We may go back up together." He smiled, then looked at her.

"I didn't know."

"Neither did we," Yasmine said. "I mean, we didn't used to. It wasn't till we were apart that we realized."

"Are you coming to the house?"

I shook my head. "It's not my place, Kader. You know that, don't you? I'll go see your father later." I glanced at Driss, who was still hanging back. "And don't worry about Driss, I'll keep an eye on him. So will Mavros."

He nodded.

"Don't forget to invite me to the wedding!"

The one thing I could give them now was a smile. I've always been good at smiles.

9.

IN WHICH INSECURITY DEPRIVES WOMEN
OF THEIR SEX APPEAL

At last it had rained. The kind of short, violent, even angry storm Marseilles often gets in summer. It wasn't much cooler, but at least the sky had cleared. The sun lapped the puddles on the sidewalks. A damp smell rose from them, a smell I loved.

I sat down on the terrace of Chez Francis, under the plane trees of the Allées de Meilhan. It was almost seven o'clock, and the Canebière was already starting to empty. In a few minutes, the stores would be pulling down their shutters, and the Canebière would be a desert, with only groups of young Arabs, riot police and a few lost tourists still circulating.

Fear of Arabs had made the people of Marseilles flee the downtown area to other neighborhoods away from the center, where they felt safer. Place Sébastopol, Boulevard de la Blancarde, Boulevard Chave, Avenue Foch, Rue Monte-Cristo. And farther east, Place Castelane, Avenue Cantini, Boulevard Baille, Avenue du Prado, Boulevard Périer, Rue Paradis, Rue Breteuil.

Around Place Castelane, an immigrant was as conspicuous as a hair on soup. Some of the bars were full of preppy high school kids and college students, who stank so much of money that even I felt out of place. People didn't usually drink at the bar here, and *pastis* was served in big glasses, just like in Paris.

The Arabs had regrouped downtown. They'd taken over from the whites who'd fled, who'd washed their hands of Cours Belzunce and Rue d'Aix, and all the narrow rundown streets between Belzunce and the Allées de Meilhan and the Saint-Charles railroad station. Streets full of hookers. Buildings unfit for human habitation, flea-ridden hotels. Successive waves of immigrants had passed through these streets, until redevelopment had pushed them out to the suburbs. The latest redevelopment was happening now, and the suburbs had moved to the very edge of the city. Septèmes-les-Vallons, and out toward Les Pennes-Mirabeau. They were farther out all the time, until they'd be out of Marseilles altogether.

One by one, the movie theaters had closed, then the bars. These days, the Canebière was just a monotonous succession of clothing stores and shoe stores. One big second-hand emporium. Only one movie theater left, the Capitole. An eight-screen complex, with a young Arab clientele. Bouncers at the entrance and inside.

I finished my *pastis* and ordered another. An old friend of mine named Corot said you only appreciated *pastis* when you got to the third one. The first one you drank because you were thirsty. The second because you were starting to like the taste. By the third, you really loved it! Thirty years ago, people came to the Canebière for an after-dinner stroll. You got home, took a shower, had dinner, then went for a walk along the Canebière as far as the harbor. You walked down the left-hand sidewalk, and came back up on the other sidewalk. When they reached the Vieux-Port, everyone had their own habits. Some kept walking past the fish auction as far as the careening basin. Others carried on toward the Town Hall and the Saint-Jean fort. Eating pistachio, coconut or lemon ice cream.

Manu, Ugo and I were regulars on the Canebière. Like all the other young men, we went there to be seen. Dressed up like princes. We wouldn't have been seen dead in espadrilles or sneakers. We put on our best shoes, Italian preferably, and had them shined on the corner of Rue des Feuillants, halfway along the route. We walked up and down the Canebière at least twice. It was where we went to pick up girls.

The girls were often in groups of four or five. They'd walk slowly, arm in arm, on their stiletto heels, but without wiggling their asses like the girls in Toulon. They had a simple, languorous way of walking that was typical of Marseilles. They talked and laughed loudly. They wanted to be noticed, wanted us to see how beautiful they were. And they really were beautiful.

We'd follow them a dozen paces behind, making comments, loudly enough to be heard. Then one of them would turn around and shout, "Did you see that one? Who does he think he is? Raf Vallone?" and they'd all burst out laughing, turn around, laugh even louder. We'd won. By the time we reached Place de la Bourse, we'd have started a conversation. On Quai des Belges, all we had to do was put our hands in our pockets and pay for the ices. Each his own girl. That's how it was done. With a look and a smile. A story that lasted, at most, until Sunday night, after endless slow dances in the half-darkness of the Salons Michel, on Rue Montgrand.

There were already quite a fair number of Arabs around in those days. Blacks, too. Vietnamese. Armenians, Greeks, Portuguese. But it didn't cause any problems. It had started to be a problem with the downturn in the economy and the rise in unemployment. The more unemployment there was, the more aware people became of the immigrants. And the number of Arabs seemed to be increasing along with the unemployment! In the Sixties, the French had lived off the fat of the land. Now they had nothing, they wanted it for themselves! Nobody else was allowed to come and steal a crumb. And that's what the Arabs were doing, stealing our own poverty off our plates!

The people of Marseilles didn't really believe that, but they'd been made to feel afraid. It was a fear as old as the city, but this time they were having a hard time getting over it. Because of the fear, they couldn't think straight, couldn't see how to reinvent themselves the way they'd always done.

It was ten after seven, and Sanchez still hadn't showed. What was the idiot playing at? I didn't mind waiting here, doing nothing. It relaxed me. My one regret was that it wasn't a good time to watch girls go by, because they were all in a hurry to get home.

They walked along quickly, eyes down, handbags pressed to their stomachs. Insecurity deprived them of their sex appeal. They'd get it back again tomorrow, as soon as they got on the bus. With that open look I loved about them. If you like a girl here, and you look at her, she doesn't lower her eyes. Even if you aren't trying to pick her up, you'd better take advantage of what she's allowing you to see and not turn away, or she'll make a scene, especially if there are people around.

A green and white Golf GTI convertible slowed down, climbed on the sidewalk between two plane trees, and stopped. Music playing. Whitney Houston, some shit like that. The driver walked straight up to me. About twenty-five. Good looking. White linen pants, a light jacket with thin blue and white stripes, a dark blue shirt. Medium length hair, well cut.

He sat down and looked me straight in the eyes. He crossed his legs, lifting his pants slightly in order to maintain the crease. I noticed his signet ring and chain bracelet. A fashion plate, my mother would have said. To me, he was a typical pimp.

"Francis!" he cried. "A *mauresque*!"

He lit a cigarette. So did I. I was waiting for him to speak, but he wasn't going to say anything until he'd had a drink. A real poser. I knew who he was. Toni. The third man. One of the guys who may have raped and killed Leila. But he didn't know I was thinking that. As far as he knew, to me he was only the taxi driver from Place de l'Opéra. He had the self-confidence of someone who wasn't in any danger, who was protected. He drank a little of his *mauresque*, then gave me a big smile. A carnivorous smile.

"I hear you wanted to see me."

"I was hoping for an introduction."

"Don't mess with me. I'm Toni, not Sanchez. He just has to see a cop and he shits in his pants. He'll say anything you want him to."

"Whereas you've got balls, right?"

"Go to hell! You don't know anything about me. You're a nobody. Just about fit to sweep up whatever shit the Arabs leave. And from what I hear, you're not even very good at that. You're sticking your nose in where it doesn't belong. I have a few friends in your station house. They say if you don't change tack, you're gonna get your legs broken. That's their advice, and I completely agree with them. Got it?"

"You're really scaring me."

"Go ahead and laugh, asshole! I could kill you, and it wouldn't make any waves."

"When an asshole gets whacked, it never makes waves. That's good for me. And for you too. If I kill you, your buddies will soon replace you."

"But that won't happen."

"Why not? Because you'd shoot me in the back first?"

His eyes became slightly glazed. I shouldn't have said that. I'd simply been dying to let him know that I knew more than he thought I did. But I didn't regret it. I'd hit the target.

"You have that kind of face, Toni," I said, to cover myself.

"I don't give a fuck what you think! Don't forget! You get the advice only once, not twice. And forget about Sanchez."

For the second time in forty-eight hours, I was being threatened. With a piece of advice I was going to get only once.

Coming from Toni, it wasn't as painful as last night, but it was just as humiliating. I'd have liked to put a bullet in his belly, right there under the table. Just to appease the hatred I felt. But I wasn't going to screw up my only lead. And in any case, I didn't have a gun on me. I didn't often take my service revolver with me. He finished his *mauresque*, as if nothing had happened, and stood up. He gave me a look that was meant to scare me. Right then, it did. The guy was a real killer. Maybe I should start carrying my gun.

Toni's full name was Antoine Pirelli. He lived on Rue Clovis Hugues, in the Belle de Mai, behind Saint-Charles station. Historically, the oldest working class neighborhood in Marseilles. A red neighborhood. Around Boulevard de la Révolution, every street name commemorated a hero of French socialism. The neighborhood had given birth to hard-line union men and militant Communists in their thousands. Some well-known gangsters too, Francis the Belgian among them. These days, the Communists and the National Front got more or less equal votes there.

As soon as I got back to the station house, I went to check the registration on his Golf. Toni didn't have a criminal record. I wasn't surprised. If he'd had one, which I was sure he had, someone had wiped it. My third man had a face, a name, and an address. With all the risks I'd run, it had been a good day.

I lit a cigarette. I couldn't seem to get out of my office. It was as if something was keeping me there, but I didn't know what. I took another look at the Mourrabed file. I read over his inter-rogation, which had been completed by Cerutti. Mourrabed didn't rent the apartment. For the past year, it had been regis-tered in the name of Raoul Farge. The rent was paid in cash every month. Regularly too, which was unusual in the projects. Cerutti thought it was more than unusual, but he'd gotten to the

Public Housing Office too late to check Farge's file. The offices closed at five. He was planning to go back tomorrow morning.

Good work, I told myself. On the other hand, it was a complete washout as far as junk was concerned. Nothing had been found either in the apartment or in his car. It must be somewhere. We wouldn't be able to get an indictment against Mourrabed over a simple assault, even a particularly nasty one. We'd have to let him walk.

It was when I looked up from my desk that it clicked. There was an old poster on the wall. The Burgundy wine route. At the bottom, the words: *Visit our cellars.* The cellar! Shit! That must be where Mourrabed stashed the dope. I radioed out. The call was picked up by Reiver, the West Indian, which annoyed me, because I was sure I'd put him on day duty. It irritated me.

"What are you doing on the night shift?"

"Replacing Loubié. He has three kids. I'm a bachelor. Don't even have a girlfriend waiting for me. It's fairer this way, don't you think?"

"OK. Get over to the Bassens project. Find out if the buildings have cellars. I'll be waiting here."

"They do," he replied.

"How do you know?"

"I know Bassens."

The telephone rang. It was Ange, from the Treize-Coins. Djamel had come by twice. He'd be back again in fifteen minutes.

"Reiver," I said. "Stay in the neighborhood. I'm on my way. I'll be there in an hour at the outside."

Djamel was at the bar, having a beer. He was wearing a T-shirt with the words *Charlie's Pizza* in black.

"You disappeared," I said, going up to him.

"I work for Charlie, on Place Noailles. Delivering pizzas." With his thumb, he pointed to the moped parked on the sidewalk. "I got a new moped. Neat machine, huh?"

"Very nice," I said.

"Yeah. It's cool and it makes me a bit of money."

"Were you looking for me the other night?"

"I have something that might interest you. The guy they whacked on the steps wasn't loaded. They planted the gun on him later."

I was so taken aback, my stomach contracted and the pain came back. I downed the *pastis* Ange had served me unasked.

"How did you find that out?"

"A friend's mother. They live over the steps. She was hanging out the washing, and saw the whole thing. But she won't say shit. Your pals have been to see her. Checking her papers and everything. She's really scared. This is all true, man, every word."

He looked at the time but didn't move. He was waiting. I owed him something and he wouldn't leave before he had it. Even to earn a few francs.

"This guy, you know. His name was Ugo. He was my friend. A long time ago. When I was your age."

Djamel nodded. He was making a mental note of it, trying to find a place for it somewhere in his head. "Yeah. From the time when you used to fuck up, you mean."

"That's right."

He noted it again, and pursed his lips. To him, whacking Ugo like that was a rotten thing to do. Ugo deserved justice. I represented that justice. But in Djamel's head, the word justice and the word cop didn't really go together. I may have been Ugo's friend, but I was also a cop, and he found that hard to forget. He'd taken one step toward me, not two. He was still a long way from trusting me.

"He seemed like a cool guy, your friend." He looked at the time again, then at me. "There's one more thing. Yesterday, when you were looking for me, there were these two guys tailing you. Not cops. My friends spotted them."

"Did they have a motorbike?"

Djamel shook his head. "Not the type. Wops, playing at being tourists."

"Wops? How do you know?"

"Because of the way they talked to each other."

He finished his beer and left. Ange served me another *pastis*. I drank it, trying not to think of anything.

Cerutti was waiting for me in my office. We hadn't been able to contact Pérol. A pity. I was sure we'd hit the jackpot tonight. We got Mourrabed out of the hole and took him with us, handcuffed and still in his flowered shorts. He wouldn't stop yelling, as if we were going to take him into a corner somewhere and cut his throat. Cerutti told him to keep his mouth shut, or else he'd be forced to slap him around.

We drove in silence. Did Auch know the gun had been planted? I'd reached the scene before him. His team was already there. Most of them, anyhow. Certainly Morvan, Cayrol, Sandoz and Mériel. It could have been a tragic mistake. The kind of thing that happened sometimes. But what if it wasn't? Whether or not he'd been armed, would they have shot Ugo? If they'd followed him on his ride to Zucca's, they must have known he was still armed.

"Shit!" Cerutti said. "There's a welcoming committee!"

Reiver's car was parked in front of the block, surrounded by about twenty kids, a mixture of races. Reiver was leaning on the car with his arms folded. The kids were circling it like Apaches, in time to the music of Khaled being played at full volume. Some had their noses pressed to the window, to see the face of

Reiver's partner, who'd stayed inside, ready to call for help. Reiver himself didn't seem too worried.

In the evening, the kids aren't bothered if we cruise the streets. But it really freaks them out when we come into the projects. Especially in summer. The sidewalk is the nicest place around. A place to talk, and pick up girls. It can get a bit noisy, but no real harm is done. We advanced slowly. I was hoping they were kids from the project. If they were, we could still talk. Cerutti parked behind Reiver's car. A few kids stepped aside, then, like flies, swarmed to our car and surrounded it.

I turned to Mourrabed. "I don't want you inciting a riot, OK?"

I got out and walked nonchalantly toward Reiver.

"Everything all right?" I asked, ignoring the kids around us.

"Cool. These kids don't bother me. I warned them, the first one who touches one of the tires will have to eat it. That right?" he said to a tall, thin black kid, with a Rasta hat pulled down over his ears, who was watching us.

He didn't bother to reply.

"OK," I said to Reiver. "Let's go."

"Cellar N488. The super's waiting. I'll stay here. I prefer to listen to Khaled. I like him." Reiver was turning out to be full of surprises. He screwed up all my statistics about West Indians. He must have guessed what I was thinking. He pointed to a block a bit farther down. "I was born over there. This is my home."

We brought Mourrabed out of the car. Cerutti took his arm and forced him to walk. The tall black kid approached.

"What did the cops collar you for?" he asked Mourrabed, pointedly ignoring us.

"Because of some fag."

Six kids were barring the entrance of the block.

"The fag doesn't matter," I said. "We're here to visit the cellar. Must be enough junk in there for the whole project to shoot up. Maybe you like that. We don't. We don't like it at all. If we don't find anything, we let him go tomorrow."

The tall black kid made a sign and the others stepped aside.

"We're following you," he said to Mourrabed.

The cellar was one vast dump. Crates, cardboard boxes, clothes, spare parts for mopeds.

"Are you going to tell us, or do we have to search?"

Mourrabed shrugged wearily. "There's nothing here. You won't find a thing."

He didn't sound very convincing. For once, he'd stopped showing off. Cerutti and the others started to search. There was a crush of people in the corridor. Not just the kids. Adults too. The whole block was gathering. At regular intervals, the light went out and someone pressed the time switch. We'd better put our hands on the stash quickly or there might be trouble.

"There ain't no junk," Mourrabed said. He'd become very nervous. His shoulders had sagged and he was keeping his head down. "It ain't here."

The team stopped searching. I looked at Mourrabed.

"It ain't here," he said, regaining some of his self-assurance.

"So where is it?" Cerruti asked, walking up to him.

"Up there. The gas main."

"Shall we go?" Cerutti asked.

"Keep searching," I said.

Mourrabed cracked. "Shit, man! I tell you there ain't nothing here. It's up there. I'll show you."

"So what's down here?"

"This!" Béraud said, holding up a Thompson sub-machine gun.

He'd just opened a crate. A real arsenal. All kinds of guns

and enough ammunition to withstand a siege. As jackpots went, this was the real thing. This was winning the lottery.

I got out of the car, making sure nobody was waiting for me with a boxing glove. But I didn't think there would be. I'd been taught a good lesson. The serious harassment would come later, if I didn't follow the advice I'd been given.

Mourrabed had been put in the cooler. We'd found a kilo of heroin in packets, which was enough junk for a rainy day, and twelve thousand francs. Enough to send him away for quite a while. Possessing arms was going to complicate his case badly. Especially as I had my own ideas about their future use. Mourrabed had clammed up, and asked for his lawyer. He responded to all our questions with a shrug of the shoulders. But his arrogance had gone. He was in serious trouble, and he wasn't sure if they'd be able to get him out of this. 'They' were the people who were using the cellar to store arms. The people who supplied him with drugs. Who may or may not be the same people.

When I opened the door, the first thing I heard was Honorine laughing happily. Then her beautiful accent:

"Hey, he must be two-timing me in paradise! I've won again!"

All three of them were there—Honorine, Marie-Lou, and Babette—playing rummy on the terrace. In the background, Petrucciani was playing *Estate*. One of his first records, and not one of his best. The later ones were more proficient technically. But this one was full of raw emotion. I hadn't listened to it since Rosa had left.

"I hope I'm not disturbing you," I said as I walked to the table, feeling a bit annoyed.

"Damn it, that's the third game I've won!" Honorine said, clearly excited.

I kissed each of them on the cheek in turn, picked up the

bottle of Lagavulin that stood on the table between Marie-Lou and Babette, and went off to look for a glass.

"There are stuffed peppers in the casserole. You can reheat them. Make sure you do it slowly. OK, Babette, you deal."

I smiled. Just a few days ago, this had been a bachelor's house, and now three women were playing rummy in it, at ten minutes to midnight! Everything was tidy. The meal was ready. The dishes had been done. On the terrace, washing was drying. There in front of me was every man's dream: a mother, a sister, and a whore!

I heard them chuckling behind my back. They seemed to have established a kind of gentle rapport. My bad mood vanished as quickly as it had come. I was happy to see them there. I liked all three of them. A pity they couldn't be combined in one woman. I'd have fallen in love with her.

"Are you playing?" Marie-Lou asked me.

10.

IN WHICH THE WAY OTHER PEOPLE LOOK AT YOU IS A DEADLY WEAPON

Honorine made stuffed peppers like no one else could. Romanian style, she called it. She'd fill the peppers with a stuffing of rice, sausage meat and a little beef, well salted and peppered, then place them in an earthenware casserole and cover them with water, add tomato coulis, thyme, bay and saw-wort, and let them cook on a very low flame, without covering. They tasted wonderful, especially if you poured a spoonful of *crème fraîche* over them at the last moment.

I watched them playing rummy as I ate. To 51. When you have 51 points in your game, a tierce, fifty, a hundred, or four aces, you put your cards on the table. If another player has already folded, you can add to your game the cards he's missing, which follow or precede his tierce or fifty. You can also take his rummy, the joker, which he may have put down to replace a missing card. The winner is the player who manages to get rid of all his cards.

It's a simple game, but it requires a certain amount of concentration if you want to win. Marie-Lou was relying on luck, and she was losing. The fight was between Honorine and Babette. Each was watching the cards the other was discarding. But Honorine had spent many afternoons playing rummy, and although she acted surprised whenever she won a game, I'd have put odds on her coming out on top. She was playing to win.

As they played, I happened to glance at the washing drying on the line. In the middle of my shirts, underpants and socks, I noticed a pair of white panties and a bra. I looked at Marie-

Lou. She'd put on one of my T-shirts. Her breasts showed beneath the cotton. My eyes traveled the length of her legs and thighs, up as far as her ass. I realized she was naked beneath the T-shirt, and started to get a hard-on. Marie-Lou caught me looking at her and guessed what I was thinking. She gave me a gorgeous smile, winked, and crossed her legs, slightly embarrassed.

There followed an exchange of looks. From Babette to Marie-Lou. From Babette to me. From me to Babette. From Honorine to Babette, then to Marie-Lou. I felt ill at ease. I stood up and went to take a shower. Under the water, I was still hard.

Honorine left around half after midnight. She'd won five games, as against Babette's four and Marie-Lou's one. As she kissed me goodnight, I was sure she must be wondering what I was going to do with two women in my house.

Marie-Lou announced that she was going to take a bath. I watched her as she went to the bathroom. I couldn't help myself.

"She's really very beautiful," Babette said, with a slight smile on her face.

I nodded. "So are you."

It was true. She'd pulled her hair back in a pony tail. Her eyes seemed huge, and her mouth bigger. She was forty, but she was more than a match for any number of young cuties. Even Marie-Lou. Marie-Lou was young, and her beauty was obvious and immediate. Babette's, on the other hand, was radiant. Enjoying life keeps you young, I thought.

"Let it go," she said, sticking her tongue out at me slightly.

"Did she say something to you?"

"We had time to get acquainted. It makes no difference. That girl has her head on her shoulders. Are you planning to help her get free of her pimp?"

"Is that what she told you?"

"She didn't tell me anything. I'm asking you."

"There'll always be a pimp. Unless she wants to drop out. If she really wants it and she's brave enough. It's not so easy, you know. The girls are kept on a very tight rein." I was talking in platitudes. Marie-Lou was a hooker. She'd turned up on my doorstep because she was fucked up, and because I wasn't crazy and represented some kind of safety. I couldn't see beyond that. Couldn't see any farther than tomorrow, which was already a long way. "I have to find somewhere for her to crash. She can't stay here. It's not so safe around here anymore."

The air was mild, like a salt-laden caress. I gazed into the distance. The lapping of the waves evoked happy memories. I tried to distance myself from the threats hanging over me. I'd landed with both feet on dangerous ground, and what made it all the more dangerous was that I didn't know which direction the blows would come from.

"I know," Babette said.

"You know everything," I replied, a touch annoyed.

"No, not everything. But I know enough to be worried."

"That's good of you. I'm sorry."

"As far as Marie-Lou is concerned, is that all there is?"

I was embarrassed by this conversation. In spite of myself, I became aggressive. "What do you want to know? If I'm in love with a hooker? It's a common male fantasy, isn't it? Fall in love with a hooker, and take her away from her pimp. Become her pimp. Have her just to yourself, as a sex object..." I suddenly felt very weary, as if I was at the end of my tether. "I haven't yet found the love of my life. Maybe she doesn't exist."

"I only have a studio apartment. You know that."

"Don't worry. I'll find something."

Babette took an envelope from her bag, opened it, and handed me a photograph. "The reason I came was to show you this."

Several men around a table, in a restaurant. I knew one of them. Morvan. I swallowed.

"The one on the right is Joseph Poli. Very ambitious. He's looking to be Zucca's successor. I'm certain the killers at the Opéra were his men. He's a friend of Jacky Le Mat. He took part in the Saint-Paul-de-Vence heist in 81."

I remembered it. Seven million items of jewelry stolen. Jacky Le Mat had been brought in for questioning, but had to be released after the main witness retracted.

"The man standing," Babette went on, "is his brother, Émile. Specializes in protection. Slot machines, discos. Looks laid back, but he's as hard-boiled as they come."

"Are they lining Morvan's pockets?"

"The guy on the left is Luc Wepler," she continued, ignoring my question.

Her description of him sent a shiver down my spine. Wepler was born in Algeria. He joined the paras very young, and soon became an active member of the OAS. In 65, he was in Tixier-Vignancourt's security team. When his man did so badly in the election, he turned away from official activism. He went back to the paras, then became a mercenary. Fought in Rhodesia, in the Comoros, and Chad. In 74, he was in Cambodia, as a military advisor to the Americans fighting the Khmer Rouge. After that, Angola, South Africa, Benin. He fought alongside Bechir Jemayel's falangists in Lebanon.

"Interesting," I said, imagining a face to face talk with him.

"Since 90, he's been active in the National Front. With his commando background, he prefers to work in the shadows. Not many people in Marseilles know him. On one side, you've got the sympathizers. Victims of the economic downturn, unemployed workers, people who feel let down by the Socialists or the Communists. They're attracted by the National

Front's radical ideas. But on the other side, you've got the militants. The really determined ones. Backgrounds in the Oeuvre Française, the GUD, the Anti-Communist Front. They're organized into action cells, and they're spoiling for a fight. Wepler deals with them. He has the reputation of being a good trainer of young people. Which means that you do it the way he wants, or you're out."

I couldn't take my eyes off the photo. Wepler's ice-cold, electric blue eyes were hypnotic. I'd known guys like him in Djibouti. Cold-blooded killers. The whores of imperialism. Its lost children. Let loose in the world, full of hatred for having been the 'cuckolds of history,' as Garel, my chief warrant officer, had said one day.

Then I noticed another familiar face. In the background, on the right. At another table. Toni. The handsome Toni.

"Do you know this one?"

"No."

"I made his acquaintance this evening."

I told her how and why I'd met him. She grimaced. "That's bad. The photo was taken at a dinner for the real fanatics. The ones who are even more rabid than the usual National Front militants."

"You mean the Poli brothers have turned fascist?"

She shrugged. "They get together for a meal and a laugh and sing Nazi songs. Like Chez Jenny in Paris, you know. It doesn't prove anything. But there's clearly a business arrangement in there somewhere. The Poli brothers must be getting something out it. I don't see why else they'd bother with these people. But there is a link. Morvan. Wepler trained him. In Algeria, First Parachute regiment. After 68, Morvan was a militant in the Anti-Communist Front, where he became head of the Action Group. That was when he met Wepler again and they became best buddies..." She looked at me and smiled, confident she was about to make an impression. "And he married the sister of the Poli brothers."

I whistled between my teeth. "anymore surprises like that?"

"Batisti."

He was in the foreground of the photo, but with his back to the camera. I hadn't even noticed him.

"Batisti," I repeated, idiotically. "Of course. So he's mixed up with these people, too?"

"His daughter Simone is Émile Poli's wife."

"The family, right?"

"The family on one side, everyone else on the other. That's what the Mafia's all about. Guérini was the same. Zucca married a cousin of Volgro, the Neapolitan. It was when there was no family in charge in Marseilles that things fell apart here. Zucca realized that. So he joined a family."

"*La Nuova famiglia*," I said with a bitter smile. "New family, same old shit."

Marie-Lou came back, her body wrapped in a big terry towel. We'd almost forgotten about her. Her appearance was a breath of fresh air. She looked at us as if we were conspirators, then lit a cigarette, poured us two large glasses of Lagavulin, and went back inside. Soon after, we heard Astor Piazzolla on bandoneon, followed by Gerry Mulligan's saxophone. One of the finest musical encounters of the last fifteen years. *Buenos Aires, twenty years after.*

The pieces of a puzzle lay scattered in front of me. Now all I had to do was put them together. Ugo and Zucca with Morvan. Al Dakhil and his bodyguards with Morvan and Toni. Leila with Toni and the two killers. But the pieces didn't fit. And what was Batisti's part in all this?

"Who's this?" I asked, pointing to a distinguished-looking man to the right of Joseph Poli.

"No idea."

"Where is this restaurant?"

"The Auberge des Restanques. Just outside Aix, on the way to Vauvenargues."

The warning lights went on instantly in my head. I forgot about Ugo, and switched to Leila. "That's not far from where Leila's body was found."

"What's the connection?"

"That's what I'm wondering."

"Do you believe in coincidence?"

"I don't believe in anything."

I'd walked Babette to her car, after making sure there was no immediate danger on the street. No car or motorbike had set off after her. I'd waited outside a few more minutes. By the time I'd come back inside, I felt reassured.

"Be careful," she'd said, stroking the back of my neck.

I'd taken her in my arms. "I can't turn back, Babette. I don't know where it's going to lead me. But I'm going on. I've never had an aim in my life. Now I have one. It may not be worth much, but it's mine."

I loved the gleam in her eyes when she freed herself from me. "The only aim in life is to stay alive."

"That's what I say."

Now I had to face Marie-Lou. I'd been hoping that Babette would stay. They could have slept in my bed, and I'd have slept on the couch. But Babette had replied that I was a big boy now, and I'd be fine on the couch, even if she wasn't there.

Marie-Lou was holding the photo. "Who are these guys?"

"Rich guys with ugly minds! All crooks, if you really want to know."

"Are you after them?"

"I might be."

I took the photo from her and had another look at it. It had been taken three months ago. It was a Sunday, a day when Les Restanques was usually closed. Babette had been given the photo by a journalist on *Le Méridional* who'd been a guest at the party. She was going to try to find out more about the participants, especially what the Poli brothers, Morvan and Wepler were cooking up.

Marie-Lou had sat down on the couch, her legs folded under her. She looked up at me. The marks on her skin were fading.

"You want me to go, right?"

I showed her the bottle of Lagavulin. She nodded. I filled two glasses and gave her one.

"I can't explain it all to you, Marie-Lou. I'm involved in something ugly. You saw what happened last night. Things are going to get complicated. It's too risky to stay here. These guys don't fool around," I said, thinking of the faces of Morvan and Wepler.

She kept looking at me. I really wanted her. I wanted to throw myself on her and have her right there and then, on the floor. It was the easiest way to avoid talking. I didn't think she'd want me to do that, so I didn't move.

"I realized that. What am I to you?"

"A hooker... But I really like you."

"Bastard!" She threw her glass at me. I'd known it was coming and dodged. The glass smashed on the tiles. Marie-Lou didn't move.

"Do you want another glass?"

"Yes, please."

I poured her another glass, and sat down next to her. The hardest part was over.

"Do you want to leave your pimp?"

"This life is the only thing I know."

"I wish you'd do something else."

"Oh yeah? Like what? Become a cashier at Prisunic?"

"Why not? My partner's daughter does that. She's your age, or just about."

"That's hell on earth!"

"And getting laid by guys you don't even know is better, is it?"

She stared at the bottom of her glass in silence, just like the other night when I'd met her at O'Stop.

"Were you thinking about it before this happened?"

"I've lost count, you know. I can't do it anymore. Fuck all these guys. That's why I got beaten up."

"I thought it was because of me."

"You were just the pretext."

By the time we finished talking, day was breaking. The story of Marie-Lou was the story of all the Marie-Lous in the world. Give or take a detail or two. Starting with her unemployed father raping her, while Mom was out working as a cleaning woman to support the family. Her brothers who didn't give a damn, because she was only a girl. Except when they saw her going out with a white guy, or, worse still, an Arab. Getting beaten for the slightest thing. Other kids are given candy, poor kids get beaten.

Marie-Lou had run away at seventeen. One evening after school. Alone, because her boyfriend, a classmate, had chickened out. So it was bye-bye, Pierrot. And farewell, La Garenne-Colombes. She headed South. The truck driver who picked her up was on his way to Rome.

"It was on the way back that I realized I'd end up a hooker. He dumped me in Lyons with five hundred francs. His wife and kids were waiting for him. He'd fucked me for more than that, but what the hell, I'd liked it! He could have screwed me for nothing. He was the first, he wasn't the worst.

"After that, all the guys I met had one thing on their minds.

It usually lasted a week. In their little minds, I was too beautiful to ever become a respectable woman. I guess it kind of scared them that I'm such a good lay. Or else they saw me as the hooker I was going to be. What do you think?"

"I think the way other people look at you can be a deadly weapon."

"You're a good talker," she said, wearily. "But couldn't you love a girl like me, huh?"

"All the women I ever loved left me."

"I could stay. I've got nothing to lose."

Her words stunned me. She was sincere. She was opening up to me, giving herself.

"I couldn't stand to be loved by a woman who has nothing to lose. That's what love is, the possibility of losing."

"You're sick, Fabio, you know that? I don't think you're very happy."

"But I don't boast about it!"

I laughed, but she didn't. She looked at me, and there seemed to be sadness in her eyes. I didn't know if she was sad for herself or for me. Her lips touched mine. She smelled of cashew oil.

"I'm going to bed," she said. "I think that's best, don't you?"

"I guess so," I heard myself saying, thinking it was too late to throw myself on her. And that made me smile.

"You know something?" she said, as she stood up. "I know one of the guys in that photo." She picked up the photo from the floor and pointed at a man sitting next to Toni. "That's my pimp. Raoul Farge."

"Shit!"

Even the best couch is always uncomfortable. It's a place you only sleep if you have to, because someone else is using your bed. I hadn't slept on mine since the last night Rosa spent here.

We'd talked and drunk till dawn, hoping once again to save our relationship. It wasn't our love that was in question. It was her and me. Me more than her. I refused to satisfy her true desire: to have a child. I couldn't give her any logical argument. I was simply a prisoner of my own life.

Clara, the only woman I'd ever made pregnant—without intending to, admittedly—had had an abortion without telling me. I wasn't reliable, she yelled at me, after she'd done it, as a way of justifying her decision. I was too interested in women. I loved them too much. I was unfaithful just looking at them. I couldn't be trusted. I was a lover. I'd never be a husband. Let alone a father. That had put an end to our relationship, obviously. I thought I'd killed the father in me, but maybe he was only taking a nap.

I loved Rosa. An angel's face surrounded by a mass of curly hair, chestnut shading to red. She had a magnificent, disarming smile, almost always slightly sad. It was her smile that first drew me to her. I could think about her now without it hurting. It wasn't so much that that I'd lost interest in her, as that she'd become unreal to me. But it had taken me a long time to get over her, to forget her body. When we were together, I just had to close my eyes and I wanted her. Images of her had obsessed me. I often wondered if I'd want her just as much if she suddenly showed up again without warning. I still didn't know.

Not true. I did know. Ever since I'd slept with Lole. You couldn't get over loving Lole. It wasn't a question of beauty. Rosa had a magnificent body, full of subtle curves and lines. Everything about her, the slightest gesture, was sensual. Lole was thinner, more willowy. Ethereal, even in the way she walked. She resembled Gradiva in the Pompeii frescoes. She seemed hardly to touch the ground. Making love to her was like letting yourself be carried away on a journey. She transported you. And, when you came, you didn't feel as if you'd lost something, but as if you'd *found* something.

That was what I'd felt, even though, in the moments that had followed, I'd completely blown it. One night at les Goudes, Manu had said: "Shit, why is it that when you come, it never lasts?" We hadn't known what to answer. But with Lole, something did last.

Ever since, I'd been living with what lasted. My one desire was to find her, to see her again. Even though I'd been refusing to admit it for three months. Even though I had no illusions. I could still feel her fingers on my skin like fire. My cheeks were still red from the shame. Since Lole, there'd been only Marie-Lou. With her, when I came it was like losing myself. An act of despair. It was despair that drove you to sleep with hookers. But Marie-Lou deserved better.

I changed position. I was sure I wasn't going to get any sleep tonight. I was torn between the persistent desire to see Lole again and the repressed desire to sleep with Marie-Lou. What did her pimp have to do with all this? Leila's death was like a stone cast into water, sending ripples in all directions, and cops, gangsters and fascists were moving within those ripples. And Raoul Farge, who was using Mourrabed's cellar to store enough weaponry to attack the Bank of France.

Shit! What were all those weapons intended for? An interesting thought suddenly occurred to me, but the last mouthful of Lagavulin put a stop to further reflection. I didn't have time to look at the clock. When the alarm went off, I didn't even feel as if I'd closed my eyes.

Marie-Lou must have been fighting monsters all night. The pillows had been rolled into balls, and the sheets were crumpled where she'd hugged them to her. She was sleeping on top of the sheet, on her stomach, with her head turned away. I couldn't see her face. I could only see her body. I felt a bit stupid, standing there with the cups of coffee and the croissants.

I'd swum for a good half hour. It cleared my lungs of all the cigarettes I'd been smoking. I felt my muscles tense as if they were about to burst. I swam straight ahead, beyond the sea wall. I didn't enjoy it. I forced myself on, and only stopped when I felt a shooting pain in my stomach that reminded me of the blows I'd received. The memory of the pain changed to fear, then panic. For a second, I thought I was going to drown.

I took a shower, and the feel of the lukewarm water on my body finally calmed me down. I drank an orange juice, then went out to buy croissants. I stopped off at Fonfon's, to grab a coffee and read the paper. Despite pressure from some of his customers, the only papers he kept were *Le Provençal* and *La Marseillaise*. Not *Le Méridional*. Fonfon deserved my custom.

There'd been a big raid last night. Several squads had taken part, including Auch's. It had been a methodical raid, covering the three main areas: bars, brothels, and night clubs. All the trouble spots had been hit: Place d'Aix, Cours Belzunce, Place de l'Opéra, Cours Julien, La Plaine and even Place Thiars. More than sixty people taken in for questioning, all of them Arabs without the right papers. A few prostitutes. A few punks. But no major gangsters. Not even a minor gangster. The captains of the squads involved had refused to make any comment, but the journalist implied that this kind of operation might be repeated. Marseilles' night life had to be cleaned up.

To anyone who could read between the lines, the situation was clear enough. The criminal hierarchy of Marseilles lacked a recognized leader. Zucca was dead, and Al Dakhil had joined him wherever bastards go when they die. The police were moving in, and Auch was trying to get his bearings. He needed to know who he was dealing with now. I'd have staked my life that Joseph Poli would be the one to come out on top. That gave me the creeps. His rise was being backed by a group of extremists. Some politician must have bet his career on it. I was sure now that Ugo had unwittingly been doing the devil's work for him.

"I'm not asleep," Marie-Lou said, just as I was leaving the coffee and croissants beside the bed.

She drew the sheet up over her. Her face was tired, and I supposed she'd slept as badly as me. I sat down on the edge of the bed, placed the tray beside her, and kissed her on the forehead.

"Are you OK?"

"That's kind of you," she said, looking at the tray. "It's the first time anyone's ever brought me breakfast in bed."

I didn't reply. We drank our coffees in silence. I watched her eat. She kept her head lowered. I offered her a cigarette. Our eyes met. Hers were sad. Mine I tried to make as gentle as I could.

"You should have made love to me last night. It would have helped me."

"I couldn't."

"I need to know that you love me. If I want to get out of this life. It's the only way I can do it."

"You can do it."

"You don't love me, do you?"

"Yes, I do."

"So why didn't you fuck me the way you'd have fucked any other girl?"

"I couldn't."

"What is it you can't do?"

She quickly slipped her hand between my thighs, grabbed

my dick through my pants, and squeezed it, squeezed it hard, her eyes still on mine.

"Stop it!" I said, without moving.

"Is this what you can't do?" She let go of my dick and just as quickly caught hold of my hair. "Or is it this? Is it in your head?"

"Yes. That's it. You'd have to stop being a hooker first."

"I have stopped, asshole!" she cried. "I have stopped. In my own little head. Why else would I come here? Here, to your house! You don't see it, do you? You must be blind! And if you don't see it, then nobody will. I'll always be a hooker." She wrapped her arms around my neck and started to sob. "Love me, Fabio. Love me. Just once. But love me the way you'd love anyone else."

She fell silent. My lips were on her mouth. My tongue found her tongue, full of words that would never be spoken. The tray went flying. I heard the cups smashing on the tiles. I felt her nails pierce the skin on my back. I almost came as soon as I entered her. Her pussy was as hot as the tears coursing down her cheeks.

We made love as if for the first time. Shyly and passionately. Without any ulterior motive. The shadows under her eyes vanished. I collapsed to the side. She looked at me for a moment, seemed about to say something, but instead just smiled at me. Her smile was so tender that I too couldn't think of anything to say. We lay like that, silently, staring into the distance, each searching for a possible happiness. By the time I left her, she'd stopped being a hooker. But I was still just a fucking cop.

And waiting for me on the other side of the door, without a shadow of a doubt, was all the world's corruption.

11.

IN WHICH THINGS ARE DONE
AS THEY ARE SUPPOSED TO BE DONE

Pérol's face said it all: there was trouble in the air. But I was ready to confront anything. "The chief wants to see you."

That was an event. It was two years since the last time my chief had sent for me. After the riot triggered by Kader and Driss, Varounian had sent a letter to *Le Méridional*, in which he talked about his life, the way the Arabs were constantly harassing him in his store, the endless robberies, and gave his own version of events. His conclusion was that the law was on the side of the Arabs. Justice was their justice. France was capitulating in the face of the invasion, because the police were with them. He finished his letter with one of the National Front's slogans: *Love France or leave it!*

OK, it didn't cause as much stir as *J'accuse*. But the local station, who'd never much liked outsiders muscling in on their territory, spent good money to produce a damning report on my squad. I was the main target. My team was good at protecting public places, everyone recognized that. But I was accused of not being firm enough inside the projects, and spending too much time negotiating with delinquents, especially immigrants and gypsies. There followed a list of the cases in which I'd been seen to be too lenient.

I was given the standard dressing down. First by my boss, then by the Big Chief. My mission wasn't to understand, but to crack down. I was there to maintain order. It was up to the judges to apply the law. In the case that had made the front page of *Le Méridional*, I'd failed in my mission.

The Big Chief had then moved on to something that, in police terms, amounted to treason: my meetings with Serge, a community organizer. Serge and I had met one evening at the station. He'd been picked up with fifteen kids in the parking lot of the La Simiane project. It was the usual thing: ghetto blaster playing, shouting, laughter, mopeds backfiring... He was with them, drinking beer. The idiot didn't even have his papers on him!

Serge was amused. He looked like a slightly ageing adolescent. Dressed like the kids. The police took him for the leader of the gang. All he'd wanted was to go somewhere with the kids where they could make noise without disturbing anyone. That was a provocation in itself, since there was nothing in the area but high rise blocks and parking lots. Admittedly, the kids were no choirboys. Four or five of them had already been collared for bag snatching and other trivial offences.

"Hey, we're the one's who'll pay for your retirement, so shut up!" Malik screamed at Babar, one of the oldest cops in the station house.

I knew Malik. Fifteen years old, four car robberies under his belt. "We don't know what to do with him," the assistant prosecutor had declared. "We've placed him in foster homes, but it never works out." Whenever they finished with him, he came back to the project. It was his home. He'd made friends with Serge. At least you could talk to Serge.

"Shit, it's true, man!" he said, seeing me. "We're the ones who pay."

"Can it!" I said.

Babar wan't a bad guy. But there was a quota in operation at the time. A hundred arrests a month. If you didn't meet it, they cut the budget and reduced manning levels.

I got on well with Serge. He was a bit too pious for my taste.

He and I would never be friends, but I liked his courage and his love for the kids. Serge had faith, and a strong sense of morality. An urban morality, he called it. We started meeting regularly, at the Moustiers, a café in L'Estaque, near the beach. We talked. He was in contact with the social workers, and he helped me to understand. Often, when we collared a kid for some trivial offence, he'd be the first person I called to the station, even before the parents.

After my interview with my superiors, Serge was transferred. Of course, it was possible the decision had already been taken. Serge sent an open letter to the newspapers, called *Cross section of a volcano*, appealing for a greater understanding of young people living in the projects. *The fire is smoldering*, he concluded, *and firefighters and arsonists are in a race to fan the flames.* It was never published. Local journalists preferred to keep on good terms with the cops, who supplied them with information.

I'd never seen Serge again. It was my fault he'd gone: guilt by association. Cops, community organizers and social workers were different jobs. They shouldn't work together. "We aren't social workers!" the Big Chief had screamed. "Prevention, dissuasion, outreach, community policing, that's all crap! Do you understand, Montale?" I understood. We preferred fanning the flames. Politically, that paid higher dividends these days. My boss had put a stop to all the community work. My mission was effectively shelved, and my squad became nothing more than the cleaning service of North Marseilles.

With Mourrabed, I was on home territory. Nobody cared about a stupid fight between a punk and a fag. I hadn't yet written my report, so no one in the station knew anything about our little ride last night, or about the spoils of war: the drugs, the arms. I had an idea what the arms were intended for. I recalled a memo I'd seen—one among many that circulated all the time—referring to armed gangs that had appeared in the suburbs. Paris, Créteil, Rueil-Malmaison, Sartrouville, Vaulx-en-Velin... Every time there was a flare-up in one of the projects, these commandos emerged. Scarves covering the lower halves of their faces, leather jackets worn inside out. And all carrying guns. A riot cop had been shot down, I couldn't remember where. The weapon, a Colt 11.45, had previously been used in the killing of a restaurant owner in Grenoble.

My colleagues were sure to be aware of all that. Loubet, certainly Auch. As soon as I came clean about what we'd discovered, the other squads would muscle in and take us off the case. As usual. I'd decided to delay that moment as long as possible. To keep shtum about what had happened in the cellar and in particular to say nothing about Raoul Farge. I was the only one who knew about his connections with Morvan and Toni.

Cerutti arrived with the coffees. I took out a piece of paper on which Marie-Lou had scribbled down Farge's telephone number, and a likely address, on Avenue de Montolivet. I gave it to Cerutti.

"Check if the number and the address match. Then go over there with a few men and pick up Farge. I don't imagine he's an early riser."

They looked at me in astonishment.

"Where did you get this?" Pérol asked.

"One of my informers. I want Farge here, by noon," I said to Cerutti. "Check if he has a record. Once we've got his statement, we'll confront him with Mourrabed. Pérol, get the asshole to talk about the junk and the arms. Especially the arms. Who supplies them? Tell him we have Farge in custody. Get someone to do an inventory of the arms, also by noon. Oh, and I also want a list of all the guns that have been used in murders in the last three months." They were more and more astounded. "It's a race against time, guys. The whole station will be on our backs soon. So get a move on! It's not that I'm bored with your company, but I can't keep God waiting!"

I was in top form.

God's justice is blind, as everyone knows. The chief didn't beat about the bush. "Come in!" he cried. It wasn't an invitation, it was an order. He didn't stand up, or offer me his hand, or even say hello. He left me standing there like a bad pupil.

"What's all this about..." He looked at the file. "Mourrabed. Nacer Mourrabed."

"A fight. Between punks."

"Is that a reason to put people behind bars?"

"There was a complaint."

"The mezzanine is piled high with complaints. Nobody died, as far as I know."

I shook my head.

"Because I don't think I read your report yet."

"I'm writing it now."

He looked at his watch. "It's been exactly twenty-six hours and fifteen minutes since you brought this punk in, and you're telling me your report still isn't ready? About a fight?"

"I wanted to check a few things. Mourrabed has a record. He's a repeat offender."

He looked me up and down. The bad pupil. Bottom of the class. His contemptuous look didn't scare me. I'd been used to looks like that ever since elementary school. I'd been insolent, a fighter, a loudmouth. I'd had my fill of lectures, both individually and as part of a group. I looked straight back at him, my hands in the pockets of my jeans.

"Repeat offender. I think you've got your hooks into this..." He looked at the file again. "Nacer Mourrabed. That's what his lawyer thinks, too."

He'd scored a point. I had no idea Mourrabed's lawyer was

already in the picture. Did Pérol know? He scored another point when he asked on the intercom for Éric Brunel to be sent in.

The name was vaguely familiar. I didn't have time to think about it. I recognized the man who now came into the office. I'd seen him in a photo, as recently as last night, sitting next to the Poli brothers, Wepler and Morvan. My heart started pounding. Things were coming full circle, and now I was really in the shit. *Total Khéops*, to quote a rap by IAM. In other words, total chaos. A complete mess. I couldn't rely on Pérol and Cerutti working fast anymore. It was up to me to gain time. Until noon.

The chief stood up and went around his desk to greet Brunel. He looked as impeccable as he had on the photo, in a navy blue double-breasted linen suit. As if the temperature outside wasn't close to 30 or 35 degrees. Clearly, he wasn't the kind of guy who sweated a lot! The chief indicated a chair. He didn't introduce me. They must already have talked about my case.

I was still standing. Since I hadn't been asked anything, I lit a cigarette, and waited. As he'd already stated on the phone, Brunel said, he found it abnormal, to say the least, that his client, who'd been arrested yesterday morning because of a fight, had not been granted the right—he insisted on the word—to call his lawyer.

"I'm within the law," I retorted.

"The law doesn't allow you to harass him. Which is what you've been doing. For several months now."

"He's one of the biggest dealers in North Marseilles."

"So you say! There isn't a single shred of evidence against him. You've already had him up before a judge, and that didn't work. Your pride was hurt, and because of that you're hounding him. As for this so-called fight, I made some inquiries of my own. Several witnesses state that it was the complainant—a junkie and a homosexual—who attacked my client as he was coming out of a bar."

I could sense that he was gearing up for a big courtroom speech, and I tried to head him off, but the chief gestured to me to keep quiet. "Carry on."

I let my cigarette ash fall to the floor.

We were treated to his 'client's' unhappy childhood. Brunel had been handling Mourrabed for just under a year. Children like him deserved a chance. He was defending several 'clients' in the same situation. Some, like Mourrabed, were Arabs, while others had completely French names. The jurors would have had tears in their eyes by now.

Now the speech started.

"At the age of fourteen, my client left his father's apartment. He no longer felt at home there. He started living on the streets. He soon learned to get by on his own, to be self-reliant. And to fight. He had to fight hard in order to survive. That's the desperate situation in which he grew into a man."

Much more of this, I told myself, and I'd blow my top. I'd throw myself on Brunel and make him eat his National Front card! But the hour hand was turning, and, thanks to these fairy tales of his, I was gaining time. Brunel was still going strong. He was on the future now. Work, family, country.

"Her name is Jocelyne. She lives in a project too. La Bricarde. But she has a real family. Her father works at the Lafarge cement works. Her mother is a cleaner at the Northern Hospital. Jocelyne was a conscientious, well-behaved student at school. At the moment, she's training to be a hairdresser. She's his fiancée. She loves him and helps him. She'll be the mother he never knew. The woman of his dreams. Together, they'll get an apartment. Together they'll build a corner of Paradise. Yes, monsieur!" he said, seeing me smile.

I hadn't been able to stop myself. It was too much:

Mourrabed in carpet slippers in front of the TV, with three brats on his knees. Mourrabed a happy wage slave!

"You know," Brunel said, appealing to my chief, "what this young man, this delinquent, told me once? One day, he said, my wife and I will live in a building with a marble plaque at the entrance, and on it the letter 'R' in gold. 'R' for Residence, like the ones around Saint-Tronc, Saint-Marcel and La Gavotte. That's his dream."

From North Marseilles to East Marseilles. That was real social climbing!

"I'll tell you Mourrabed's dream," I interrupted, just about ready to throw up. "A big car, a suit and a ring. His dream is to be like you. But he doesn't have your gift of the gab. So instead he sells junk. Supplied by guys as well dressed as you."

"Montale!" the chief screamed.

"What about it?" I cried too. "I don't know where his sweet little fiancée was the other night. But I can tell you what he was doing at the time. Fucking a sixteen-year-old runaway! After beating up a guy whose hair was a tad too long. And for good measure, he had two of his buddies to help him. Just in case the... homosexual, as you call him, knew how to fight. Personally, I have nothing against Mourrabed, but I wouldn't have minded seeing him knocked out by a fag!"

And I stubbed out my cigarette with my foot.

Brunel had remained unruffled, a discreet smile hovering on his lips. He was making a mental note of me, imagining what his buddies could do to me. Cut my tongue off and shove it down my throat. Blow my brains out. He adjusted the knot on his tie, even though it was already impeccable, and stood up, looking sincerely contrite. "In the light of such opinions, monsieur . . ."

My chief stood up at the same time, also looking shocked by my words.

"I demand that my client be released immediately."

"If you'll allow me," I said, picking up the office phone. "I have to check one more thing."

It was seven minutes after twelve. Pérol picked up at the other end.

"Just in time," he said. He gave me a quick rundown.

I turned to Brunel.

"Your client is about to be charged," I said. "With assault, corruption of a minor, possession of drugs, and possession of arms, at least one of which was used in the homicide of a young girl named Leila Laarbi. Captain Loubet is dealing with that case. An accomplice is currently being interrogated. Raoul Farge. A pimp. I hope he's not another one of your clients, Monsieur Brunel."

I managed not to smile.

I called Marie-Lou. She was sunbathing on the terrace. I had a vision of her body. I've always been amazed by blacks tanning themselves. I've never been able to see the difference. But apparently, they can. I told her the good news. Farge was in my office, and wasn't about to leave anytime soon. She could take a taxi, go home, and pack her bags.

"I'll be there in an hour and a half," I said.

It was this morning, after we'd laughed and picked up the broken cups and had another coffee on the terrace with Honorine, that we'd decided she should go away. She'd go back to her place to pack, and then she'd settle in the country for a bit. A sister of Honorine's lived in Saint-Cannat, a little village twenty kilometers from Aix, on the road to Avignon. She and her husband owned a little land, with vines and cherry and apricot trees. Neither was in the first flush of youth. They were happy to have Marie-Lou stay there for the summer. Honorine was delighted to be able to do a good turn. Like me, she'd grown fond of Marie-Lou.

"And you'll have time to go see her, won't you?" she asked, winking at me. "It's not the middle of nowhere."

"I'll go there with you, Honorine."

"You don't need me, handsome. I'm too old to play the chaperone."

We both laughed. I'd have to sit her down sometime and tell her I was in love with someone else. I wondered if Honorine would like Lole. But to me, Honorine was like my mother, and I'd never been able to talk to my mother about girls. The only time I'd ever dared was when I'd just turned fourteen. I told her I thought Gélou was really beautiful and was in love with her. In return, I got a slap. For the first time in my life. Honorine might have reacted the same way. You didn't mess around with cousins.

Taking Farge into custody reduced the risk for Marie-Lou. Someone might be watching her place, but he wouldn't do anything without contacting Farge. All the same, I preferred to be there. Farge was denying the whole thing, except where the evidence was staring him in the face. He admitted he was the person who rented the two-room apartment where Mourrabed was crashing. But he couldn't stand the projects anymore. Too many Arabs and blacks. He'd sent his notice to the Public Housing Office. Of course we found no trace of his letter. But the story made it possible for him to declare that he didn't know Mourrabed. He was just a squatter, he kept repeating. "They go there to get their fix! That's the only thing they know how to do. Apart from raping our women." I thought of Leila and Toni and the two killers, and almost punched him.

"Say that again," I said, "and I'll make you eat your own balls."

He had no record. White as snow, our Farge. As with Toni, someone had done a bit of cleaning up. We'd find a way to make him confess where the arms came from. Maybe not us, but Loubet. I was ready to hand Farge over to him. I went to see him, with the Astra special in my pocket. I told him what I'd found at Mourrabed's place. He looked at the gun, which I'd placed on his desk.

"The third man is still on the streets. So if you have time..."

"You're certainly persistent," he said, smiling slightly.

"Luck."

By sending Farge to Loubet, I was kicking the ball into touch. Getting Auch off my back. And Morvan. Loubet was respected in a way that I wasn't. He didn't like people interfering in his investigations. He'd do his job.

I didn't tell him about Toni. He'd been driving the taxi. That didn't make him a killer, or a rapist. At most, he'd have to explain his connection to the two killers. Since they were both dead, Toni could make up any story he liked. Since all I had was a belief, but no proof, I preferred to keep one length ahead of everyone else.

"Having a few Arabs under your belt gives you a thrill, does it?" Mourrabed the 'squatter' yelled, suddenly angry.

"I don't have a problem with Arabs. I have a problem with you."

I told him I'd met his lawyer and that unfortunately he couldn't do anything for him right now. Out of pure spite, I added that I could phone his fiancée, if he liked.

"Your lawyer spoke very highly of Jocelyne. But if you're still thinking of marriage, I think you've blown it!"

Improbably, his eyes misted over. He was a picture of misery and despair. The hatred had gone. It would come back, though. After a few years of prison, it would come back more violent than ever.

He finally cracked. After all the threats, the phony allegations, and the slaps. Farge was not only supplying him with drugs but regularly bringing him guns. The arms thing had been going on for six months. His job was to sell them to a few buddies who really had balls. But he never touched them himself. All he did was find customers and make a bit of commission. It was Farge who ran the show. With another guy. A tall, well-built guy, with very short hair. Blue eyes, like steel. Wepler.

"Can I have some decent clothes?"

You could almost have felt sorry for him. His T-shirt was haloed with sweat and his shorts were stained yellow where he'd pissed himself. But I didn't feel any pity for him. He'd long since crossed a boundary. And his personal background was no excuse. No point in calling Jocelyne. She'd just gotten married, to some asshole who worked for the post office. She was just a bitch. The fag was none other than her brother.

There was no welcoming committee at Marie-Lou's. The apartment was just as she'd left it. She packed her bags quickly. Like someone going on vacation, she was in a hurry to get away.

I carried her cases to her car, a white Fiesta parked at the top of Rue Estelle. Marie-Lou was packing a final bag with objects she cared about. This wasn't a vacation, it was a farewell. I went back up the street. A motorbike, a Yamaha 1100, was parked before the bridge that crosses Cours Lieutaud. Marie-Lou lived just after the bridge, in a building that clung to the stairs leading up to Cours Julien. There were two of them on the bike. The passenger got off. A tall, blond guy, very muscly. When he moved his biceps, the sleeves of his T-shirt came close to bursting. I followed him.

Marie-Lou was coming out. Muscles went straight up to her and grabbed her arm. She struggled, until she saw me coming.

"Is there a problem?"

Muscles turned around, ready to punch me, but recoiled when he saw me. I don't think it was because I impressed him all that much, physically. No, it was something else. I realized what it was. He was my friend the boxer.

"I asked you a question."

"And who are you?"

"That's right, we weren't introduced the other night, were we?"

I opened my jacket. He saw the holster and the gun. Before leaving the station, I'd put on the holster, checked my gun and loaded it. Watched anxiously by Pérol.

"We have to talk."

"Later."

"This evening?"

"I promise. But I have an urgent appointment. With one of Farge's girls. She was the tip-off."

He made no comment. I'd proved to him yet again that I was an outstanding cop, but completely crazy. We really did have to talk. This business with Mourrabed had landed us both in the garbage.

"Put your hands against the wall and spread your legs," I said.

I heard the motorbike take off. I approached Muscles and relieved him of the wallet sticking out of the back pocket of his jeans. I couldn't believe they'd beaten me up like that because of Marie-Lou.

"Your pal Farge is inside. What did you come for the other night?"

He shrugged, and all his muscles moved. I recoiled. The guy could lay me flat just by clicking his fingers.

"Why don't you ask him?"

He didn't really believe me. And I sure didn't scare him any. I wouldn't be able to take him in on my own. Even with my gun. He was just waiting for the right opportunity. I placed the barrel against his skull. A few people passed, but no one stopped.

"What should I do?" Marie-Lou asked, behind me.

"Go to the car."

Time passed. It seemed like a century. Finally, what I was hoping for happened. A police siren could be heard on Cours Lieutaud. It came closer. There were still some good citizens around. Three cops arrived. I showed them my badge. I was a long way from home, but to hell with manners.

"He was bothering a young lady. Take him in for resisting arrest. Hand him over to Lieutenant Pérol. He'll know what to do with him. Go on, you. I'll speak to you later."

Marie-Lou was leaning on the hood of the Fiesta, waiting and smoking. A few men turned around to look at her as they passed. But she didn't seem to see anyone. Or even to feel their eyes on her. She had that look I'd first seen on her face this morning, after we made love. A distant look. She was already a long way away.

She cuddled up to me. I buried my face in her hair, breathing in its cinnamon smell one last time. Her breasts felt hot against my chest. She moved her fingers down my back. I slowly freed myself, and placed my finger on her mouth before she could say a word. Goodbye, so long, whatever. I didn't like departures. I didn't like returns either. I just liked things to be done as they were supposed to be done.

Gently, taking my time, I kissed her on the cheeks. Then I walked away down Rue Estelle. I had an appointment with Batisti at five o'clock.

12.

IN WHICH WE SEE A MICROCOSM OF THE WORLD'S CORRUPTION

We jumped onto the ferry just as it was leaving the pier. In the case of Batisti, it wasn't so much that he jumped, more that I'd pushed him. I'd pushed him hard, without letting go of him. He ended up in the middle of the cabin. I thought he was going to lose his balance and fall, but he steadied himself against a bench. He turned, looked at me, and sat down. He lifted his cap and mopped his forehead. "The wops!" I said, as I went to pay.

I'd spotted them the moment Batisti had joined me by the ferry pier on Place aux Huiles. They were following him at a distance of a few yards. Dressed like tourists. White linen pants, flowery shirts, sunglasses, and bags slung across their shoulders. As Djamel had said, they were playing their roles to the hilt. I recognized them immediately. They'd been having lunch behind us the other day at the Bar de la Marine. They'd gone when Batisti had left. It was Batisti they were tailing. The only reason they'd followed me to the Panier was because they'd seen me with him. At least that was what I reckoned, and it made sense.

The wops weren't trailing me. Neither was anyone else. I'd made sure of that before coming to meet Batisti. When I left Marie-Lou, I went down Rue Estelle and turned onto Rue Saint-Ferréol, Marseilles' biggest pedestrian-only street. All the big stores were concentrated here. Nouvelles-Galeries, Marks and Spencer, La Redoute, Virgin. They'd replaced the beautiful movie houses of the Sixties, the Rialto, the Rex, the Pathé

Palace. There wasn't even a bar anymore. At seven o'clock, the street became as sad and empty as the Canebière.

I'd plunged into the stream of pedestrians. The middle classes, managers, civil servants, immigrants, the unemployed, the young, the old: after five o'clock, the whole of Marseilles walked along this street. Everyone rubbed shoulders naturally, unaggressively. This was the true face of Marseilles. It was only at the ends of the street that the divisions reappeared. The Canebière, the implicit frontier between the north and south of the city, at one end. And Place Félix-Baret at the other end, a stone's throw from Police Headquarters, where a van full of riot police was always parked. The gateway to the rich parts of town. Beyond it, the bars, including the Bar Pierre, which for a century have been the most sophisticated meeting places for gilded youth in the downtown area.

With the riot police constantly watching, there was always the feeling of a city at war. Beyond those limits, the enemy was watching, with fear or hate depending on whether your name was Paul or Ahmed. The way you looked was considered reasonable grounds for being arrested.

I'd walked aimlessly, not even window shopping. I was trying to get my thoughts in some kind of order. I was starting to pick apart the thread of events leading from Manu's death to Ugo's. I still couldn't make sense of them, but at least I could put them in some kind of order. For the moment, that was enough for me. The teenage girls on the street seemed much prettier than the ones I'd known. Their faces were a map of their racial history, and the city's. They walked with confidence and pride in their beauty. They were Marseilles girls, and had that languid Marseilles way of walking, and that almost impudent look if your eyes lingered on them. Someone, I couldn't remember who, had called them mutants, which seemed a good word to me. I envied young men today.

On Rue Vacon, instead of continuing on to the Quai de Rive-Neuve, as far as the ferry pier, I turned left and went down into the underground parking garage on Cours d'Estienne d'Orves, where I lit a cigarette and waited. The first person to appear was a woman of about thirty. Salmon-colored linen suit, plump body, heavy make-up. When she saw me, she recoiled, clutched her bag to her chest, and walked off very quickly in search of her car. I finished my cigarette and went back upstairs.

Batisti was still sitting on the bench, mopping his forehead with a big white handkerchief. With his short white shirt over blue cotton pants, his espadrilles, his sailor's cap pulled down tight over his head, he looked like a retired naval officer. A good old Marseilles citizen. Batisti was looking at the pier as it receded into the distance. The two wops seemed uncertain what to do. Even if they found a taxi, which would be a miracle, they wouldn't get to the other side of the harbor in time. They'd lost us. For the moment.

I leaned against a window, ignoring Batisti. I wanted him to soak in his own juice. At least while the crossing lasted. I loved that crossing. Looking at the channel between the two forts, Saint-Nicolas and Saint-Jean, which guard the entrance to Marseilles. Facing the open sea, not the Canebière. By choice. Marseilles, gateway to the East. To foreign lands, adventure, dreams. Marseilles people don't like traveling. Everyone thinks of them as sailors and adventurers, or imagines their fathers or grandfathers went around the world at least once. At most, they'd been as far as Noilon or Cap Croisette. In middle class families, the children weren't allowed near the sea. The port allowed business to flourish, but the sea itself was dirty, the source of vice, and plague. As soon as the weather turned fine, you went to live inland. Aix and the surrounding countryside, with its cottages and country houses. The sea was left to the poor.

When I was a child, the harbor was our playground. We'd learned to swim between the two forts. One day or another, to prove you were a man and impress the girls, you had to swim there and back. The first time, Manu and Ugo had to come and fish me out. I was sinking, and couldn't catch my breath.

"You were afraid."

"No, I wasn't. I was just out of breath."

I'd gotten my breath back. But I had been afraid.

Manu and Ugo were no longer around to come to my rescue. They'd sunk and I hadn't been able to fish them out. Ugo hadn't made any attempt to see me. Lole had gone away. I was alone, and I was about to plunge into the shit. Because I had to make things right with them. With our broken youth. If you have a debt to a friend, you have to pay it. I'd be the only one finishing the crossing. If I got there. I still had a few illusions about the world. A few tenacious old dreams too. I'd know how to live now, I thought.

We were approaching the pier. Batisti stood up and walked anxiously to the other end of the ferry. He threw me a glance. There was no emotion in it. It was coldly indifferent, devoid of fear, hatred, or resignation. On Place de la Mairie, there was no sign of the wops. Batisti followed me without speaking. We crossed the square and climbed Rue de la Guirlande.

"Where are we going?" he said at last.

"Somewhere quiet."

On Rue Caisserie, we turned left. We reached Chez Félix. Even without the wops around, I'd always planned to take him there. I took his arm, turned him around, and showed him the sidewalk. He shivered, despite the heat.

"Take a good look! This is where they gunned down Manu. I bet you've never been here!"

I made him go in. A few old guys were playing *belote* and

drinking Vittel with mint. It was noticeably cooler inside. This was the first time I'd been here since Manu died. But Félix made no comment. From the handshake he gave me, I could tell he was pleased to see me again.

"You know, Céleste still makes *aïoli*."

"I'll be back. Tell her that."

Céleste made better *aïoli* than anyone I knew, except Honorine. The cod was desalted just right, which is rare. Most people leave it to soak for too long, and give it only two soakings. It was best to soak it several times. Eight hours the first time, then three times two hours. It was also a good idea to poach it in simmering water, with fennel and pepper grains. Céleste also used a particular olive oil to give the *aïoli* a 'lift.' It came from the Rossi mill, at Mouriès. She used others in cooking and in salads. Oils from Jacques Barles of Éguilles, Henrii Bellon of Fontvieille, and Margier-Aubert of Auriol. Her salads always tasted different.

I hadn't often seen Manu at Chez Félix. Since the time I'd called him a loser, he'd done his best to avoid me. But he did make one attempt to smooth things over. Two weeks before he was killed, he came in and sat down opposite me. It was a Friday: *aïoli* day. We had a few rounds of *pastis*, then two bottles of Saint-Cannat rosé. We were trying to get back to the way we'd been, to forget our grudges. But there was still resentment.

"The point the three of us have reached, there's no going back."

"We can always admit we made mistakes."

"Don't be stupid, Fabio. It's too late. We waited too long. We're in it up to our necks, and we can't get out."

"Speak for yourself!"

He looked at me, without malice, but with a rather weary irony. I couldn't look him in the eyes. I knew he was right. I was no better than he was.

"OK," I said. "We're in it up to our necks."

We clinked glasses, and finished the second bottle.

"I made a promise to Lole. A long time ago. A promise I've never been able to keep. To shower her with money. And take her away from here. To Seville, or somewhere else down there. Now I'm going to do it. I'm onto something good. For once."

"Money isn't everything. For Lole, it's love—"

"Let it go! She waited for Ugo. I waited for her. Time has shuffled the cards. Which one of us was right?" He shrugged. "I don't know. Lole and I have been together, what, ten years now, but there's no passion there. Ugo was the one she loved. And you."

"Me?"

"If you hadn't been built like a girl, she'd have come to you. One day or another. Whether or not Ugo had been around. You're the strongest of us. Your heart's in the right place."

"Now, maybe."

"No, it always was. Of all of us, you're the one who's suffered the most. Because of that. Your heart. If I get in any trouble, take care of her." He stood up. "I doubt we'll ever see each other again. We've said all there was to say. Let's leave it at that."

He'd walked out very quickly. Leaving me to pick up the tab.

I had a beer, Batisti a glass of *orgeat*.

"I hear you like hookers. That's not very nice. Cops who go with hookers. You were given a warning. Period."

"You're a jerk, Batisti. I cornered the hitter just an hour ago. The guy who sent him, Farge, has been in my office since this morning. And trust me, we're not talking hookers. We're talking drugs. Possession of arms. In an apartment he was renting in the Bassens project."

"Ah!" he said, laconically.

I was sure he already knew. About Farge, and Mourrabed, and my meeting with Toni. He was waiting for me to tell him more. Once again, that was why he'd come. To worm information out of me. I knew it. And I also knew where I wanted to take him. But I didn't want to lay all my cards on the table. Not right away.

"Why are the wops tailing you?"

"I don't know."

"Listen, Batisti, let's not beat about the bush forever. I can't say you're in my good books, but it'll save time if you tell me."

"Why bother to save time? You're going to get yourself killed in the end anyhow."

"I'll think about that later."

Manu had been at the center of all this shit. After he died, I'd talked to a few informers and gone around the different squads, asking questions. No one had heard the slightest rumor that there'd been a contract out on him. I'd found that surprising, and had come to the conclusion that he'd been gunned down by some punk as revenge for a stunt he'd pulled in the past. He'd been unlucky, that was all. I'd satisfied myself with that. Until noon today.

"It was Manu who did the job at Brunel's, the lawyer. He did a clean job. That was his style, I guess. This time it was even better than usual, because there was no chance he'd be disturbed. That was the night you were all having dinner at Les Restanques. But Manu didn't have a chance to get paid for the job. Two days later, he was dead."

I'd pieced the story together when I typed up my report. At least the sequence of events. But not always what they meant. I'd questioned Lole about the famous job Manu had mentioned to me. He didn't usually confide in her. But this time he'd told her everything had gone well. It was a great job, and at last he was going to make a lot of money. They'd bought a round of champagne that night, to celebrate. The job had been child's play. Open the safe of a lawyer on Boulevard Longchamp, and steal all the documents inside. The lawyer's name was Éric Brunel. Zucca's right hand man.

Babette had given me the info when I'd called her after finishing my report. We'd arranged to talk on the phone before my appointment with Batisti. Brunel must have been double-crossing Zucca, and the old man must have suspected. He'd sent Manu to clean up, or something like that. Zucca and the Poli brothers weren't on the same planet. Or even the same family. There was too much money involved. Zucca couldn't allow himself to be double-crossed.

According to a Roman contact of Babette's, the Neapolitans weren't too happy about Zucca's death. They'd get over it, of course. They always did. But it put the brakes on some important deals that were going through. Zucca had apparently been in the middle of negotiations with two big French companies. The laundering of drug money was an essential factor in Marseilles' economic recovery. Businessmen and politicians both agreed about that.

I told Batisti what I knew. I was hoping for some reaction. A silence, a smile, a word. Anything to help me understand. I still couldn't figure out Batisti's part in all this. I didn't know where he stood. Babette thought he was more closely linked to Zucca than to the Poli brothers. But there was Simone. The only thing I was sure of was that he'd pointed Ugo in Zucca's direction. I couldn't let go of that. It was the one thing connecting Ugo's death to Manu's. And somewhere in that sordid mess, Leila had found herself trapped. I still couldn't think of her without seeing her body covered with ants. Even her smile had been eaten by ants.

"You're well informed," Batisti said, without blinking an eyelid.

"I don't have anything else to do! I'm just an unimportant neighborhood cop, as you know. Your buddies, or anyone else for that matter, can wipe me off the map without making any waves. And all I want to do is go fishing. I like an easy life, with no one bothering me. I really can't wait to get back to my fishing!"

"Go fishing. No one will come looking for you. Even if you do fuck hookers. That's what I told you the other day."

"But it's too late! I keep getting these nightmares, you know what I mean? I keep thinking about my old friends and how they got themselves whacked. I know they weren't saints..." I paused for breath, and looked Batisti straight in the eye. "But the girl they raped in the back room of Les Restanques didn't even have a part in this movie. I know she was only an Arab. And to you and your kind, Arabs don't count, do they? They're like niggers, just animals, no souls. Isn't that right, Batisti?"

I'd raised my voice. At the table behind us, the cards remained suspended in mid-air for a fraction of a second. Félix looked up from the comic book he was reading. An old, yellowing issue of *Les Pieds Nickelés*. He collected them. I ordered another beer.

"*Belote*," one of the old guys said.

And life resumed its course.

I'd hit home, but Batisti wasn't going to let it show. He was an experienced operator. He tried to stand, but I put my hand firmly on his arm. One phone call from him, and Fabio Montale would end the evening in a gutter. Like Manu. Like Ugo. But I had too much anger in me to let myself be suckered into getting killed. I'd put almost all my cards on the table, but I still had a rummy in my hands.

"Not so fast. I haven't finished."

He shrugged. Félix put the beer down in front of me. His eyes went from Batisti to me. Félix wasn't a violent guy. But if

I'd said to him, "Manu was killed because of this jerk," old or not, he'd have smashed his face. Unfortunately, with Batisti, things couldn't be settled with fists.

"I'm listening," he said, in a brusque tone. I was starting to annoy him, which was fine by me. I wanted him to fly off the handle.

"I don't think you have anything to fear from the two wops. My guess is, they're protecting you. The Neapolitans are looking for a successor to Zucca. I think they contacted you. You're still in the Mafia phone book. Under 'advisors.' Maybe you're their choice for the top job." I was watching his reactions. "Or Brunel. Or Émile Poli. Or your daughter."

He had a kind of twitch, at the corner of his mouth. Twice. I must be getting closer to the truth. "You've gone completely crazy. Where do you get this stuff from?"

"No, I'm not crazy, and you know it. Stupid yes. I don't understand any of it. Why you had Zucca whacked by Ugo. How it was all set up. How Ugo came to show up out of the blue. Or why your pal Morvan was waiting for him once he'd done the job. Or what rotten game you're playing. It's all a mystery to me. Especially why Manu died and who killed him. I can't do anything to you. Or the others. But there's still Simone, and I'm going to bust her."

I knew I'd hit the bull's eye. His eyes turned an electric gray. He squeezed his hands together so hard, I thought his knuckles were going to snap. "Don't touch her! She's all I've got!"

"And she's all I've got too. Loubet is handling the girl's murder. I have everything I need, Batisti. Toni, the gun, the scene. I just pass it all on to Loubet, and in less than an hour he brings in Simone. The rape happened at her place. She owns Les Estanques, doesn't she?"

That was the latest piece of information Babette had given me. Of course, I had no proof for any of the things I was saying. But that didn't matter. Batisti didn't know that. I was taking him somewhere he didn't expect to be. Exposed ground.

"I thought she was stupid to marry Émile. But children never listen. I've never been able to stand the Poli brothers."

It didn't feel so cool in the bar now. I'd have liked to take off, to be on my boat, on the open sea. Sea and silence. I'd had more than I could take of human beings. All these stories were like a microcosm of the world's corruption. On a grand scale, it gave rise to wars, massacres, genocide, fanaticism, dictatorship. As if the first man had been so fucked coming into the world, he'd immediately started hating. If God exists, we're all sons of bitches.

"They have a hold over you through her, am I right?"

"For years, Zucca was an accountant. Numbers were his thing, not guns. Gang wars, feuds: he stayed away from all that. That helped him score points. When the Mafia wanted to set up a branch in Marseilles, they chose him to be their liaison. He was good at handling business. Chairman of the board. That's what he was these last few years. A businessman. If only you knew..."

"I don't want to know. It doesn't interest me. I'm sure it'd only make me vomit."

"You know, I preferred working with him than the Poli brothers. They were like shopkeepers. They didn't have his caliber. I think Zucca would have eliminated them one day or another. They were getting too big for their boots. Especially after they came under the influence of Morvan and Wepler.

"They think they're going to clean up Marseilles. They're dreaming of setting the town alight. Starting in North Marseilles. Kids going on the rampage, looting. Wepler's handling all that. Using the dealers and their networks to build up the pressure among the kids. Looks like they're getting there."

Violence on one side, fear and racism on the other. If it worked, their fascist friends would end up in City Hall. And then they'd be left in peace. The same way Carbone and Spirito, the two big bosses of the pre-war Marseilles underworld, had been protected by Sabiani, the all-powerful deputy mayor. They'd be able to carry on with their business, and they'd be in a position of strength to confront the Italians. They could already see themselves getting their hands on Zucca's fortune.

I'd heard enough to disgust me for a hundred years. Fortunately, I'd be dead before then! And what was I going to be able to do with all this? Nothing. I couldn't see myself taking Batisti with me and forcing him to tell the whole story to Loubet. I had no evidence against any of them. The only one I could charge was Mourrabed. The bottom of the list. An Arab. The fall guy. As usual. Babette wouldn't even be able to get an article out of it. She had a strict code of ethics. Facts, and nothing but. That was how she'd made a name for herself in the press.

Nor could I see myself in the role of judge, jury and executioner. I couldn't see myself in any role anymore. Not even as a cop. I couldn't see anything. I was dizzy with it all. The hatred, the violence. Gangsters, cops, politicians. With poverty as the breeding ground. Unemployment, racism. We were all like insects caught in a spider's web. We struggled, but the spider would eat us in the end.

But I still had to know.

"Where did Manu fit into all this?"

"He never touched Brunel's safe. He negotiated with him. Against Zucca. He wanted to make more money for himself. Much more. I think he was going off the rails. Zucca didn't forgive him. When Ugo called me from Paris, I realized that I had my revenge."

He'd talked fast, as if letting it all out. Too fast.

"What revenge?"

"Huh?"

"You mentioned revenge."

He looked up at me. For the first time, he was being sincere. His eyes clouded over. He stared into the distance, to a place where I didn't exist. "I really liked Manu, you know," he stammered.

"But not Zucca, right?"

He didn't answer. I wouldn't get anymore out of him. I'd touched a sore spot. I stood up.

"You're still jerking me around, Batisti." He kept his head lowered. I leaned over him. "I'll keep going. Keep nosing around. Until I know everything. None of you are getting away with this. That includes Simone."

I was threatening him for a change, and it felt good. They hadn't left me a choice of weapons. He looked at me at last, and smiled maliciously. "You're crazy."

"If you want to have me killed, you'd better hurry up about it. To me, you're a dead man, Batisti. And I like that thought. Because you're nothing but a piece of shit."

I left Batisti with his glass of *orgeat*.

Outside, the sun hit me full in the face. I had the feeling I was coming back to life. Real life. Where happiness is an accumulation of insignificant everyday things. A ray of sunlight, a smile, washing drying at a window, a boy dribbling with a tin can, a song by Vincent Scotto, a slight breeze lifting a woman's dress...

13.

IN WHICH THERE ARE SOME THINGS YOU CAN'T LET PASS

I stood outside Chez Félix for a few moments, motionless, my eyes blinded by the sun. I could have been killed there and then, and I'd have forgiven everyone everything. But there was no one waiting for me on the street corner. The appointment was somewhere else. I hadn't fixed it yet, but I'd be there.

I walked back up Rue Caisserie and cut across Place de Lenche. I walked past a bar called the Montmartre, and couldn't help smiling. I smiled every time I passed it. The Montmartre was so out of place here. I turned onto Rue Sainte-Françoise and went into the Treize-Coins. I gestured to Ange to bring me a bottle of cognac. I drank the first glass straight down. He stood there in front of me, with the bottle in his hand. I gestured to him to pour me a second glass, and downed it as quickly as the first.

"Are you all right?" he asked, a bit worried.

"Great! Never felt better!" I said, holding out my glass to be filled again. I took it and went and sat down on the terrace. There was a bunch of Arabs at the next table.

"But I'm French, you jerk. We were born here. I've never been to Algeria."

"Oh, you're French, are you? We're the least French of all the French. That's what we are."

"If the French don't want you anymore, what are you going to do? Wait till they shoot you? Me, I'm taking off."

"Oh, yeah? And where are you going? You're out of your mind!"

"Well, I don't give a shit. I'm from Marseilles. I'm staying here. Period. If they want me, they know where to look for me."

They were inhabitants of Marseilles more than they were Arabs. They felt the same way about it as our parents had. The way Ugo, Manu and I had fifteen years ago. One day, Ugo had said, "In my house and Fabio's house, they speak Neapolitan. At your house, they speak Spanish. At school, we learn French. But what are we, when you get down to it?"

"Arabs," Manu had replied.

We'd burst out laughing. And now they were here, too. Reliving our poverty. In the same houses as our parents. Taking it at face value as a kind of paradise and praying for it to last. "Don't forget," my father had said to me. "When I first came here, there were mornings when my brothers and I didn't know if we'd have anything to eat at noon, and yet somehow we always ate." That was the history of Marseilles, and always had been. A utopia. The only utopia in the world. A place where anyone, of any color, could get off a boat or a train with his suitcase in his hand and not a cent in his pocket, and melt into the crowd. A city where, as soon as he'd set foot on its soil, this man could say, "This is it. I'm home."

Marseilles belongs to the people who live in it.

Ange came over to my table with a *pastis* in his hand and sat down.

"Don't worry," I told him. "It'll all work out. There's always a solution."

"Pérol has been looking for you for two hours."

"Where the fuck are you?" Pérol screamed.

"At Ange's. Get over here. With the car."

I hung up, and quickly drank my third cognac. I felt a whole lot better.

I waited for Pérol on Rue de l'Evêché, at the bottom of the Passage Sainte-Françoise steps. It was the only way he could come. By the time he arrived, I'd had a smoke.

"Where are we going?"

"To listen to Ferré, if that's OK with you."

In his bar, the Maraîchers à la Plaîne, Hassan, an Arab, never played raï, rock, or reggae. Just French *chanson*, almost always Brel, Brassens and Ferré. He liked to catch his customers off guard.

"Hello, strangers," he said, when he saw us come in.

Here everyone was a stranger and a friend, whatever the color of their skin, hair or eyes. Hassan's clientele was mostly young: high school kids and college students. The kind who cut classes, preferably the most important ones. They'd discuss the future of the world over a glass of draft beer, then, after past seven, make up their minds to change it. Nothing ever got changed, but it was a nice way of killing time. Ferré was singing:

We're no saints.
Our miracle's Cinzano.
No complaints,
We'll always pray to Pernod.

All I could do was drink. It was too late in the day for *pastis*. Glancing at the bottles, I opted for a Glenmorrangie. Pérol chose draft beer.

"Haven't you ever been here before?"

He shook his head. He was looking at me as if I was sick. A hopeless case.

"You ought to get out more. You know, Pérol, we should go out some evening, just you and me. Otherwise, you lose touch with reality. You know what I mean? You lose your sense of reality, and hey presto, you don't know which shelf you left your soul on. The shelf where you put your friends. The shelf where you put your women. Stage right, stage left. Or in the shoe box. You turn around and you find you're stuck in the bottom drawer, with the accessories."

"Stop it!" he said, though without raising his voice.

"You know," I continued, ignoring his anger, "I think a few bream would be nice. Grilled with thyme and bay. And just a drizzle of olive oil on top. You think your wife would like that?"

I wanted to talk about cooking. To list all the dishes I could make. Cannelloni, cooked slowly with ham and spinach. Tuna salad with new potatoes. Marinaded sardines. I felt hungry.

"Are you hungry?"

Pérol didn't reply.

"Pérol, you know something, I've forgotten your first name."

"Gérard," he said, smiling at last.

"OK, Gérard. Let's have another drink, then we'll go grab a bite to eat. What do you say?"

Instead of answering my question, he told me about the mess things were in over at the station house. Auch had come to claim Mourrabed, because of the arms. Brenier wanted him because of the drugs. Loubet refused to let him go, because, goddammit, he was investigating an actual crime. Immediately, Auch had turned on Farge, who'd been playing the fool, over-confident about being protected, and hit him. If he didn't explain how the arms had come to be in his cellar, Auch screamed, he'd blow his brains out.

Then Muscles, who I'd sent to Pérol, ran into Farge in the corridor, and started screaming that he was the one who'd sent him to break the hooker's teeth. As soon as the word 'hooker' reached the floor below, Gravis showed up. Pimps were his department. And he knew Farge like the back of his hand.

"That was when I decided to say how surprised I was that Farge didn't have a record."

"Good thinking."

"Gravis screamed that the station was full of idiots. Auch screamed that they'd make a new record for Farge right away. And he passed Farge on to Morvan for a guided tour of the basement."

"And what happened?" I asked, even though I could guess the answer.

"Couldn't handle it. Had a heart attack, forty-five minutes later."

How much longer did I have to live? I wondered what dish I'd like to eat before I died. Maybe fish soup. With a good spicy sauce, made with sea-urchin flesh and a little saffron. But I wasn't hungry anymore. And I'd sobered up.

"How about Mourrabed?"

"We read over his confession, and he signed it. Then I passed him to Loubet. OK, now you tell me your story. I need to know what you're mixed up in. I don't want to die an idiot."

"It's a long story. Let me just go take a leak."

In passing, I ordered another Glenmorrangie. It was the kind of drink you didn't even notice you were drinking. In the toilet, some joker had written: *Smile, you're on Candid Camera.* I gave my smile No 5. Don't worry, Fabio. You're the fairest of them all. The strongest too. Then I put my head under the faucet.

By the time we got back to the station house, Pérol knew the whole story. In the smallest detail. He'd listened without interrupting. It did me good to tell him the story. It didn't really help me to see things more clearly, but I had the feeling I knew where I was going.

"Do you really think Manu planned to double-cross Zucca?"

It wasn't impossible, given what he'd told me. It wasn't so much the job itself that had excited him, it was all the money he was going to make from it. But at the same time, the more

I thought about it, the less likely it sounded. Pérol had put his finger on it. I couldn't see Manu hustling Zucca. He sometimes did crazy things, but he was like an animal, he could smell real danger. And besides, it was Batisti who'd found him the job, and Batisti was the father he'd chosen for himself. The only guy he trusted, more or less. Batisti wouldn't have done that to him.

"No, Gérard, I don't think so."

But I still didn't see who could have taken him out.

There was one other question I couldn't answer: how had Leila gotten to know Toni?

I'd been planning to ask him. It was academic now, but I felt strongly about it. It gnawed away at me, like jealousy. Leila in love. I'd come around to the idea, but it wasn't easy to admit that a woman you desire is in bed with another guy. I may have made my decision, but it just wasn't as simple as that. With Leila, I might have been able to start from scratch, to reinvent, to rebuild my life. Free of the past, free of memories. It was an illusion. Leila was the present and the future. I belonged to my past. If I was to have a happy tomorrow, there was unfinished business I had to get back to. Lole. And the past we'd shared.

Leila and Toni was something I couldn't grasp. It was definitely Toni who'd picked up Leila. The super from the college residence had called during the afternoon, Pérol told me. His wife had remembered seeing Leila in the parking lot talking to the driver of a Golf convertible, then getting in. She'd even thought, "Hey, all right for some!"

Behind the railroad tracks of the Saint Charles station, stuck between the exit from the northern freeway, Boulevard de Plombières and Boulevard National, the Belle de Mai neighborhood was the same as ever. The way of life there hadn't changed. A long way from downtown, even though it was only a few minutes away. There was still a village spirit there, just as there was in Vauban, the Blancarde, the Rouet, or the Capelette, where I'd grown up.

As children, we often went to the Belle de Mai. To fight, usually over girls. There was always a scrap going down. And a stadium or a waste land where we could lay into each other. Vauban against the Blancarde. The Capelette against Belle de Mai. The Panier against the Rouet. After a dance, a fair, coming out of the movies. It wasn't like *West Side Story*, Latinos versus WASPs. Every gang had its share of Italians, Spaniards, Armenians, Portuguese, Arabs, Africans and Vietnamese. We fought over a girl's smile, not because of the color of our skins. It created friendships, not hatreds.

One day, behind the Vallier stadium, I got really badly roughed up by a wop for eyeing his sister as we were coming out of the Alhambra, a dance hall in the Blancarde. Ugo had picked up a couple of girls there, and it made a change from the Salons Michel. We later discovered that our fathers were from neighboring villages. Mine from Castel San Giorgio, his from Piovene. We went off to grab a beer. A week later, he introduced me to his sister, Ophélia. We were *paese*, which made it different. "If you manage to keep her, I take off my hat to you! She's just a tease." Ophélia was worse than that. She was a bitch. She was the girl Mavros had married. And look what a hard time she'd given him.

I'd lost all notion of time. I parked my car almost outside the apartment building where Toni lived. His Golf was parked about fifty yards up the street. I had a few smokes and listened to Buddy Guy. *Damn right, he's got the blues.* A fantastic recording. Backed by Marc Knopfler, Eric Clapton and Jeff Beck. I was still hesitating to pay Toni a visit. He lived on the second floor, and there was a light in his apartment. I wondered if he was alone or not.

Because I was alone. Pérol had gone off to Bassens. Things were about to turn ugly. There was going to be trouble between the neighborhood kids and Mourrabed's buddies. A bunch of really scary characters had appeared on the scene, provoking the kids in the project. They'd let the cops take Mourrabed in. They were well organized, that was obvious. The tall black kid had already been beaten up. Five of them had cornered him in the parking lot. The Bassens kids didn't like anyone muscling in on their territory. Especially not dealers. Knives were being sharpened.

Cerutti couldn't handle it on his own. Even with the help of Reiver, who'd hotfooted it there, ready to do the night shift after his day shift. Pérol had rounded up the teams. There was no time to lose. A few dealers had to be collared, on the pretext that Mourrabed had turned them in. The rumor needed to be spread that he was a squealer. That ought to calm things down a bit. We wanted to avoid the Bassens kids getting into fights with these scumbags.

"Go grab a bite to eat, take a breather, and don't do anything stupid," Pérol had said. "Leave it to me." I hadn't told him my plans for this evening. Not that I had any. I just felt that I needed to make a move. I'd made threats. I didn't want to be like a hunted animal anymore. I had to force them to show their hand. To do something stupid. I'd told Pérol we'd meet up later and put our heads together. He'd suggested I sleep at his house, it was too risky going back to Les Goudes. I could believe that.

"You know, Fabio," he'd said after listening to me, "of course these things don't mean the same to me as they do to you. I never knew your friends, and you never introduced me to Leila. But I understand where you're coming from. I know it isn't just a question of revenge. It's the feeling there are some things you can't let pass. If you did, you wouldn't be able to look at yourself in the mirror afterwards."

216 - JEAN-CLAUDE IZZO

Pérol didn't talk much, but now he'd got started, he could be at it for hours.

"Don't get yourself worked up, Gerard!"

"It's not that. I'll tell you something. You're on to something big. You can't hit out on your own and hope to get off scot-free. I'm with you. I'm not going to drop you."

"I know you're a friend. Whatever happens. But I'm not asking you for anything, Gérard. You know what they say? Beyond this point, your ticket is no longer valid. That's where I am now. And I don't want to drag you into it. It's too dangerous. I think we'd be forced to do things that weren't very clean. In fact, I'm sure of it. You have a wife and daughter. Think of them, and forget about me."

I opened the door. He grabbed my arm. "No can do, Fabio. If they find you dead tomorrow, I don't know what I'll do. Something even worse, maybe."

"I'll tell you what you should do. Make another kid. With the woman you love. Then I'll be sure there's a future for the world."

"You're just a bullshit artist!"

He'd made me promise to wait for him. Or to join him, if I decided to make a move. I'd promised. That had reassured him, and he'd left for Bassens. He didn't know I wouldn't keep my word. No way! I stubbed out my last smoke and got out of the car.

"Who is it?"

A woman's voice. Young and anxious. I heard laughter. Then silence.

"Montale. Fabio Montale. I'd like to see Toni."

The door half opened. I must have switched channels again! Karine was as surprised as I was. We stood there looking at each other. Neither of us could say a word. I went in. There was a strong smell of dope.

"Who is it?" I heard someone say at the end of the corridor. Kader's voice.

"Come in!" Karine said. "How did you know I live here?"

"I came to see Pirelli. Toni."

"He's my brother. He hasn't been here in ages."

That was the answer! At last I had it. But it didn't explain anything. I still couldn't understand Leila and Toni. They were all here. Kader, Yasmine, Driss. Around the table. Like conspirators.

"Allah is great," I said, pointing to the bottle of scotch on the table.

"And Chivas is his prophet," Kader replied, grabbing the bottle. "Have a drink with us?"

They must have drunk quite a lot. Smoked quite a lot too. But I didn't get the feeling they were having a ball. Quite the opposite.

"I didn't know you knew Toni," Karine said.

"We don't really know each other. You see, I didn't even know he'd moved."

"So it must be ages since you last saw him..."

"I was passing and saw a light, so I came up. Old friends, you know."

They were staring at me. Obviously, Toni and me as old friends wasn't something they could get their heads around. But it was too late for me to change tack. Their brains were working overtime.

"What did you want with him?" Driss asked.

"A favor. I needed to ask him a favor. Anyhow," I said, finishing my drink, "I won't bother you anymore."

"It's no bother," Kader said.

"I've had a long day."

"Collared a dealer, I hear?" Jasmine said.

"News travels fast."

"Arab telephone!" Kader said, with a laugh that sounded false.

They were waiting for me to explain what I was doing there, looking for Toni. Jasmine pushed a book toward me, still in its gift wrapping. I read the title without even picking it up. *Death Is a Lonely Business* by Ray Bradbury.

"You can have it. It was Leila's. Do you know it?"

"She often mentioned it. I've never read it."

"Here," Kader said, handing me a glass of whisky. "Sit down. There's no rush."

"We bought it together," Jasmine said. "The day before..."

"Oh," I said. The scotch was burning my insides. I still hadn't eaten anything all day. I was starting to feel exhausted. The night wasn't over yet.

"Have you got any coffee?" I asked Karine.

"I just made some. It's still hot."

"It was for you," Jasmine went on. "That's why it's gift wrapped. She wanted to give it to you."

Karine came back with a cup of coffee. Kader and Driss didn't say a word. They were waiting to hear the rest of the story, even though they already seemed to know the ending.

"I couldn't figure at first what it was doing in my brother's car," Karine said.

That was it. It left me speechless. These kids had knocked me for six. They weren't smiling now. They looked solemn.

"On Saturday night, he came to take me out for a meal. He does that regularly. Talks to me about my studies. Gives me a little money. A big brother, right? The book was in the glove compartment. I can't remember what I was looking for. 'What's this?' I said. It took him completely by surprise. 'What? That? Oh, yeah, that... It's... It's a gift. It was for you. I was planning... to give it to you later. But you can open it now.'

"Toni often gave me gifts. But a book, well, that was a first. I didn't know how he'd known what to choose... I was touched. I told him I loved him. We went to eat and I put the book in my bag, still in its wrapping.

"I put it there on the shelf when I got back. Then it all happened. Leila, the funeral. I stayed with them. We slept at Mouloud's. I'd forgotten all about the book. At noon today, Jasmine came by, and she saw it. We couldn't figure it out. We called the boys. We had to clear it up. Do you understand?" She'd sat down. She was shaking. "Now, we don't know what to do."

And she burst into tears.

Driss stood up and took her in his arms. He stroked her hair tenderly. Her tears were almost like a nervous breakdown. Jasmine went to her, kneeled, and slipped her hands into Karine's. Kader was motionless, his elbows on the table, dragging manically on his joint. His eyes were completely absent.

I felt dizzy. My heart started pounding. No, it wasn't possible! Something Karine had said had startled me. She'd referred to Toni in the past tense.

"Where is Toni?"

Kader stood up like an automaton. Karine, Jasmine and Driss watched him as he went and opened the French door to the balcony. I stood up and went closer. Toni was there. Lying on the tiled floor.

Dead.

"We were going to call you, I think."

14.

In which it's better to be alive in hell than dead in paradise

The kids were at the end of their tether. Now that Toni's body was there in front of them again, they were cracking. Karine was still crying. Now Jasmine started, followed by Driss. Kader seemed to have gone off the rails completely. The dope and the whisky hadn't helped. He gave little staccato laughs every time he looked at Toni's body. As for me, I was starting to coast. And this wasn't the time for that.

I closed the balcony door, poured myself a glass of scotch, and lit a cigarette. "OK," I said. "Let's start again from the beginning."

But I might as well have been talking to deaf-mutes. Kader started laughing even more frantically.

"Driss, take Karine to the bedroom. She needs to lie down and get some rest. Jasmine, see if you can find some tranquilizers, Lexomil, anything, and give one to each person. And take one yourself. Then make me some more coffee."

They looked at me as if they were Martians newly landed.

"Go on!" I said, gently but firmly.

They stood up. Driss and Karine disappeared into the bedroom.

"What are we going to do?" Jasmine asked. She was starting to recover. Of the four, she was the strongest. You could see that in every precise, self-assured gesture. She may have smoked as much as the others, but it was obvious she'd drunk less.

"Get this one back on his feet," I replied, indicating Kader.

I lifted him from his chair.

"He won't fuck with us anymore, right?" he said, laughing. "We fucked his ass, the jerk."

"Where's the bathroom?"

She pointed at the door. I pushed Kader inside. There was a very small tub. The room smelled of vomit. Driss had already been in here. I grabbed Kader by the neck and forced him to lower his head. I opened the cold water faucet. He struggled.

"Don't mess me around, or I'll throw you in!"

I rinsed his head thoroughly, and wiped him with a towel. By the time we came back to the living room, the coffee was ready. We sat around the table. In the bedroom, Karine was still crying, and Driss was talking to her. I couldn't hear what he was saying, but it was like soft music.

"Shit!" I said to Kader and Jasmine. "You could have called me!"

"We didn't mean to kill him," Kader replied.

"What were you expecting? That he'd apologize? He was the kind of guy who'd have slit his own mother's throat."

"We could see that," Jasmine said. "He threatened us. With a gun."

"Who hit him?"

"Karine, first. With the ashtray."

A big glass ashtray, which I'd been filling with cigarette butts since I arrived. The impact had knocked Toni to the floor. He'd let go of his gun. Jasmine had kicked it under the wardrobe. It was still there. Toni had rolled over onto his stomach and tried to get up. Driss had jumped on him and taken him by the throat, crying, "Bastard! Bastard!"

"Kill him!" the others yelled. Driss squeezed with all his might, but Toni kept struggling. Karine was screaming, "He's my brother!" She wept and implored and pulled Driss by the arm, to get him to let go. But Driss wasn't there anymore. He was letting out all his rage. Leila wasn't only his sister. She was his mother. She'd raised him, pampered him, loved him. They couldn't do that to him. Take away both of the mothers he'd known in his life.

His hours of training with Mavros were paying off.

With a loser like Sanchez—or with a gun in his hand—Toni was a winner. But in this case, he didn't stand a chance. He knew it as soon as he felt Driss's hands on his throat, squeezing. Toni's eyes begged for mercy. His pals hadn't taught him about this. Death gradually seeping into his body. The absence of oxygen. The panic. The fear. I'd had a taste of all that the other night. Driss was easily as strong as Muscles. No, I wouldn't have liked to die like that.

Karine still clung weakly to Driss. She'd stopped shouting. She was sobbing now, and saying, "No, no, no." But it was too late. Too late for Leila, who she loved. Too late for Toni, who she loved. Too late for Driss, who she loved even more than Leila or Toni. Driss had stopped hearing anything. Not even Jasmine crying, "Stop!" He was still squeezing, with his eyes closed.

Was Leila smiling at Driss? Was she laughing, like the day she and I decided to go swimming at Sugitton? We'd left the car on a flat area of the Ginestre pass, and had taken a path through the Puget massif to reach the Gardiole pass. Leila wanted to see the sea from the top of the Devenson cliffs. She'd never been there before. It was one of the most beautiful places in the world.

Leila was walking ahead of me. She was wearing fringed denim shorts and a white sleeveless top. She'd pulled her hair back under a white cotton cap. There were beads of sweat running down her neck. At moments, they glistened like diamonds. I'd been watching as the sweat went inside her top and down the hollow of her back as far as her waist. Her buttocks swayed.

She was pressing forward with all the ardor of youth. I saw the way the muscles of her lower legs tensed as she moved. She was as graceful climbing in the hills as she was walking on the street in high heels. I was overcome with desire for her. It was early, but the heat had already released the strong resinous odor of the pines. I imagined that resin smell between Leila's thighs. The taste it might have on my tongue. At that moment, I knew I was going to put my hands on her buttocks. She'd have stopped walking. I'd have held her tight against me. Her breasts in my hands. Then I'd have stroked her stomach and unbuttoned her shorts.

I'd stopped walking. Leila turned and smiled.

"I want to walk in front," I said.

As I passed her, she patted me on the ass, and laughed.

"What are you laughing at?"

"You."

Happiness. One day. Ten thousand years ago.

Later, on the beach, she'd asked me about my life, the women in my life. I've never been able to talk about the women I've loved. I wanted those loves to stay intact inside me. Talking about them brought back the screaming matches, the tears, the slammed doors. And the nights that followed, the bedsheets as rumpled as my heart. I didn't want to do that. I wanted to preserve the best part of those loves. The beauty of the first glance. The passion of the first night. The tenderness of the first awakening. I'd answered vaguely, as vaguely as I could.

Leila had looked at me strangely. Then she'd talked about her lovers. She could count them on the fingers of one hand. The description she gave me of the man of her dreams and what she expected of him turned into a fully-fledged portrait. It scared me. It wasn't a portrait I liked. I wasn't that man. Neither was anyone. I told her she was just a shallow teenager.

That amused her at first, then made her angry. For the first time, we quarreled. A quarrel exacerbated by the desire we both felt.

We dropped the subject, and walked back in silence. We'd both put away, somewhere inside us, our desire for each other. We'd have to answer its call one day, but this wasn't the day. The pleasure of being together, and getting to know each other, was more important. We knew that. The rest could wait. Just before we reached the car, she slipped her hand in mine. Leila was a fantastic girl. Before we said goodbye that Sunday, she kissed me on the cheek. "You're a great guy, Fabio."

Leila was smiling at me.

I saw her at last. On the other side of death. The men who'd raped and killed her were dead. The ants could do what they wanted with her corpse. Leila was untouchable. She was in my heart now, and I'd carry her with me always, on this earth that every day gives men a chance.

Yes, she must have been smiling at Driss at that moment. I knew I'd have killed Toni. To wipe out the horror. With my bare hands, like Driss, and just as blindly. Until the shit he'd been responsible for had risen to his throat and choked him.

Toni pissed on him. Driss opened his eyes, but didn't take his hands from Toni's neck. Toni had a glimpse of hell. The black hole. He struggled one last time. His body jerked. His last breath. Then he stopped moving.

Karine stopped crying. Driss straightened up. His arms dropped to his sides, over Toni's body. They didn't dare move or speak. Their hatred had gone. They were drained. They didn't even realize what Driss had just done. What they'd let him do. They couldn't accept that they'd just killed a man.

"Is he dead?" Driss asked at last.

Nobody replied. Driss retched, and ran to the bathroom. That was an hour ago, and since then, they'd been getting drunk and smoking joints. From time to time, they looked at the body. Kader stood up, opened the French door to the balcony, rolled Toni's body outside with his foot, just to get him out of sight, and closed the door.

Every time they were on the point of calling me, one of them would suggest something else. But each suggestion meant touching the body, and they didn't dare do that. They didn't even dare go out on the balcony. Three quarters of a bottle of scotch and quite a few joints later, they considered setting fire to the place and getting the hell out. That gave them a fit of the giggles, which felt good. It was then that I knocked at the door.

The telephone rang. Just like in a bad TV episode. Nobody moved. They looked at me, waiting for me to make a decision. In the bedroom, Driss had stopped talking.

"Shouldn't we answer?" Kader asked.

Quickly, nervously, I picked up the phone.

"Toni?" A woman's voice, sensual, husky, warm, arousing.

"Who's that?"

Silence. I could hear the sound of plates and forks. Schmaltzy music in the background. A restaurant. Les Restanques? Maybe it was Simone.

"Hello." A man's voice, with a slight Corsican accent. Emile? Joseph? "Is Toni there? Or his sister?"

"Can I take a message?"

They hung up.

"Did Karine call Toni this evening?"

"Yes," Jasmine replied. "To get him here. She said it was urgent. There's a number she uses to contact him. She leaves a message, and he calls back."

I went into the bedroom. They were lying side by side. Karine had stopped crying, and Driss had fallen asleep holding her hand. They looked adorable. I wished they could go through life with the same tender abandon.

Karine's eyes were wide open and wild. She was still in hell. There was a song by Barbara—I couldn't remember which one—in which she sang: *It's better to live in hell than to be dead in paradise.* Or something like that. Which did Karine want at that moment?

"What's the number you used to call Toni earlier?" I asked in a low voice.

"Who just called?"

"Friends of your brother, I think."

A look of fear came into her eyes. "Are they coming here?"

I shook my head. "Don't worry," I said. "Do you know them?"

"Two of them. One really evil-looking, the other tall and well built. Military kind of guy. In fact, they're both really evil-looking. The military guy has these weird eyes."

Morvan and Wepler.

"Have you seen them often?"

"Just once. But I can't forget them. I was having a drink with Toni on the terrace of the Bar de l'Hotel de Ville. They came and sat down at our table, didn't ask if we minded. The military guy said, 'She's cute, your sister.' I didn't like the way he said it. Or the way he looked at me."

"How about Toni?"

"He laughed, but I think he felt uncomfortable. 'We have to talk business,' he said to me. That meant I had to split. He didn't even dare kiss me. 'I'll call you,' he said. I could feel the other one looking at me as I walked away. I felt ashamed."

"When was that?"

"Last week. Wednesday, at noon. The day Leila gained her master's. What's going to happen now?"

Driss had let go of Karine's hand and turned over. He was

snoring slightly. From time to time, a small tremor shook his body. I felt bad for him. For all of them. They'd have to live with this nightmare. Could they do it? Karine and Driss? Kader and Jasmine? I had to help them, to free them from the terrible images that would haunt their nights. I had to do it fast. For Driss, first of all.

"What's going to happen now?" Karine repeated.

"We have to get out of here. Where do your parents live?"

"In Gardanne."

It wasn't far from Aix. The last surviving mining town in the region. Doomed, like all the men working there.

"Is that where your father works?"

"They fired him two years ago. He's active in the CGT Defense Committee."

"Do you get on OK with them?"

She shrugged. "They never noticed me growing up. Or Toni. Their idea of educating us was to build a better world. My father..." She paused for thought. "When you've suffered a lot, had to count every sou, that's all you see of life. All you think about is changing it. It was an obsession. Toni might have understood, I think. But instead of just saying, 'Sorry, I can't buy you a moped,' my father would make a speech. Tell him he hadn't had a moped when he was that age. Tell him there were more important things in life than mopeds. A whole big scene. It was always the same. Whether it was about clothes, pocket money, cars. My father would give a speech. The workers, the capitalists, the Party.

"The third time the cops came to the house, my father threw Toni out. After that, I don't know what became of him. No, that's not true, I do know. And I didn't like what became of him. The people he saw. The things he said about Arabs. I don't know if he really thought that way. Or if it was..."

"And Leila?"

"I wanted him to meet my friends, to get to know other people. Jasmine, Leila. They'd met once or twice. Kader and Kriss too. And a few others. I invited him to my birthday party last month. He liked Leila. You know how it is. You dance, you drink, you talk, you flirt. He and Leila talked a lot that night. I'm sure he wanted to sleep with her. But Leila didn't want it. She crashed here, with Driss.

"He saw her again after that. Four or five times, I think. In Aix. A drink on a terrace, a meal, a movie. It didn't go any farther than that. Leila was doing it for me, I think, more than for him. She didn't really like Toni. I'd told her a lot about him. Told her he wasn't what he seemed. I pushed them together. I told myself she could change him. I couldn't. I wanted a brother I wouldn't be ashamed of. A brother I could have loved. Like Kader and Driss." Her eyes moved off into the distance—towards Leila, and Toni—then came back to me. "I know she loved you. She often talked about you.

"She wanted to call you. After her master's. She was sure she was going to get it. She wanted to see you again. 'I can do it now,' she said to me. 'Now that I'm a big girl.'"

Karine laughed, then her eyes filled with tears again and she huddled against me.

"It's all right," I said. "It's going to be fine."

"I don't understand any of what's happened."

We'd never know the truth. All there could ever be was speculation. The truth was part of the horror. I supposed Toni had been seen with Leila in Aix. By one of the gang. Probably by one of the worst of them. Morvan or Wepler. White suprematists, guys who believed in ethnic cleansing and final solutions. They must have put Toni to the test. Like an initiation. To move him up a level.

The paras liked that kind of crazy stunt. Fuck a guy from the next room. Go to the Legionnaires' bar, kill one, and bring back his *képi* as a trophy. Kill a teenager who looked like a fag. They'd signed a pact with death. Life was cheap. Their own and everyone else's. Particularly everyone else's. In Djibouti, I'd come across even bigger maniacs. They'd go to the neighborhood around the former Place Rimbaud and find a hooker. Leave her for dead, with her throat cut. Mutilated, sometimes.

Now, our former colonies were here. Capital: Marseilles. Here, like there, life didn't matter. The only thing that mattered was death. And violent sex. It was a way to express your hatred of being nothing but a ghost waiting to fight. The unknown soldier of the future. One day or another. In Africa, Asia, the Middle East. Or even two hours from home. Wherever the West was threatened. Wherever there were foreigners hungry to fuck our women, our pure white women, and soil our race.

That was what they must have asked Toni to do. Bring them the Arab girl, so that they could fuck her. One after the other. Toni first. He must have been the first. He wanted her, and he was angry because she'd rejected him. A woman was just a piece of ass. They were all whores. Arab girls had whores' asses. Like those Jewish bitches. Jewish girls' asses were higher and rounder. Arab girls' asses were a bit lower, right? Black girls too. Black girls' asses, you're telling me! Really worth the effort!

Then the other two had had their turn. Not Morvan, or Wepler. No, the other two apprentice Nazis. The two who'd died on Place de l'Opéra. I don't suppose they'd been up to it, when the time came to kill Leila. Fucking an Arab girl was one thing. Shooting her down without your hand shaking couldn't have been so easy.

Morvan and Wepler were voyeurs. That's what I imagined. They were the MCs. Had they jerked each other off as they watched? Or had they fucked each other afterwards, nostalgic for the SS and the virile love of warriors? And when had they decided that whoever survived that night would be the one who put his bullet closest to Leila's heart?

Had Toni felt any pity for Leila as he fucked her? For a moment at least. Before he too fell headlong into the horror of it all. Into what could never be undone.

I recognized Simone's voice. And she recognized mine. The number where Karine had left messages for her brother was indeed Les Restanques. She'd called him there this evening.

"I'd like to speak with Emile. Or Joseph."

The same nauseating music. Caravalli and his magic violins, or some crap like that. But not so many noises of plates and forks. Les Restanques was emptying. It was ten before midnight.

"Émile," the voice said. The same voice as before.

"Montale. No need to draw you a picture, you know who I am."

"I'm listening."

"I'm coming over there. I want to talk. A truce. I want to make you an offer."

I had no plan. The only thing I wanted was to kill them all. I knew it was a fantasy, but it was what I needed to keep going, to do what had to be done. To move forward. To survive another hour, another century.

"Are you coming alone?"

"I haven't been able to raise an army yet."

"Where's Toni?"

"He swallowed his tongue."

"You'd better have a good excuse. Because to us you're already dead."

"Idle talk, Émile. Kill me, and you'll all be collared. I've sold the story to a newspaper."

"No paper would dare print it."

"Here, no. In Paris, yes. If I don't call in two hours, it'll be in the final edition."

"All you have's a story. No proof."

"I have everything I need. All the things Manu stole from Brunel's safe. The names, the bank statements, the check books, the purchases, the suppliers. The list of bars, clubs and restaurants paying protection money. Better still, the names and addresses of all the local businessmen who support the National Front."

I was laying it on thick, but I probably wasn't too far from the truth. Batisti had been playing me for a sucker all down the line. If Zucca had had the slightest suspicion about Brunel, he'd have sent two of his own men to the lawyer's office to put a bullet in his head. Only then would they have cleaned up. Zucca was too old to fuck around. There was a line, a straight line, and you did-n't deviate from it. That was how he'd gotten where he was.

And Zucca would never have entrusted Manu with a job like that. He wasn't a killer. It was Batisti who'd sent Manu to Brunel's. I didn't know why, I didn't know what kind of game Batisti was playing. Babette was categorical that he wasn't in the business anymore. Manu had fallen for it. You didn't turn down a job for Zucca. He trusted Batisti. And the kind of money he was being offered wasn't to be sneezed at.

These were the conclusions I'd reached. They were shaky, and they raised even more questions than they answered. But I couldn't stop now. I'd come too far. I needed to have them, all of them, in front of me. I needed to know the truth. Even if it killed me.

"We're closing in an hour. Bring the papers."

He hung up. So Batisti had the documents. And he'd had Zucca killed by Ugo. But Manu?

Mavros arrived twenty minutes after I called him. That was the only solution I could think of. Call him and hand over to him. Let him take care of Driss and Karine. He hadn't been sleeping. He'd been watching Coppola's *Apocalypse Now*. For the fourth time, by my reckoning. He loved that movie, even though he didn't understand it. I remembered the song by the Doors. *The End.*

We were all moving to a pre-ordained end. You just had to open the papers and read the international news, or the crime reports. We didn't need nuclear weapons. We were killing each other with prehistoric savagery. We were just dinosaurs, and the worst thing of all was that we knew it.

Mavros didn't hesitate. Driss was worth the risk. He'd liked the boy ever since I'd introduced them. These things couldn't be explained, anymore than you could explain what attracted you sexually to one person rather than another. He'd put Driss in the ring. He'd make him fight. He'd make him think. Think about the left fist, the right fist. The reach of the arm. He'd make him talk. About himself, about the mother he never knew, about Leila. About Toni. Until he came to terms with what he'd done, what love and hate had pushed him to do. You couldn't live with hate in your heart. You couldn't box either. There were rules. A lot of the time, they were unfair. But if you obeyed them, you had a chance of saving your skin. And however rotten the world was, staying alive was still the best thing you could do. Driss would listen to Mavros. Mavros knew what it meant to fuck up. At the age of nineteen, he'd been sent down for a year for assaulting his trainer, who'd fixed a match he ought to have won. By the time they'd pulled him off, the guy was almost dead. And Mavros hadn't been able to prove that the fight was fixed. In the joint, he'd had time to think about these things.

Mavros winked at me. We both agreed that we couldn't let any of the four take a murder rap. Toni wasn't worth it. He'd deserved what he'd gotten tonight. I wanted them to have a chance. They were young, and they loved each other. But even with a good lawyer, no excuse would hold up. Self-defense?

Not easy to prove. Leila's rape? No evidence against Toni. At the trial, or even before, Karine would crack under pressure and tell it the way it had happened. And then it would be just an Arab from North Marseilles killing a young man in cold blood. A punk, maybe, but a Frenchman, the son of a worker. The two accomplices were Arabs too, and they had a girl, the victim's younger sister, under their spell. I couldn't even be sure that Karine's parents, on the advice of their lawyer, wouldn't press charges against Driss, Karine and Jasmine and plead extenuating circumstances for their daughter. I could already see the picture. I didn't trust my country's justice anymore.

When we picked up Toni off the floor, I knew I was placing myself outside the law, and that I was taking Mavros with me. But it was too late now. Mavros had already arranged everything. He'd close the gym until September and take Driss and Kader to the mountains. He had a little chalet at Orcières, in the Upper Alps. Hikes, swimming and bike rides were on the program. School was out for Karine, and Driss had almost overdosed on the garage and axle grease. Kader and Jasmine would leave for Paris tomorrow. With Mouloud, if he wanted to go. He could live with them. Kader was sure the three of them could make a living from the grocery store.

I'd driven Toni's Golf up to the door. Kader was outside, keeping watch. Not that there was any risk. The street was deserted. Not a cat, not even a rat. Just us, doctoring reality, since we couldn't change the world. Mavros opened the rear door of the car and I slid Toni's body inside. I went around the car, opened the other door, and sat Toni up. I used the seat belt to keep him upright. Driss came toward me. I didn't know what to say. Neither did he. So he took me in his arms and hugged me. And kissed me. Then Kader, Jasmine and Karine did the same. Nobody said a word. Mavros put his arm around my shoulder.

"I'll keep in touch."

I saw Kader and Jasmine get in Leila's Panda, and Driss and Kader climb into Mavros' four-wheel drive. They drove off. Everyone was leaving. I thought about Marie-Lou. Good morning, heartache. I sat down at the wheel of the Golf, and glanced in the rear view mirror. The street was still deserted. I put the car in first gear. *Que será, será!*

15.

IN WHICH HATRED OF THE WORLD
IS THE ONLY SCENARIO

I was thirty minutes late, which is what saved my life. Les Restanques was all lit up as if it were the 14th of July. By about thirty revolving lights. Police vans, ambulances. The thirty minutes had been taken up in driving Toni's Golf to the third level down in the Centre Bourse underground parking garage, wiping off all prints, finding a taxi, and going back to the Belle de Mai to pick up my car.

It wasn't easy to find a taxi. If I'd gotten Sanchez as a driver, that really would have taken the cake. Instead, I got a carbon copy, with a National Front pennant above the meter thrown in as a bonus. If I'd been spotted on foot on Cours Belzunce, I might have been stopped by a police car. Walking alone at that hour was a felony in itself. But no police car passed. I could easily have been murdered. But I didn't bump into any murderers either. Everyone was sleeping peacefully.

I parked on the other side of the Restanques parking lot. On the road, with two wheels in the grass, behind a Radio-France car. The news had spread quickly. All the journalists seemed to be there, contained, with difficulty, by a cordon of gendarmes in front of the entrance to the restaurant. Babette must be somewhere. Even though she didn't cover day to day events, she liked to be around when stories broke. Old habits died hard.

I saw her, standing slightly to the left of a crew from France 3. I walked up to her, put my arm around her shoulder, and whispered in her ear, "What I'm about to tell you will give you the biggest scoop of your career." I kissed her on the cheek. "Hello, gorgeous."

"You're late. The massacre's over."

"I was nearly in it. So I'm feeling quite pleased with myself!"

"Quit fooling!"

"Do you know who's been killed?"

"Émile and Joseph Poli. And Brunel."

I grimaced. That meant the two most dangerous ones were still at large. Morvan and Wepler. Batisti too. If Simone was still alive, Batisti must also be alive. Who'd done this? The Italians would have slaughtered everyone. Morvan and Wepler, working for Batisti? The possibilities made my head spin.

Babette took my hand and drew me away from the journalists. We went and sat down on the ground, our backs against the low wall of the parking lot, and she told me what had happened. Or at least, what she'd been told had happened.

Two men had walked in just as the restaurant was closing around midnight. The last couple of customers had just left. There was nobody in the kitchen. Only one of the waiters was still around. He'd been wounded, but only slightly. According to him, he was more a bodyguard than a waiter. He'd dived under the counter and opened fire on the attackers. He was still inside the restaurant. Auch had wanted to question him immediately, like Simone.

I told her everything I knew. For the second time that day. Ending up with Toni and the Centre Bourse parking lot.

"You're right about Batisti. But way off track about Morvan and Wepler. It's your two wops who did this. For Batisti. In agreement with the Camorra. But first read this."

She handed me a photocopy of a press cutting. An article about the Tanagra massacre. One of the gangsters taken out then had been Batisti's elder brother, Tino. It was common knowledge that Zucca had ordered the operation. People were lining up to succeed Zampa. Tino had been top of the list. Zucca had beaten him to it. And Batisti had retired. With revenge in his heart.

Batisti had backed all the horses. He'd dropped out, given up his stake in the business, but seemed to have come to an understanding with Zucca. He had family ties with the Poli brothers, which also meant ties of friendship with Brunel then, later, with Morvan and Wepler. And he was on good terms with the Neapolitans. He'd had those three irons in the fire for years. The conversation I'd had with him at Chez Félix took on new meaning.

It was when O Pazzo was arrested that he started to plan his revenge. Zucca wasn't so untouchable anymore. Babette's contact in Rome had called back that evening. He had new information. In Italy, the judges had stopped beating about the bush. Heads were rolling every day, and some vital information had come out. The reason Michele Zaza had been busted was because his Marseilles branch was rotten. It had to be cut off urgently. A new man was needed to start business over again with. It was only natural that Batisti had been contacted by the *Nuova Famiglia* to carry out the changes.

He was clean. The police no longer had him under surveillance. His name hadn't been linked to anything in fifteen years. From Simone, via the Poli brothers, Batisti had learned that the net was closing in around Zucca. Auch's squad was on permanent stakeout near his house. He was followed even when he was walking his poodle. Batisti informed the Neapolitans, and sent Manu to Brunel's office to collect any compromising documents, in order to make sure they changed hands.

Zucca was planning to escape to Argentina. Reluctantly, Batisti had resigned himself to that. Then Ugo showed up. So fired up with hatred that he didn't realize he was being set up. I couldn't really make heads or tails of it all, but I was sure of one thing: Ugo, sent by Batisti, had whacked Zucca without Auch's men intervening. They'd killed him afterwards. They would have taken him out whether he'd been armed or not. But one question remained unanswered: who had killed Manu, and why?

"Batisti," Babette said. "Just like he's had the others killed. The big clean-up."

"You think Morvan and Wepler are dead, too?"

"Yeah, that's what I think."

"But there are only three bodies."

"They'll arrive soon enough, special delivery!" She looked at me. "Come on, Fabio, smile."

"I don't believe that explains Manu. He wasn't involved in any of that. He was planning to take off once the job was done. He'd told Batisti. You see, Batisti screwed me all down the line. Even over that. He genuinely liked Manu."

"You're an incurable romantic, honey. It'll be the death of you."

We looked at each other. We were both bleary-eyed, like people on the morning after a wild night.

"Total chaos, eh?"

"You said it, gorgeous."

And I was in the middle of the quagmire. Wading in other people's shit. Just a banal gangster story. One more story, and surely not the last. Money and power. The story of mankind. With hatred of the world as the only scenario.

"Are you all right?"

Babette was shaking me gently. I'd dozed off. I was exhausted, and I'd drunk too much. I remembered that when I left the kids I'd taken the bottle of Chivas with me. There was still a fair amount left. I gave Babette what was intended as a smile and got painfully to my feet.

"I need fuel. I have what we need in the car. Want some?"

She shook her head. "Stop drinking!"

"I prefer to die like that. If you let me."

In front of Les Restanques, the show was still in full swing. The bodies were being brought out. Babette went off to see what she could find out. I took two large swigs of scotch. I felt the alcohol move down into my insides and spread heat all through my body. My head started spinning. I leaned on the hood. I could feel my guts coming up into my throat. I turned to the hard shoulder, intending to throw up on the grass. It was then that I saw them. Two motionless bodies, lying in the ditch. Two more corpses. I swallowed my guts back down, and they tasted disgusting.

I slid cautiously into the ditch and crouched by the bodies. They'd been shot in the back, with a tommy gun. Whoever had done it was a crack shot. No more tourism or flowery shirts for them. I stood up, my head humming. The corpses had indeed arrived by special delivery, only not the ones we'd expected. All our theories fell apart. I was about to extricate myself from the ditch when I noticed a dark patch a little distance away in the field. I glanced back at Les Restanques. Everyone was busy. Waiting for a statement, an explanation from Auch. Three strides, and I was standing over a third corpse, lying face down. I took out a Kleenex and moved the head slightly so that it faced me, then held my cigarette lighter next to it. Morvan. His .38 Special in his hand. His career was over.

I caught Babette by the arm. She turned.

"What's up? You've gone white."

"The wops. Dead. And Morvan too. In the ditch and the field... Near my car."

"Shit!"

"You were right. Batisti and the wops were doing a spring clean."

"And Wepler?"

"Still at large. What I suspect happened is that when the shooting started, Morvan tried to get the hell out, and they ran after him. Forgetting all about Wepler. From the little you told me about him, he's the kind who'd stay in hiding, waiting for me to arrive so that he could make sure I was really alone. When the two wops showed up, he must have been puzzled but not especially worried. By the time he realized what was going down, everything exploded. When they came out, running after Morvan, he got them in the back."

Flashbulbs started popping. Besquet and Paoli came out, supporting a woman. Simone. Auch followed ten paces behind. His hands buried in the pockets of his jacket, as usual. Looking solemn. Very solemn.

Simone crossed the parking lot. A very thin face, with finely-drawn features, framed by shoulder-length black hair. Slender, quite tall for a Mediterranean woman. Class. She was wearing an unbleached linen suit that set off her tan. She looked exactly the way her voice sounded. Beautiful and sensual. And proud, like all Corsican women. She stopped, overcome with sobs. Calculated tears, for the benefit of the photographers. She turned her distraught face to them. She had huge, magnificent black eyes.

"Do you like her?"

It was much more than that. She was exactly the type of woman Ugo, Manu and I had gone for. Simone looked like Lole. I finally understood.

"I'm getting out of here," I said to Babette.

"Not without an explanation."

"I don't have time." I took out one of my cards. Under my name, I wrote Pérol's home number. On the back, an address. Batisti's. "Try to reach Pérol. He could be at the station, or home. Just find him and tell him to meet me at this address. As soon as possible. OK?"

"I'm going with you."

I took her by the shoulders and shook her. "No way! I don't want you mixed up in this. But you can help me. Find Pérol for me. Ciao."

She caught my jacket. "Fabio!"

"Don't worry. I'll pay for the calls."

Batisti lived on Rue des Flots-Bleus, above Pont de la Fausse-Monnaie, in a villa overlooking Malmousque, the farthest headland in the harbor. One of the ritziest neighborhoods in Marseilles. The villas, built on the rock, had a magnificent, sweeping view of the harbor, from La Madrague de Montredon on the left to well after L'Estaque on the right, and the islands—Endoume, Le Fortin, La Tour du Canoubier, Le Château d'If—as well as the Frioul islands, Pomègues and Ratonneaux, straight ahead.

I drove with one foot on the floor, listening to an old recording by Dizzy Gillespie. I reached Place d'Aix just as *Manteca* was starting. It was a piece I loved, one of the first to fuse jazz and salsa.

The streets were deserted. I turned toward the harbor, and drove along Quai de Rive-Neuve, where a few groups of young people were still hanging out at the entrance to the Trolleybus. I thought again of Marie-Lou. The night I spent dancing with her. The pleasure I'd had that night had taken me back years. To a time when everything was an excuse to stay up all night. I must have aged one morning, coming home to sleep. And I didn't know how.

I was struggling through another sleepless night. In a sleeping city where there wasn't a single hooker to be seen on the streets, even in front of the Vamping. I was about to play Russian roulette with the whole of my past life. My youth and my friendships. Manu, Ugo. And all the years that followed. The best and the worst. The last months, the last days. Staking them on a future in which I could sleep peacefully.

The stakes weren't high enough. I couldn't confront Batisti with what amounted to the daydreams of an angler. What cards did I have left? Four queens. Babette: friendship found. Leila: a missed opportunity. Marie-Lou: a promise given. Lole: lost but still awaited. Clubs, spades, diamonds, hearts. So much for the love of women, I told myself as I parked about a hundred yards from Batisti's villa.

He was probably waiting anxiously for a call from Simone. After my call to Les Restanques, he must have made up his mind very quickly. To take us all out in one fell swoop. Acting in a hurry wasn't Batisti's usual style. He was cold and calculating, like all people who bear a grudge. But the opportunity had been too good to miss. It wouldn't come again and it coincided neatly with the aim he'd set himself when he'd buried Tino.

I walked all the way around the outside of the villa. The front gate was closed and there was no way I could get through a lock like that. Not to mention that it was probably connected to an alarm system. I couldn't see myself ringing the bell and saying: "Hi, Batisti, it's me, Montale." I was stuck. Then I remembered that all these buildings could be reached on foot, along old paths that went all the way down to the sea. Ugo, Manu and I had explored every inch of this area. I went back to my car, and drove down, with the engine off, as far as the Corniche. I engaged the clutch, drove another five hundred yards and turned left along Vallon de la Baudille. I parked and continued on foot up the steps of Traverse Olivary.

I was directly to the east of Batisti's villa, facing the perimeter wall. I walked along it until I found what I was looking for. The old wooden door leading into the garden. It was covered in Virginia creepers. It couldn't have been used in years. There was no lock, no latch. I just pushed open the door and walked in.

The ground floor was lighted. I walked around the outside of the house. A fanlight was open. I jumped, steadied myself, and slipped inside. The bathroom. I took out my gun and entered the house. In the big living room, Batisti sat in shorts and a leather undershirt in front of the TV screen. A video was playing. *Don't Look Now... We're Being Shot At*. He'd dozed off and was snoring quietly. I crept up to him and put my gun to his temple. He jumped.

"A ghost."

He blinked, realized who I was, and turned white.

"I left the others at Les Restanques. I don't care for family parties. Or for Saint Valentine's Day. Do you want the details? The body count, that kind of thing?"

"And Simone?" he stammered.

"On top form. You have a very beautiful daughter. You should have introduced us. I like that kind of woman too. Shit! Manu gets everything, and his friends get nothing."

"What the fuck are you talking about?" He was fully awake now.

"Don't move, Batisti. Put your hands in the pockets of your shorts and don't move. I'm tired, and I can easily lose control." He did as I said, but I could see the wheels in his head turning. "Don't build up your hopes. Your two wops are dead too."

"Tell me about Manu. When did he meet Simone?"

"Two years ago. Maybe more. His girlfriend was away at the time, I can't remember where. Spain, I think. I'd invited him for a *bouillabaisse*, at l'Épuisette, in the Vallon des Auffes. Simone joined us. Les Restanques was closed that day. They got on well, but I didn't realize. Not straight away. I didn't mind about Simone and Manu. True, I've never been able to stand the Poli brothers. Especially Émile.

"Then the girl came back. I thought it was over between him and Simone. I was relieved. I didn't want any trouble. Émile was a violent guy. But I was wrong. They were still seeing each other, and—"

"Spare me the details."

One day I said to Simone, "Manu's doing one more job for me and then he's taking off for Seville, with his girlfriend."

"Oh!" went Simone, "I didn't know." I realized it wasn't over between them. But it was too late, I'd blown it."

"Are you telling me she killed him?"

"He'd told her they'd be going away together. To Costa Rica, or somewhere in that part of the world. Ugo had told him it was a great place."

"Are you telling me she killed him?" I repeated. "Say it, for fuck's sake!"

"Yeah."

I hit him. I'd been wanting to do it for a long time. Then I hit him a second time, and a third. Crying all the while. Because I knew I couldn't press the trigger. Or even strangle him. There was no hate left in me. Only disgust. Could I hate Simone for being as beautiful as Lole? Could I hate Manu for fucking the ghost of a lost love? Could I hate Ugo for breaking Lole's heart?

I'd put down my gun, thrown myself on Batisti, and lifted him. I just kept hitting him. He was completely limp now. I let go of him and he sank to the floor, on all fours. He looked up at me like a dog. A scared dog.

"I could shoot you, but you're not worth it," I said, though that was exactly what I wanted to do.

"You said it!" a voice yelled behind us. "Lie down on the floor, asshole. Legs apart, hands on your head. You, old man, stay where you."

Wepler.

I'd forgotten about him.

He walked around us, picked up my gun, checked it was

loaded, and removed the safety catch. His arm was dripping with blood.

"Thanks for showing me the way, asshole!" he said, kicking me.

Batisti was sweating buckets. "Wait, Wepler!" he begged.

"You're worse than all the Chinks put together. Worse than the fucking Arabs." With my gun in his hand, he walked up to Batisti and put the barrel against his temple. "Get up. You're a worm, but you're going to die standing up."

Batisti got to his feet. He was an obscene sight, in his shorts and undershirt, with sweat pouring down his body over rolls of fat. And fear in his eyes. Killing was easy. Dying was something else.

The shot rang out.

And the room echoed with several reports. Batisti collapsed on top of me. I saw Wepler take a couple of steps, as if performing a ballet. There was another shot, and he went through the glass door.

I was covered in blood. Batisti's rotten blood. His eyes were open, looking at me.

"Ma...nu.." he stammered. "I... loved..."

A gush of blood spattered my face. And I vomited.

Then I saw Auch. And the others. His squad. Then Babette running to me. I pushed away Batisti's body. Babette kneeled.

"Are you OK?"

"Where's Pérol? I told you to get Pérol."

"He's had an accident. They were chasing a car. A Mercedes with gypsies in it. Cerutti lost control of the car on the coast highway, above the Bassin de Radoub. It skidded. Pérol died immediately."

"Help me," I said, holding out my hand to her.

I felt dizzy. Death was everywhere. On my hands. On my lips. In my mouth. In my body. In my head. I was a walking corpse.

I swayed. Babette slipped her arm under my shoulder. Auch came toward us. His hands in his pockets, as usual. Sure of himself, proud, strong.

"How are you feeling?" he said, looking at me.

"Can't you see? Ecstatic."

"You're just a pain in the ass, Fabio. In a few days, we'd have collared all of them. You had to go fuck it up. Now all we're left with is a pile of corpses."

"Did you know? About Morvan? About everything?"

He nodded. He was pleased with himself, when all was said and done. "They just kept making mistakes. Starting with your buddy. That was too much."

"You knew about Ugo too? You let him do it?"

"We had to see things through. It would have been the haul of the century. Arrests all over Europe."

He offered me a cigarette, and I punched him in the face, with a strength I'd found somewhere in the deepest of the black, damp holes where Manu, Ugo and Leila were rotting. I was screaming.

After that, it seems, I fainted.

EPILOGUE

Nothing changes, and it's a new day

I woke around noon, wanting to take a leak. The answerphone display told me there were six messages. I really didn't give a shit. I immediately sank back into the blackest darkness, as if I'd smashed my head on an anvil. By the time I resurfaced, the sun was setting. There were eleven messages now, but they could all wait. In the kitchen, there was a note from Honorine. *Didn't notice you were sleeping. I put some farci in the fridge. Marie-Lou called. Everything's fine. She says hi. Babette brought back your car. She says hi too.* She'd added *What's wrong with your phone? Is it out of order? Anyhow I say hi too.* And then another postscript: *I read the newspaper.*

I couldn't stay like this for long. Beyond the door, the earth was still turning. There were a few less bastards in the world. It was another day, but nothing had changed. Outside, it still smelled bad. I couldn't do anything about that. Neither could anyone. It was called life: a cocktail of love and hate, strength and weakness, violence and passivity. And people were waiting for me. My bosses, Auch, Cerutti. Pérol's wife. Driss, Kader, Jasmine, Karine. Mouloud. Mavros. Djamel maybe. Marie-Lou who said hi. And Babette and Honorine who also said hi.

But I could take my time. I needed silence. I didn't want to move, let alone talk. I had a *farci*, two tomatoes and three courgettes. At least six bottles of wine, including two white Cassis. A pack of cigarettes, barely started. Enough Lagavulin. I could hold out another night and a day. Maybe one more night after that.

Now that I'd slept, and had recovered from the exhaustion of the last twenty-four hours, the ghosts were about to launch their attack. They started with a dance of death. I was in the tub, smoking, a glass of Lagavulin next to me. I'd closed my eyes for a moment, and there they all were. Formless, decomposing masses of gristle and blood. Supervised by Batisti, they were busy exhuming the bodies of Manu and Ugo. Leila's too, tearing her clothes off. I wanted to go down and save them, get them away from these monsters. I couldn't open the grave, though, and I was afraid of putting my foot in the black hole. But Auch was standing behind me, with his hands in his pockets, and kicking me in the ass, pushing me forward. I was falling, falling into the slimy hole. I pulled my head out of the water, and breathed hard. Then I sprinkled myself with cold water.

I stood at the window, naked, a glass in my hand, looking out at the sea. I was in luck: it was a starless night. I didn't dare go out on the terrace for fear of meeting Honorine. I was washed and scrubbed, but the smell of death still clung to my body. It was in my head too, which was worse. Babette had saved my life. So had Auch. I loved one and hated the other. I still didn't feel hungry. And even the sound of the waves was getting on my nerves. I took two Lexomil and went back to bed.

I did three things when I got up the next morning about eight. I had coffee with Honorine on the terrace. We talked about this and that, the weather, the drought, the forest fires that were starting up early this year. Next, I wrote a letter of resignation. I kept it brief. I didn't really know who I was anymore, but I certainly wasn't a cop. Then I swam, for thirty-five minutes. Unhurriedly, without forcing. As I came out of the water, I looked at my boat. It was still too early to take it out.

I should have been fishing for Pérol and his wife and daughter, but now there was no need. Maybe I'd go out tomorrow. Or the day after. I'd get back my taste for fishing. And for simple pleasures. Honorine was watching me from the top of the steps. She was depressed to see me like this, but she wouldn't ask me any questions. She'd wait for me to speak, if I wanted to. She went back inside before I climbed the steps.

I put on walking shoes and a cap, and took a backpack with a thermos of water and a terry towel. I needed to walk. The road through the *calanques* had always had a calming effect on me. I stopped off at a florist's shop at the Mazargue crossroads, and chose a dozen roses to be delivered to Babette. *I'll call you. Thanks.* Then I set off for the Gineste pass.

I got back late. I'd walked from one *calanque* to the next. Then I'd swum and dived and climbed. Concentrating on my legs and arms and muscles. And on my breathing. In, out. Putting one leg, one arm in front of the other. Then another leg, another arm. Sweating out all the impurities, drinking, sweating again. Pumping oxygen back into my blood. Now I could return to the land of the living.

Mint and basil. The smell filled my lungs, which were now as good as new. My heart started pounding. I took a deep breath. On the low table were the mint and basil plants I'd watered every time I'd been to Lole's place. Next to them, a canvas suitcase, and another, smaller one in black leather.

Lole appeared in the doorway leading to the terrace. Wearing jeans and a black sleeveless top. Her coppery skin gleamed. She was just the way she'd always been. The way I'd never stopped dreaming about her. Beautiful. She'd moved through time, untouched. Her face lit up in a smile. Her eyes rested on me.

Her eyes. On me.

"I called. There was no reply. About fifteen times. So I took a taxi and here I am."

Here we were, face to face. Just a few feet between us. Neither of us moved. Her arms hung by her sides. It was as if the surprise of finding ourselves in this situation had rooted us to the spot. We were alive, and we were too scared to move.

"I'm glad. That you're here."

I talked.

I came out with more trite phrases than I ever knew existed. How hot it is! Would you like to take a shower? How long have you been here? Are you hungry? Thirsty? Do you want to put on some music? Would you like a scotch?

She smiled again. No more small talk. She sat down on the couch, in front of the mint and basil plants. "I couldn't leave them there." Another smile. "Only you could have done that."

"Someone had to. Don't you think so?"

"I think I'd have come back, whatever you did, or didn't do."

"Watering them was my way of reviving the spirit of the place. It was you who taught us that. If the spirit is alive, the other person can't be far away. I needed you. Without you, I couldn't live, couldn't move forward, open doors. I was living an enclosed life. Out of laziness. You always make do with less. One day you make do with what you have, and you think that's happiness."

She stood up and came toward me. With her ethereal walk. My arms were open. All I had to do was hug her to me. She kissed me. Her lips had the velvety quality of the roses I'd sent that morning to Babette, and they were more or less the same dark red. Her tongue searched for mine. We had never before kissed like this.

The world was falling back into place. Our lives. Everything we'd lost or forgotten, all our failures, finally had a meaning. With one kiss.

That kiss.

I reheated the *farci*, and drizzled olive oil over it. We ate it with a bottle of Terrane, a Tuscan red that I'd been keeping for a special occasion. The souvenir of a journey to Volterra with Rosa. I told Lole everything that had happened. In detail. It was like scattering the ashes of someone who's died, to be borne away on the wind.

"I knew. About Simone. But I didn't believe in Manu and Simone. anymore than I believed in Manu and Lole. I didn't believe in anything anymore. When Ugo showed up, I knew it was all going to end. He didn't come back for Manu. He came back for himself. Because he was tired of chasing after his own soul. He needed a good reason to die.

"You know, if Manu had stayed with Simone, I'd have killed him myself. Not out of love, or jealousy, but for the principle of the thing. Manu had lost all his principles. Anything he could have was good. Anything he couldn't have was bad. You can't live like that."

I packed some sweaters and blankets and the bottle of Lagavulin, and took Lole by the hand and led her to the boat. I rowed out as far as the sea wall, then started the engine and set sail for the Frioul islands. Lole sat down between my legs, her head on my chest. We shared the bottle, passed each other cigarettes. We didn't talk. Marseilles was getting closer. I left Pomègues, Ratonneaux and the Chateau d'If on the port side and continued straight ahead toward the channel.

Once past the Sainte Marie sea wall, beneath the Pharo, I cut the motor and let the boat drift. We'd wrapped ourselves in blankets. My hand rested on Lole's stomach. Her soft skin glistened.

At last Marseilles was revealed. From the sea. The way the Phocian must have been seen it for the first time, one morning many centuries ago. With the same sense of wonder. The port of Massilia. I know its happy lovers, a Marseilles Homer might have written about Gyptis and Protis. The traveler and the princess. In a soft voice, Lole recited:

O procession of Gypsies
May the sheen of our hair guide you...

One of Leila's favorite poems.

Everyone was invited. Our friends, our lovers. Lole placed her hand on mine. It was time for the city to burst into flame. White at first, then ocher and pink.

A city after our own hearts.

About the Author

Jean-Claude Izzo was born in Marseilles, France, in 1945. Best known for the Marseilles trilogy, Izzo is also the author of *The Lost Sailors*, *A Sun for the Dying*, *Garlic, Mint & Sweet Basil,* and one collection of short stories, *Living Tires*. Izzo died in 2000 at the age of fifty-five.